The People In Between: A Cyprus Odyssey

Gregory S. Lamb

The People In Between: A Cyprus Odyssey

Copyright © 2010 Gregory S. Lamb

ISBN-13: 978-1461138747

DEDICATION

For individuals, family members, friends and relatives of refugees and displaced populations, whoever and wherever they may be.

ACKNOWLEDGMENTS

I had a lot of help from several of my friends and close relatives who read and re-read my multiple drafts. Their patience and editing skills made it possible to finally publish this story.

My wife Cindy and our three sons, Ian, Eric, and Owen, endured my time away during the years I lived and worked in Cyprus. I can't thank my wife Cindy enough for her dedication, patience, and gentle methods for offering editorial suggestions along with her extensive editing. My son Eric also took the time out of his busy life to give me some valuable insights from a reader's perspective.

My friend and former U-2 Squadron mate Paul Memrick was the first to read this story and I can't thank him enough for the encouragement to continue working on it until I got it right.

This story couldn't be possible if not for the suffering of the Cypriot people and the pains that resulted from displacement and loss that accompanies human conflict. Many of my Cypriot friends were a tremendous source of inspiration. I'd name them here, but they know who they are.

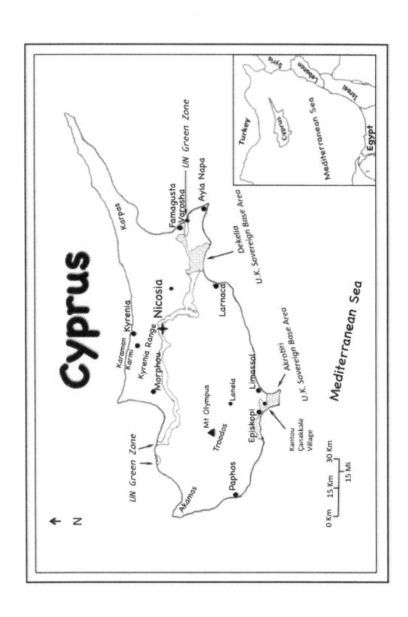

PROLOGUE

Kantou/Çanakkale Cyprus

March 1964

Hanife Yilmaz and her younger sister Didem began to panic. They were returning from the village school when the commotion started. There was turmoil and confusion everywhere. Plumes of smoke from exploding bombs and the sounds of automatic rifle fire echoed throughout the outskirts of Limassol. Their family home was on the far side of Çanakkale village north west of Limassol. Hanife took hold of her younger sister by the shoulders and spun her around so they were face to face. She wanted to make sure the ten-year-old would follow her instructions.

"It isn't safe to go home right now," Hanife repeated to Didem who was shaking with fright. Tears were streaming down her young cheeks. "Kostas will look after you. Do what he says. He will make sure you are safe. Now go to the cafe and wait for me there. I won't be long." The owner of the village cafe was a Greek Cypriot neighbor and close friend to the Yilmaz family.

"Hanife I am scared. Where are *Anne* and *Baba*? I want them," cried Didem.

"Don't worry, I will bring *Anne* with me back to the cafe when I return, now go."

"Will you be long?"

"Not long. Now go hurry! *Anne* and *Baba* will be angry with us if we don't do what we were told." Hanife waited in the road until she was sure Didem was safe in the cafe with Kostas.

Weeks earlier, in the capital city of Nicosia, inter-communal violence between Greek and Turkish Cypriots erupted over the island's collapsing government. The violence was blamed on members of the subversive organization called EOKA, which stood for the National Organization of Cypriot Fighters. Originally EOKA formed by the Greek military leader Georgios Grivas, to push back against British colonial rule but following Cypriot independence in 1960, EOKA went underground. In the most recent episode of violence, a resurgence of EOKA fighters ravaged the village of Evdim and burned homes belonging to the minority population of Turkish Cypriots.

At the start of the New Year, optimism grew among the mixed population of Kantou, the name given to the village by the Greek Cypriot residents. The Turkish Cypriot people living there called the same village Çanakkale. All of the residents hoped that the U.N. Security Forces sent to the island would end the violence and restore peace, but not this day.

As Hanife turned the corner towards home, she could see smoke and flames licking the windowsills. The heat of the fires within the house scorched what was left of the geraniums in the window boxes that Hanife's mother was tending when the girls left for school. A Greek Cypriot neighbor boy that the girls grew

2

up with shouted toward Hanife in a frightened voice.

"Hanife, run! I'm right behind you. The soldiers were just here. They will come back. There is nothing here for you."

"No, Hristos, I have to find my *Anne*. I told Didem to wait in the cafe. *Anne* told us if something like this happened, we were supposed to get our things and go there."

"There is nothing. Everything inside is burning. Your mother must have run when the soldiers came and threw the bombs." Hristos sounded angered and frustrated that the peace of his native village had turned into something so horrible.

Hanife took a look around and noticed some of the homes of the Greek Cypriot villagers were also burning. She wasn't able to comprehend all of what she saw so she focused on finding her mother.

Ignoring Hristos's pleas, Hanife charged around the side of the family home to look for her mother in the back garden. Behind the Yılmaz home were the family's lands. These lands passed down to them through generations were terraced and planted in carob and olive groves. Orange and fig trees lined the side yards of the once lovely home and its traditional garden. Now all of it is turning to ruin in the rubble left behind by the EOKA bombs.

"*Anne - Anne - Anne!!!*" Hanife cried in horror, frozen in place at the rise above the first terrace as she recognized her mother still wearing the kitchen apron from her morning chores.

The woman was face down on the rocks. Her long black raven hair covered her battered face. Hanife felt a sudden grip on her shoulder. It was the older boy Hristos with his firm hand. He turned her toward him and bored his dark green eyes into Hanife's.

"We must go. It isn't safe here for any of us anymore." He said gently. Hanife could see he was still wavering from his own fear.

"She fell, I need to help her. We need to help her get up. Then we can bring her to the cafe. Kostas will know what to do."

"Hanife, your mother will not be coming to the cafe with us. I saw what happened. There was shooting. I am scared too. We need to go. They will be coming back."

Hristos words caused Hanife to become even more worried. She was shuddering from the realization of seeing and knowing her mother was gone forever.

When Hristos and Hanife returned to the main road leading to the village cafe, the street out front was full of chaos. People from the village were scrambling to board the Bedford bus from Limassol. They brought along as many of the treasured belongings from their homes that they could carry. Just when they were close enough to see and hear what was going on, the bus started to leave.

"Didem! Didem!" Hanife yelled to her younger sister at the

top of her lungs.

"Kostas. Wait. Please, Kostas my little sister! She's my responsibility!" Hanife and Hristos were both still running toward Kostas as the bus began to roll away from the cafe. Hanife could see her younger sister being pulled into the bus by the other Turkish Cypriots fleeing their village, as Kostas lifted the crying and exhausted Didem to the window.

That horrifying afternoon in April of '64 was the last time Hanife saw her younger sister. She had no idea of the whereabouts of her father or older brother, but she knew she had lost her mother forever. She was alone and terrified.

CHAPTER 1

Greek South

Cyprus

Early Spring 2001

The April sun and warm humid breezes of the East Mediterranean are the trademarks of spring on the island of Cyprus. The salt air mixed with the scent of oleander filled the interior of the rented car Nora picked up at the airport terminal. Kiraz "Nora" Johansson was on her way to meet her twin brother at a lunch spot on the beach just below the ruins of the ancient city of Curium.

It had only been a few days earlier when she was amidst the noise and traffic of downtown Washington, D.C. She was gratified to have finally arrived in Cyprus, a place she'd never visited until now. Nora was feeling a familiar sense of freedom and adventure, which she thrived on.

Having returned from an eight month stint teaching English in Azerbaijan, Nora had been home in her one-room flat in Arlington, Virginia for less than twenty-four hours when she received a phone call from her brother Nils.

"Hi Sis, how's things?

"Wow Nils, what a surprise to hear from you. I've been away. Where are you calling from?"

"First you go. You said you've been away. Where this

time?"

Her brother's bitter and sarcastic tone had gotten worse in recent years. Nora knew he hated talking on the phone, but wanted to give him a chance to explain the reason for his call.

"A long story. I'm not sure you want to hear all of it."

"Come on Sis, I want to hear all about what you've been up to, but that isn't why I called. We can maybe catch up later OK?"

"Alright. Where are you calling from anyway, France again? It feels like it's been ages."

"Akrotiri, Cyprus," he replied, "I have a proposition for you," he said.

Cyprus, thought Nora. It took a few moments for the images and flashes of world history to register before she reacted to her brother's proposal. "Oh Nils, last time I wrote something on your suggestion, there wasn't a single journal, or magazine that would touch it. I still don't understand what got between us back then." She hesitated a beat then said, "I'm glad you called."

Nilsson "Onur" Johansson was on his first deployment as a U.S. Air Force Intelligence Officer in spring of 1999. He was assigned to NATO to monitor and report on the effects of the NATO air campaign supporting Kosovo's independence from the former Yugoslav Republic. Something sparked his emotion when the frequency of reports from non-government organizations, suggested that collateral damage from air strikes were on the rise. These reports from the NGOs made it into the international media and conflicted dramatically with the daily intelligence reports Nils had to analyze and report on.

He saw an opportunity for a different kind of story to hit the presses. He wanted to see his twin sister do something more meaningful than chasing what he thought were lost causes with the Peace Corps, so he encouraged her to pursue her passion for journalism and urged her to do some freelance writing. He gave her a file containing the details of alleged collateral damage that dispelled some of the accusations of reckless actions by NATO pilots. Nora ignored the file and its contents and went off on a tangent about refugees and forced population movements. The conflict was short lived and even though Nora thought her reporting was timely, the magazine editors told her it wouldn't hold the interests of their reading audience.

"No, no nothing like that. If you remember, last time things didn't work out too well. Anyway, I know it is spur of the moment." He paused then asked, "Did Dad ever mention anything about an artist friend of his who lives here on the island?"

"I don't remember if he ever did, so no I guess not."

"Well, this Brit named Gavin Hart is an old friend of his. I got a call from Gavin this morning and he asked me if I knew anyone who would be interested in temporarily running his gallery in Laneia Village. He is leaving at the end of the week.

Are you interested?"

"Hmmm, tempting offer. For how long?"

"He said he's going to be away for two, maybe three weeks. Hey, it is an easy job and a free place to stay in a beautiful spot. I've been up there a couple of times already. It's a lovely place really, and you won't have to do much more than water the plants and maybe sell a painting or two. So what do you say? It'll be good for us to catch up. You can maybe even do some writing during your stay."

Nora didn't have to ponder the prospect for long. Cyprus, she thought to herself. It was a perfect opportunity to get to know the place where her mother grew up. Nora and Nils were born to Hanife and Sven Johansson on Offutt Air Force Base Nebraska in 1977. They discovered later that their mother, Hanife suffered from the rare disease, preeclampsia that manifested itself during her pregnancy. Giving birth to twins was just too much for her and she died of sudden heart failure during labor. It was a miracle that both twins survived.

"Nils, you still know how to persuade me. OK, I will come."

"Good, I'll email you some directions. I have a connection through work that will get you a good discount for a hire car while you're here."

When she arrived at Larnaca International Airport, Nora's luggage wasn't waiting for her at baggage claim. She filled out the paperwork for the one and only bag she checked when she departed Dulles seventeen hours ago. With nothing else to do, she decided to head directly to Curium Beach, where Nils had arranged for them to meet when she arrived.

There were very few cars traveling on the new freeway that stretched from Larnaca to Paphos. It was a Tuesday morning. The tourist season hadn't started and there were still a couple hours before the mid-day meal. Nora was glad she chose to travel in light khaki slacks, practical slip on loafers, and a loose long sleeved button down white cotton shirt. Her matching Khaki blazer was draped over the seat next to her. A small satchel containing a bottle of water, a toothbrush, and a few other practical travel items sat on the seat beside her. In spite of her young age, Nora was a seasoned traveler.

Though it was her first visit to Cyprus, Nora was no stranger to driving on the left side of the road. The traffic system in Cyprus is one of a few remnants left over from the island nation's history as a former British Colony. Cyprus was granted independence from Britain in 1960 with a complicated arrangement of government divided between Turkish and Greek Cypriot representation.

On the road to Curium, while passing through Limassol, some of the more prominent buildings could be seen flying both the white Cypriot flag along side the national flag of Greece. Just west of Limassol, she exited the A-6 and followed the signs to what was once the main coastal road, now called the B-6, which took her to Curium. She drove by groves of lemon and grapefruit trees and passed a sign. It read, "Entering the Sovereign Base Area of Akrotiri." That explains the boundary labeled SBA on the road map she got at the car rental agency, she thought. Nora wasn't aware that Cyprus's two SBAs were a condition of the British when they conceded their colony to the Cypriots.

A short distance further just before the B-6 began a winding climb to the ancient Curium site and amphitheater, Nora spotted the small sign her brother's instructions told her to look for, beneath a stand of eucalyptus trees. The sign directed her onto a dusty gravel road made from chalk white limestone leading to Curium's beach.

Chris's Blue Beach Tavern is located at the far west end of Curium Beach, which extends between the western shoreline of the Akrotiri peninsula and the headlands of Episkopi with her steep cliffs overlooking the sea. In the morning hours, the air was nearly still. A slight westerly breeze began its seasonal ritual of filling in full strength by mid-afternoon. It was a phenomenon that occurred every day from spring through the fall season.

On her right as Nora drove toward the beach, there were some cordoned off areas where new archeological excavations were underway below the white cliffs of the ancient city. Nora spun the rented Astra into an almost vacant car park adjoining the lovely beach tavern. Looking no worse for wear, she grabbed her satchel from out of the now dusty rental car and walked up to the patio of the tavern.

At twenty-three years old, Nora carried herself with the confidence of a more experienced woman. She wore her wavy auburn hair in a short-cropped style emphasizing her deep green eyes rimmed by a ring of brown with colors that changed with the different hues of light. With facial features more Anatolian than European and her naturally dark complexion, she made the impression that she spent much of her time out of doors. Nora was a fit young woman. Not the gym rat type like many of her contemporaries who she went to college with, but rather because she walked nearly everywhere when she could and almost always with purpose. Her narrow waist and hips slightly wider than her shoulders suited the way she carried herself with a strong posture. Her long legs and short torso made her appear slightly taller than her 5'4", and though not a stunning exotic beauty, she still got double takes from most men when she walked past.

The patio of *Chris's* was empty all but for one of the umbrella tables near the back corner. Amidst a stack of wind surfing board bags, towels and a table top full of sunglasses, sat a young looking woman with wet dark hair wearing a wetsuit with the upper half rolled down to expose her brown arms and shoulders and lime green bikini top.

Nora approached one of the empty tables that had a commanding view of the shoreline. When she sat down, she pulled off her sunglasses and set them on the table and took in the sound of the waves lapping against the sandy beach. Twenty meters off-shore she could see there was a group of wind surfing sailors spread out and cruising back and forth along the length of Curium's broad beach. A young lean Cypriot boy with black curly hair came out from beneath the covered section of the patio adjacent to where she was sitting.

"*Kalimera*," said the young boy who couldn't have been more than 16 years old. Covering only some of his bronzed skin, he was wearing faded blue beach shorts and a white tank top with a colorful beach scene printed on it with the words *Chris's Blue Beach* scrolled across the top. The boy stood beside the table waiting for Nora to say something.

"Good morning to you also. This spot is so beautiful this morning."

The boy spoke with a strong Greek Cypriot accent when he replied, "Of course. This is Cyprus. Everyday is the same this time of year. We love it. You are American. I can tell because I have met many Americans on this beach, but mostly the English and tourists from Europe come here. This table, almost everyday my American friend comes to. Maybe you know him." He paused then asked, "Is there anything I can bring you? A Coke, Cypriot coffee, something you like to eat? You just say."

"A coffee would be nice."

"What kind? We have Nescafe, filter coffee, or our specialty, Cypriot coffee."

"I'll try your specialty then. Thank you."

"Super, how do you like? Sweet, medium sweet, without sugar, you tell me what you like and I will bring you a nice coffee."

"Medium will be fine. Thank you."

"In Cyprus we say *metreo*. You would like a Cypriot Coffee, *metreo*. Oh key, I'll be right back. I bring you. You will see." He said with a broad grin and rushed off.

Nora took in the expansive view of the beach while she waited for her coffee to arrive. The wind was picking up and the sound of the windblown waves against the sandy shore created a peaceful sort of white noise. Down the beach more sun seekers started to show up. The umbrella tables on the patio began to fill with locals stopping in for lunch before heading back to whatever activities they engage in during the weekdays.

Lost in thought, Nora sensed a presence approaching from behind and looked over her right shoulder thinking it would be the Greek Cypriot boy bringing her coffee.

"Nils! You surprised me! I wasn't expecting you so soon. My flight got in early and my baggage didn't make it, so I came straight here. What a lovely spot."

Dressed in beige colored pressed cotton slacks, tan colored

leather slip on shoes, and a black knit polo shirt, Nils looked the part of a young professional with unspecified responsibilities like so many of the foreigners and expatriates who live and work on the island. If Nora Johansson comes across as the outgoing, cheerful, adventurous spirit of a young twenty something, her twin brother is the polar opposite.

Nils Onur Johansson is different in every way. He is tall, lean and fair, with a shock of blond hair and blue eyes more like his father than his deceased mother. He's the calculating type and though not in his nature, occasionally gloomy. While growing up together Nora and Nils shared a close relationship, which seemed to have drastically changed since their final years of high school. Tragedy changes people.

"Kiraz, Hi. You know you're sitting in my favorite spot."

"Nils are you teasing me? You know I don't use that name. Am I supposed to get up and move or something? You can have your chair if you like."

"No that's alright Nora, I didn't mean for you to have to get up. I've always kind of liked the name 'Kiraz.' It has a nice ring and makes people curious. You know, they might wonder where and how our parents came up with it. How's the malaria? A good thing it isn't keeping you from traveling."

"It was hepatitis and I have been treated for it and I am fine now thanks." She wasn't going to let the jab at her name pass easily. "Kiraz is Turkish for 'Cherry,' but you already knew that didn't you?"

Nils gave her a short laugh taking in her auburn color and olive skin tone, "I get your drift. Hepatitis. It's kind of like cholera which has been pretty much eradicated in the developed world."

"What is with you? I haven't seen you in gosh I don't know, almost a year, and we are back to bickering over things we cannot change. Can we just stop this? It has been a long day already."

"It's our way maybe. Did you see him?"

"Who?"

"Dad. Did you see him before you came?"

"The day after you called I stopped by his place on the way to the airport. He is looking much better. It is good to see him in his own place. Hospitals are so depressing. What about you, when did you see him last?"

"Every freakin day Nora. I am surrounded by the presence of the great Sven Kjell Johansson every single day. His picture is pasted on the walls of the office along with a string of the other commanders who followed, but his is the first."

Sven Johansson, Lieutenant Colonel, USAF was on a fast track to General. Before his career was cut short, he left a legacy with the small U-2 reconnaissance unit at RAF Akrotiri. Sven was a Captain at the time and had just returned from duty in Vietnam where he flew RB-57s. He and his back seater were shot down over hostile territory in 1969. After giving the order to bail out, Sven stayed with his aircraft just long enough to send a coded message to search and rescue forces before ejecting himself. As a result he became separated from his back seater by several kilometers.

His crew mate, who was also his best friend, and husband to his sister Ronella, was captured by the North Vietnamese shortly after they both parachuted into the jungles of Laos. Captain Stone was later reported to have died in captivity as a POW in North Vietnam. Sven on the other hand, spent two weeks evading captors before connecting to a Special Operations Group recon unit who found him near the Ho-Chi-Min trail on the west side of the North Vietnamese border.

After Vietnam, Sven was the first to deploy and fly U-2 missions from Akrotiri. He was a member of the U-2 reconnaissance operation at RAF Akrotiri deployed to support an international set of agreements leading to the monitoring of the hostilities between Egypt and Israel in August of 1970.

Nora was never one to let her brother off the hook without getting to the bottom of his caustic comments. "You sound like you are still so bitter. What did he ever do to deserve the way you treat him?"

"It's what he didn't do Nora. What did you guys talk about anyway?"

"I wasn't able to stay long, so the conversation was pretty

short. He asked about Azerbaijan. I didn't have much to share because he seemed like he wanted to talk about the past. He seemed different and maybe concerned that his time was getting short. When I told him I was coming here he said, 'Enjoy Cyprus, there is a lot to be learned there.' He went on and told me that if I could understand the history here it would open a window to understanding so much more. I'm not sure I know what he meant."

Nils shook his head from side to side with a smirk. "That sounds just like him. Always talking in riddles. That is, whenever he says anything at all. What about you Nora, all the flitting around that you do. How's your love life anyway? No. On second thought, don't answer that. Let me guess. Too busy traveling and solving the social problems of the world. Too sophisticated for any mortal man to...."

Nora wasn't going to let her brother's comment go unchecked, so she just stared at him with a look that let him know she wouldn't let herself become rattled by his prying. Instead she said to him, "Well it is nice to see you...."

Just then, breaking the icy atmosphere under the umbrella at their table, the young Greek Cypriot boy arrived with Nora's coffee. His toothy smile broke the tension as he set the small cup and saucer along with a small clear glass of water in front of Nora. The boy noticed Nils right away when Nils took up a chair at the table with Nora.

"Hi my American friend. Will you be having your usual?" It was the first time he saw Nils with a woman and wasn't sure what to make of it.

"Jeri! Yes of course. Let me introduce my sister. Nora, this is my good friend Jericho. His mom and dad have been running this place on a seasonal basis along with his older brothers for quite awhile. Jeri said his mom used to serve Dad here back in those days in the 70s when everything changed."

"Nice to meet you Jericho." Nora extended her hand.

"Pleased to meet you. Call me Jeri. We take extra special good care of our American friends here. I will bring you something that I know you are sure to like to go with your coffee. My mother baked it last night."

Jeri swiftly departed and checked on a few of the other guests at the tables around them, Nora took a sip of the coffee and looked across and over her brother's shoulder at the sparkling sunlight reflecting from the wave faces on the sea. She set the cup down and picked up her sunglasses to relieve her tired eyes from the brightness of the midday sun. The silence between her and her brother was short lived, as was the initial tension from their first encounter in many months. Moments later, Jeri returned to the table with a small plate for Nora holding a slice of fresh baklava and a tiny fork. In front of Nils he set down a small stainless bowl of shredded cabbage salad with oil and vinegar and slice of fresh bread.

As he departed, Jeri said to them both, "Enjoy your lunch. It is good to see families together." He turned to Nora and said to her, "You are going to love it here. This is Cyprus and everyone who comes here falls in love." He then turned to Nils, winked, and walked away.

"How long will you be able to stay?" Nils knew that Gavin Hart was only planning to be gone for a few weeks but wasn't sure about his sister's plans.

"I haven't thought beyond taking care of Mr. Hart's gallery. My ticket home is for an open return, but I definitely need to be back before the summer ends. When I got back from Azerbaijan I received notice from Georgetown University that I got accepted into their Masters Program for the State Department's Foreign Service. It's a full ride scholarship with a job commitment. My dreams come true."

"Well congratulations sis. I take it you'll be living the dream then. Maybe you'll finally meet your 'one and only' when you get back to school. Perhaps a professor or maybe a young undergrad? I can picture how that conversation will go when you have to tell them you'll be leaving for post soon."

"You're just trying to get a rise out of me I know. What about you and Josette? Have you made amends?"

Nils met Josette, the mother of his son, during his first overseas assignment while stationed at Istres, France. Their attraction was purely physical with little else in common. Right before his departure for a brief assignment to NATO in Brussels, Josette informed Nils that she was pregnant with his child. Seven months later on his way to Cyprus, Nils returned to southern France to see his son Martin for the first time. There was no wedding and Nils didn't think there would ever be one.

Exasperated and feeling a little bad for poking at his sister's soft emotions, Nils replied, "Nora, I saw Martin on my way here. I would really love to be situated so that I could be a proper father to him, but he is with Josette and she is with her family in France. Before I left for Brussels, she told me she was pregnant, she said she would never leave France. It was a lot to take in such a short span of time. "

Nora was relieved that Nils was showing signs of opening up to her. It reminded her how close they were for so many years. "Do you have a picture of him? I would like to see what the son of a Swedish Turk Cypriot and a French mother looks like."

Nils pulled his wallet from his shirt pocket and removed a small photo of a stunning young bronzed and bare shouldered brunette woman holding a chunky little boy baby with a shock of blond hair and a drooling grin. "It isn't the best picture I have of him, but it is the one I carry around with me," he said as he passed the photo over to Nora.

"He's adorable. Nils, he really is something." She knew not to say anything else about his relationship Josette or how they would hopefully one day be together. The fact that Nils chose to carry around a picture with Josette and his son together in the same shot, was indication that Nils still had feelings for her. She took one more glance at the picture and handed it back to her brother before taking the last sip of her coffee.

"Do you want to share this last bite of baklava with me? It is really tasty."

Nils tucked the photo back into his wallet and shirt pocket and resumed picking at the remains of his salad. To his sister's offer of the baklava he replied, "No thanks. You go ahead, it doesn't really mix well with the salad dressing. I gotta head back soon anyway. Are you going to be alright getting your luggage sorted out?"

"I gave the airline Gavin's address in Laneia. I hope that won't pose too much of a problem. They said they would have it delivered before dinner."

"Well, good luck. I really have no experience with how things work at Larnaca Airport. Since you had no trouble getting here, I take it you have the rental car I recommended you pick up from *Petsas?*

"Yeah, thanks. That was no problem. They were really good to me there. They even went over the map with me and showed me how to get here according to your instructions. We covered the route from here to Laneia also. I saw the exit for the B-8 going to Troodos on the way here. How long do you think it will take to drive from here to Laneia anyway?"

"It's not a bad drive now that the highway is finished. When I first got here, you had to drive into Limassol and get on the two-lane road to the mountains from there. It seemed to take forever back then. Shouldn't take much more than an hour to get up there now. I saw Gavin when I first got here. It was at the end of last summer and he seemed tired from all the activity that comes with the tourist season. Until he called last week, I hadn't heard from him since that visit."

"Well I'm glad it won't be a bad drive. I'm pretty tired from the flight and the time change. The dry sunny weather sure helps though. So, I guess you're off then?"

Nils pushed his chair back and said, "I'll go in and settle with Jeri before I head back." He rose from the table and passed behind his sister on his way to find Jeri. As Nora got up, he gave her a brotherly hug and said, "I'm glad you came. Really, it's been too long and maybe we need the time together. I don't know?" He turned and headed to the covered part of the tavern and toward the bar area to pay the tab. Nora grabbed her bag, turned and took one last gaze at the early afternoon beach scene and Mediterranean beyond before walking the few dusty yards through the car park to her rented Astra.

As she was opening the door to the car she heard the crunching of footsteps rapidly approaching and turned to see that it was Nils.

Catching his breath Nils stopped short in front of his sister.

"Nora, I almost forgot to ask you. Tomorrow evening there is a cocktail party on back lawn of the Officers' Mess at the base. I would really like you to be my date."

"Oh, Nils I don't know, I just got here. There's the jet lag and I don't even know what Mr. Hart will need from me yet. I don't even know if I will have clean clothes to wear by tomorrow. Can I get back to you?"

Nils knew he could appeal to his sister's sense of spontaneity. "What's the harm, it's just me. If you are worried about clothes, you can stop on your way up to Laneia and pick up what you need. Just say yes. I will have everything arranged at the gate when you arrive. Show up there at around half five in the evening and I will escort you."

He jotted something on a strip of paper and handed it to her. "This is my mobile phone number. I should be at the gate waiting for you as long as you can make it there by quarter to six. If you are later, you can ring me from the gate and it shouldn't take but five minutes for me to reach you."

Nils didn't wait for an answer as he nodded and gave his sister a rare smile before dashing across the car park to his vehicle, leaving her standing next to the open door of the car.

"Nils wait! I just...I mean...."

"Alright Nora, I gotta run. See you tomorrow eve. It will be fun, trust me," shouted Nils through the open window of his car as he sped out of the car park and back to the business of his day on Akrotiri.

On her way to Laneia at the outskirts of Limassol and just before reaching the turnoff from the ring road, Nora noticed a small European style billboard with an image of a woman pushing a shopping cart. The advertisement was for a department store called *Orphanides*. She took the exit and pulled into the paved car park of what looked like a smaller Mediterranean version of Wal-Mart. At the opposite end of the parking area from the main store she noticed there was a McDonalds. "You just can't get away from these things," she thought to herself.

Nora was glad that her first impression of Cyprus was shaped by the time she spent on Curium's beach because as she walked through the glass doors of the *Orphanides* department store, she was assaulted with the sights and sounds that she thought she'd left behind in the malls of Arlington, Virginia. Nora never really learned to enjoy shopping for clothes. During college and during the times she spent overseas as an exchange student and with the Peace Corps, she discovered that a small wardrobe of good quality clothing of neutral colors would go a long way and with appropriate accessories she could meet the demands of any dress code. The added benefit to this practice was that she had more time available for other pursuits and activities that were more interesting than shopping for clothes.

With fatigue setting in, Nora wanted to get the chore of

grabbing some necessities over with quickly. From the shelves of the toiletry aisle she recognized the same name brands for toothpaste and the small sized bottles of shampoo that were available back home. Filling a small basket with the things she needed took no time at all. A clean simple cotton blouse, a change of underwear and maybe some fresh socks took a bit longer, but Nora didn't give the process of selection much thought as she headed for the cashier and grabbed another plastic bottle of water from the small fridge next to the checkout counter.

With her purchases complete she was able to get back on the road, hoping to meet up with Gavin Hart in his gallery before the business day was finished. She realized right then that she had no idea what the gallery's business hours were but quickly came to the conclusion that it didn't matter anyway. She was going to be spending the night in Laneia one way or the other.

CHAPTER 2

Gavin Hart

The road leading to Troodos narrowed and began a climb up a steep ridge. Nora rolled down the front windows to enjoy the fresh cooling breeze that swirled through the car. The road she was on crested and followed a ridge. There was no guardrail or barrier between her and the steep valley to her left. From her vantage point, she took in what seemed like endless terraces of olive groves, carob trees, and the odd lemon tree.

The brightness reflecting off the chalky white color of the rocky soil strained her tired eyes in spite of the Polaroid sunglasses she was wearing. Ahead of her and above in the far distance she could trace the road's winding path into the pine trees towards the rocky slopes of Mount Olympus.

She saw a small signpost on the right that said Laneia 8 km, so she took the sharp turn leading away from the main road toward the village. The terrain was similar to what she had been seeing along the way so far, but as the road took a 90 degree turn to the right, overlooking the terraced slopes below, she was able to take in the expansive view of the Eastern Mediterranean and a good deal of the southern coast line.

Just before she approached what appeared to be the village center where the roads crossed in front of a public fountain, Nora saw what looked like a vintage tour bus. Dusty and dilapidated, it looked like it was once painted an olive green and dark red, and bore the corroding metal letters "Bedford," marking the manufacturer's name across the hood. The bus sported a placard above the windscreen that was rusted but she could still make out the names of the villages the bus must have served in its day, "Paphos-Evdimou-Troodos."

Nora turned left at the intersecting roads in front of the Laneia village fountain. There was a small cafe built of white stones on the opposite corner. The wooden doors and blue painted window shutters were propped open. Instead of cheap white plastic chairs, there were dark wooden four-legged chairs, all of the same basic size, but in varying condition and age, surrounding the five tables in front of the cafe. A sign above the entry had the brand name and logo for *Nescafe* next to in Greek stenciled in baby blue on the stone and concrete of the main structure.

Under the bright sun the geraniums were in full bloom. The bright purple blooms of bougainvillea cascading over the whitewashed walls of the village buildings contrasted against the orange tiled roofs enhancing the dramatic color of the deep blue sky above. Nora knew she was going to enjoy Laneia village.

She drove slowly for another hundred meters up along the village road following the directions Nils gave her. She soon found herself in a more residential area of the village. The road was not paved and there were no sidewalks. The homes were close together and rose up about a half a level from the walled terraces that enclosed each of the family gardens.

There were fig trees in the front and side gardens, and window flower boxes decorated the multi-leveled homes. The smaller single floored buildings all had a front porch with table and chairs beneath overhanging roofs. The village road became very narrow as Nora drove to a "T" intersection. Instead of a street name, bolted to the wall in front of her was a wooden sign in the shape of an arrow pointing to the left that read Hart Gallery. There were other signs mounted all over the same wall pointing to the abodes of other artists and craftsman living in the village.

Nora made a very cautious left turn in the narrow confines and decided that at the first opportunity, she would leave the rental car and walk the remaining distance to the gallery. Just beyond an opening in a low rock wall, Nora parked the car.

Before getting out she grabbed her only bag and stuffed in the contents from the *Orphanides* shopping errand. She slung the bag over her shoulder, locked the car door and strode back the ten meters or so to the opening in the wall, which also served as the entry to the Hart Gallery.

On either side of the gallery entry, large clay terracotta vessels and other Cypriot antiquities adorned the grounds leading into the main building on Gavin Hart's property. Next to the gravel pathway there was green vegetation that couldn't really be called a lawn. In the small yard there were other pieces of vintage artifacts, one looked like part of a marble statue no taller than Nora's waist.

The colors from the flowers in the garden, combined with their sweet aroma along with the singing from several small birds hopping between the branches of a lemon tree, made the place seem like a fantasy. To top things off, lounging beside the statue was a very large ginger colored tiger striped cat lying stretched out on its side. Nora knew she had found the right place and continued up the two small steps leading beneath the overhanging tiled roof to the open double doors of the main gallery.

The floor throughout the main room was a dark hard wood. As she walked in, there were pane glass windows facing south and west and a small wooden desk with a single drawer just to the left of the entry. The walls, or at least what she could see of them, were white washed. There were oil paintings of all sizes hanging on every wall. Most of them were landscapes. There were a few with figures sitting or standing near the shore in coastal village.

Near the back and to the right there was a single hardwood step and an arched passageway leading to another room. Nora could see there were lights on in the room around the corner to the right. As she stepped closer to the back room, the floor creaked several times.

"Right then! I can hear you. I will be with you momentarily." The voice from the back was just loud enough for Nora to make out the rough British accent, which sounded to her as if it came from an aged man.

"…Or you can come on back if you like." He said this slowly and deliberately as if he were concentrating on something.

"It's me, Nora Johansson," she said, as she stepped up into the back room. This space was bigger and longer, but not as wide as the first room. It had a row of windows at one end. The walls were adorned with watercolor paintings illustrating local scenes. Nora looked in both directions to find her host.

"Oh Miss Johansson, so good of you to have finally made it. I was expecting you yesterday." A large man, just over six feet, with greying dark curly hair tied in a ponytail and a scruffy beard stood before an easel holding a small artist's sponge in his right hand. There was a lamp in the back corner aimed at the canvas board in front of him and a window just in front of the easel that looked out into the front garden.

"Please forgive me while I finish up here. I was preparing to leave earlier today and I must have gotten the dates mixed up with respect to your arrival. I called your brother this morning because I was worried. He said you'd be here in the afternoon. Such a relief...as it were." He put the sponge down and wiped both his hands down the sides of his khaki trousers. He was wearing a baggy blue denim shirt with the long sleeves rolled up above the elbow. On his feet were dark brown sandals that looked like Birkenstock knock offs. He stretched his hand out to Nora.

"Gavin Hart. Pleased to meet you young lady. Your dad and I go back a long way."

"Mr. Hart, I guess you already know me then. My full name…."

"Yes, Kiraz. I know quite a bit about you indeed, and please call me Gavin. I knew your mother also, but not well. We met when your father introduced us during one of their visits to Laneia years ago before I had all of this. Enough about that for now. Where are your things? I can help you get settled."

"Please Mr. Hart, I mean Gavin. Nobody calls me Kiraz. I go by Nora," she said.

"Right then. Nora it is. Allow me to help you get situated."

"The airline misplaced my luggage. They promised it would be delivered sometime this evening."

Gavin gave her an exaggerated guffaw, "Really, they 'promised'? Where did you tell them your bags would need to be delivered?"

"I gave them your address here in Laneia. I also gave them your telephone number. Should I have done something else?"

"No. Under the circumstances there wouldn't be anything else you could do. They won't be calling and your things won't be delivered here either. Not a worry though. I'll tell you

what…I will call the airline. We will see what can be arranged."
Gavin turned around and switched off the lamp.

"Come this way," he said as they made their way toward the
room with the telephone. Nora stopped short before returning
to the lower main gallery room. In front of her were a series of
watercolor paintings in tones of sky blue, sand, and olive greens.
The color hues in each of the paintings seemed to bathe every
scene in sunshine. She thought the artist was a master at
contrasting the landscapes with the cobalt shades of the sea that
washed the Cypriot coast.

Gavin stepped behind the small wooden desk near the entry
doors, and located the antiquated old British black rotary phone.
Before picking it up he noticed Nora still on the upper landing
looking mesmerized by the watercolor painting hanging in front
of her on the wall.

"You see something you fancy?" he asked trying to get
Nora's attention back to the task at hand.

"No…I mean yes. These look familiar." There were three
paintings in all, illustrating what appeared to be a secluded bay
with a few small buildings and an empty stretch of beach. Each
of them portrayed the same scene but from a different location.
In one of them there was a pair of figures near the edge in the
lower left. A man was standing on a flat rock where a woman sat
with her skirt pulled into her lap while her bare feet dangled in
the aquiline sea. The impression suggested the man was holding

the woman's sandals.

"I know this place, these colors and these scenes," Nora said to herself.

Since she was still staring at the paintings on the wall, Gavin walked back over to her. He gently eased her by the shoulders and turned her toward him. Nora could see he was smiling from the corners of his deep-set dark eyes.

"Your dad and mum made a most unusual couple. I met them in the late summer of 1970. August actually. The tourist season here on the mountain was coming to a close. I had a flat, or more like a room above the coffee house around the corner. Back then I spent my days with an easel, brush, and pallet, mostly here in the village with some of the other fledgling artists that wound up in Laneia. None of us had a car in those days. Did you see the 'Cyprus Village Bus' parked beside the stone wall as you came into the main square?"

"Yes. It looks as if it hasn't been working for years. All the tires are flat."

"That bus, young lady is one of the village treasures. There is a small group of tractor mechanics that bought it and plan to restore it so that it can be used as a tourist vehicle. Anyway, that is the very bus that I used to take into Limassol or over to Paphos during the week when I wanted to get away and do some painting."

"What has that got to do with meeting my parents?" Nora

could see that the artist was getting lost in the past. His mind seemed to be wandering through the days of his youth.

"Oh, I'm sorry I do digress. Where were we? Yes the luggage. Let us make that call to the airport shall we?"

"No, not yet. Please you were about to tell me about the paintings and meeting my parents." Nora felt she was getting closer to the thought that was nagging in her memory and learning why these paintings seemed so familiar. She couldn't move herself from looking at them.

"Oh, yes. Late August, maybe it was September. I remember the first impression your dad made. I was sitting on the low wall near the fountain in the village square doodling as I call it. During the fall season in the late afternoon, the colors can be spectacular. I had a small board on my lap and I heard the distinct accent of an American so I looked up. Standing there over my shoulder was this tall blond man. On his arm was the most beautiful, petite, dark haired Cypriot woman slightly younger than him. Both watching what I was doing. I looked up at them and simply said hello.

Your dad introduced himself. He told me his name was Sven and then proudly introduced the young woman, Hanife. I don't remember the whole conversation. It was a long time ago, but I can tell you why you may know these paintings.

As she looked on at my doodling, Hanife said she loved the colors. She said they reminded her of the Cyprus that makes her feel like she is 'home.' I don't know what she may have meant by that. As I said earlier, I didn't know your mother. Your dad asked me if I ever did any work on commission. At the time nobody had ever asked me that, but I said, yes of course. You know, starving artist and all of that."

Nora was enjoying the story about Gavin meeting her parents. It transported her to a different time. She was thrilled to be in the same village where all of them met. "Where is this place Gavin? The place in the paintings I mean."

"Melanda Bay. I didn't know the place until that week when I met your mum and dad. I could tell the both of them were 'together.' Your mum had a glow about her. She held your father's arm and leaned into his shoulder as we chatted. Your father was proud and confident to have the affection of such a lovely lady.

Nora, please do not take this the wrong way, but your mother was…well, I couldn't keep my eyes from her. She had fine features, a triangular and very petite chin and the most shiny, silken waves of dark chestnut brown hair. Beautiful teeth too, and rare for a local girl in those days. Her eyes, yes she had big walnut colored almond shaped eyes. You have your mother's eyes Nora, only not as dark." He looked at her and nodded.

"Please Gavin, go on. I really love hearing about how they were. You were so lucky to have seen them both together."

Gavin's eyes misted and he looked away from her, "I'm sorry

Nora. I heard what happened to your mum. Your dad came to visit shortly after you were born. Maybe a month later. Business he told me. I never got to congratulate him on becoming the father of twins. He was choked up when he told me about your mother. Sad story that. Again, Nora, I am sorry you never got to meet your mother. From what I knew of her, she was a wonderful and beautiful woman."

"You were saying about my dad and mom in the village the day you met."

Collecting himself again with a renewed smile Gavin continued, "Well then, your dad, he asked me if I had ever been to Melanda Bay. I told him I'd never heard of it. Then he asked how much it would cost if I painted a scene of Melanda Bay for him. I quoted a price. I don't remember what it was. He gave me directions so that I could find the place, handed me fifty Cypriot pounds, which was more money than I had seen in one go up to that time. He said he would be back in a week or two to pick up the painting and would give me the rest of the commission at that time."

Now almost completely transfixed, with a whispering monotone, Nora said, "I know it now. I know this place, this painting. It hung in our dining room when I was very young. I remember imagining being inside the scene, playing in the sand close to the water under the warmth of the sun. Over the years, I don't know what my dad did with the painting. We moved a few times and then when I came home from school only at the holidays, it seemed like I was visiting someone else's home. Once we left for college Nils and I really had no where we thought of as home."

Gavin stood and touched his hand to Nora's shoulder. "Let's make that phone call shall we? We will sort out your things and I can show you the rest of the place and where you will be staying."

"That would be nice. I must say I am really very tired."

Gavin made the call to the airline. Looking over to Nora he said, "Right, how many bags did you have?"

"Just the one."

"Yes, that is correct, just the one bag…." Amidst the unfamiliar Greek, that Nora heard Gavin using her entire name to confirm with the airline desk clerk, that the bag they were discussing was indeed hers.

When he was finished with the call he glanced at what looked like an ancient wristwatch and noticed it was getting on past six o'clock. He then looked to Nora, "Good news, your bag just arrived. Bad news is that at this hour it doesn't make a lot of sense to head all the way back to Larnaca to pick it up. Even if we left right now, it would be well past ten o'clock by the time we returned. Besides, I have another deal to strike with you."

"What might that be?" As he lead Nora out of the main gallery building to a staircase leading to an upstairs apartment and guest room, Gavin explained that he was scheduled to leave for the UK mid-morning and proposed that Nora accompany him to the airport, leave him off and retrieve her bag in one trip. "Ok that sounds like it will work out. Will we have enough time to go over all the details for running the gallery while you are away?"

"We can get to that. Nothing to it really." Gavin pushed open a door immediately to the right of a narrow hallway at the top of the stairs.

In the guest room there was a small dark wood table with an antique lamp and matching chair, it looked like it served as a desk. The single bed rested on a heavy dark wood frame matching a small shoulder high wardrobe cabinet propped against the right-hand wall. Next to the bed was a modern standing lamp for reading. It looked slightly out of place in the otherwise traditionally furnished Cypriot home.

Gavin leaned on the doorjamb with his back to the wall and watched while Nora pushed aside the sheer lace curtains shading a pair of French doors. She turned the door latch, pushed them both open and stepped onto a small wooden balcony with a view to the south and west looking down the ridge slope to the sea with the center of Laneia village off to the left.

"What do you think?"

"About the room, the view, or my running your gallery while you're away? Sorry, I am really beat. If we are going to head off to the airport in the morning I feel like there won't be enough time to go over everything."

"Its OK. Even though you might be completely knackered, you don't want to let yourself nod off just yet, as you know with the jet lag you'll be a mess at about two in the morning. The loo is just across the hall here. If you want to freshen up, there are fresh towels, soap and a washrag in the cupboard next to the shower. I will leave you to it. I will be downstairs if you need anything. In fact I'll put the kettle on. A brisk cup of herb tea will do you good. Then we can go over the essentials, like feeding the cat and keeping the place from burning down while I'm gone."

"Thanks Gavin. I'll be down in a bit."

Nora took a refreshing shower, first with lukewarm, then cold, and then satisfyingly warm water. After she dried off, she located the few things she bought at the *Orphanides* and put them on feeling slightly rejuvenated. She unwrapped the towel from atop her head and ran a comb through her hair while it was still damp, and let it dry naturally. She had learned the futility of traveling with a blow dryer, especially in austere locations during her internships and time with the Peace Corps.

By the time she came down stairs the sun had set. She found Gavin sitting in a large kitchen area with a cup of tea sitting on a thick wooden butcher-block table in front of him. The only light came from a hanging lamp in the corner where it illuminated a large countertop lined with small jars of native herbs and spices.

Hearing her approach, Gavin looked up from the yellow pad of paper he was jotting notes on. "Feeling better I imagine. You certainly look relaxed."

"Yes much better."

"There's a cup on the counter behind you. Tea bags are in the tin near the back wall there and you'll find the kettle on the stove just there. Mind the hot water when you pour, I just switched off the flame."

Nora prepared the tea before pulling up a chair across from Gavin.

"Milk? Sugar?"

"No, nothing thanks. This will be fine just as it is. It feels good to be in one place. I should have commented earlier on what a lovely spot this is. It is so quiet."

Gavin lifted the pen he was using to write on the yellow pad. He rolled it between his fingers staring at it and said, "I didn't get to ask you how your father is doing. When did you see him last?"

"He's doing as well as can be expected. I saw him yesterday...I mean the day before I left to come here, whenever that was. He was just home from a recent treatment. He looks so old and frail."

Sven Johansson contracted an aggressive form of skin cancer

on his left arm, shoulder and neck while he was working as a civil servant working in the planning division at Offutt AFB. The cause was attributed to the time he spent flying the U-2 at the edge of the atmosphere, unprotected from the sun's damaging rays.

He kept this news from his children because he didn't want to burden them with serious family issues as they headed out the door for college. He was immediately medically retired from his civil service position following the initial diagnosis.

With Nils and Nora out of the house, he decided it would be easier on everyone if he moved closer to the Bethesda Naval hospital in D.C. where he was receiving treatment. Before that, he had been living next door to his younger sister Ronella to provide close moral support after her husband was declared MIA. It turned out that his sister "Roni" provided him with a great deal of support while he raised his children as a single father. Roni finally met a Swedish gentleman she could call her soul mate at around the same time Sven left for D.C., which made his decision to move on a lot easier.

"I'm sorry. You know, he was here in Cyprus shortly after he was diagnosed. I'm not sure exactly why he came back. Maybe to keep some sort of spiritual connection. He told me he didn't think he had much time. That was over six years ago. A lot was happening in his life back then. I guess it is good that doctors can sometimes be wrong…or maybe that stubborn old

Sven just can't be beaten by melanoma."

"Gavin, he looks like he's been beaten by life in general. The treatments have taken their toll. I'm just glad he's in his own place and able to take care of himself. The man doesn't have many friends."

"Well, he's a good man and a good friend of mine. You tell him that for me when you head back home in a few weeks. Right, well you are indeed looking quite knackered and we need to go over a few things here. Tomorrow morning will be on us before you know it."

He put his pen down, pushed the yellow pad across the table and turned it so Nora could follow his explanation of each of the items he wrote down.

Starting at the top he pointed to each of them, "This is the number where I can be reached, but please, don't call unless the place is crumbling in an earthquake." Pointing to the next item, "This address belongs to a young bloke here in the village by the name of Aydın. His place is two doors down from the coffee house on the opposite side of the street. He can assist with anything with regards to the property. Water heater, gas line, plumbing problem and the like. He also knows my business quite well should there be any inquiry about art shows from the local hotels. Best you just get a name and number if anyone is interested in an exhibition and I will sort that out when I return. Oh, and I nearly forgot, Aydın can be a trusted interpreter if you have difficulty making any type of arrangement with the local villagers. Everyone here knows him and for whatever reason, they all seem to like him.

For meals, you can find anything you'll need right here in the village. There is a morning market in the square on Mondays. The coffee house has a wallboard that never seems to get updated but sometimes there are useful announcements about local events. You can always ask Elias, the coffee house owner, if you need anything and he will know where to direct you.

There aren't really any eating establishments here. You'll see tables and chairs in front of a few of the village homes. When the doors and windows are open, the smell of baking bread is the hint that you could buy a dinner just by asking.

Just replace whatever you use in the house. The phone is good for use anywhere on the island. You'll need to locate a phone box to use an overseas calling card. There is one in the square across from the fountain. The smoke shop doesn't have a sign, but you'll recognize it by the postcard rack out front when it is open. You can get a calling card there. Well, I think that should be enough to make your stay a pleasant one."

"Thanks, I think I can do this, but what about the art, the gallery?"

"Right, the art. I wish I could tell you not to sell anything, but then how would I make a living?" He pushed his chair back and went to the sink to rinse out his tea mug. "Come, I will show you just what to do."

Nora rose from her chair and picked up her mug cradling it in both hands to steady the remaining liquid, still steaming hot and not quite ready to drink much of it. She followed Gavin out of the kitchen and back into the main gallery. Small recessed state of the art spotlights in the wood ceiling illuminated each of the oil paintings when he switched on the lights. The room looked amazing. Each of the pieces took on a life that Nora didn't notice when she walked through the same room earlier in the day.

Gavin reached for a medium sized painting framed in a dark hardwood. It was a landscape of some dark rock crags set on a hillside overlooking the sea with wildflowers in the foreground. He lifted the framed oil painting from the wall and flipped it over.

"All the pieces have a tagger on them. I have taken the pains to be sure that the tags on all the paintings are at the lower left corner at the back. In the drawer of the desk you'll find a small portfolio with photographs of everything that is for sale along with the prices. Get to know the content of the portfolio and you won't have to remove the painting from the wall to find out the value I put on it. I only accept cash. Cypriot or British Pounds. No exceptions, and the prices are not negotiable under any circumstances."

"Clear enough," said Nora still looking at the price when

Gavin flipped the frame back over and mounted it back in its place on the wall. The tag specified £350. "What sort of customers do you usually get who can afford to pull that kind of cash from their wallet?"

"Oh, all sorts really. You'd be surprised what tourists carry on them when they come up here. Young Russian men who want to impress their women sometimes buy several pieces. I've also had local restaurants and hotels commission projects. Most of the buyers are repeat visitors. People who browse and discover something they like, often return later to purchase it. The arrangement is simple and my rules have worked for me so far."

"OK, that sounds good and the money? Is there a local bank where I should be making deposits? Gavin really, I'm not too thrilled at the prospect of having a bunch of cash around for the taking."

"Oh, girl, you've spent too much time in the big city. First off, the season hasn't started yet. I don't expect much in the way of sales while I'm away. If you are at all uncomfortable, Aydın can show you the bank where I keep an account. It really isn't like the Wild West here on Cyprus. You'll see."

They walked back out of the main gallery. Gavin switched off the lights and they both headed back into the adjoining cottage. Gavin reached for Nora's tea mug, "I'll take this for you. I know you're probably ready to sleep off some of the jet lag by now. I'll see you in the morning. Sleep well."

"Thanks. You'll wake me then?"

"If necessary, yes, but I suspect I'll find you down here before the sun rises. Sleep well."

CHAPTER 3

Aydın Kostas

Nora had finally fallen back asleep after having spent what seemed like an eternity staring at the ceiling at three a.m. She awoke to the songs of local thrushes, finches, and Spanish sparrows. Sunlight poured through the lace curtains drawn across the balcony doors. She also heard kitchen sounds coming from below and decided she was awake enough for what the day had in store.

After freshening up and getting dressed she saw Gavin in the kitchen. "Good morning." She noticed that Gavin was dressed smartly in dark creased slacks, an ironed shirt, and polished leather street shoes. His small roller bag was already packed and standing by the open door.

"*Kalimera.*" Gavin was standing at the counter shifting portions of eggs, and a stir-fry of potatoes and local vegetables between the stove and the two plates he was preparing on the counter. "I take it you slept rather well. You are looking bright this morning."

"Yes thanks. You're sure looking all spiffed up this morning. I am famished though. With the traveling, my times are all mixed up and I wasn't really hungry when I arrived."

"Well young lady you are in luck. I hope you like fresh scrambled eggs. The potatoes are from the winter garden and the rest is from the local market." He then opened the small refrigerator beneath the counter to the left of the stove and pulled out a ceramic pitcher. He grabbed two beakers from the shelf over the counter and set them both, along with the pitcher, on the wooden table in the center of the room.

"This is some squash I made from fresh lemon and orange."

Just then they both heard the sound of a young man whistling as he walked briskly up the path to the covered porch in front of the open kitchen door. "Ah yes, Aydın. *Kalimera*, you are just in time."

"*Ghiasas* my friend!" In one hand Aydın held a tray. On it there were three small cups of Cypriot coffee. In his other hand he held a loaf of local bread producing an aroma that suggested it came fresh from the oven just moments earlier.

Nora never formed the habit of taking notice of young men. Sure she had relationships in her young life, but none lasted and she rarely made the effort. Her brother Nils thought her lack of interest stemmed from the absence of role models. Even though there was a regular female presence around in the form of their aunt Roni, the relationship they witnessed as children was a tense one between an adult brother and a sister rather than a healthy marriage.

When Aydın set his morning treasures on the table, his toothy smile lit up the entire room and Nora couldn't help but notice that the young man standing in front of the table looked like he'd just stepped out of a photo shoot from GQ magazine. Aydın Galen Kostas stood just under six feet tall. Covering his lean form were starched faded jeans and a crisp white cotton shirt that complimented his long dark curly hair and Mediterranean facial features.

Gavin turned and set both plates of breakfast items on the table and said, "Aydın, this is Nora. Nora, meet Aydın, the young man I mentioned last night who can assist you with just about anything here in Laneia. As you can see, he is pretty reliable with the morning coffee."

"*Kalimera* Miss Nora. Pleased to meet you."

"*Efharisto, Posise?*"

"Fine, thank you, such a surprise, an American that speaks Greek!"

"Just a few words Aydın. That's all, I love languages and try to learn a few polite expressions whenever I travel abroad."

With an even bigger smile, Aydın said, "That is so nice. Most tourists in Cyprus don't bother. Almost everyone speaks English anyway."

"Aydın, please sit down. Have you had breakfast yet?" asked Gavin.

"Yes I have, thanks, I just wanted to bring the coffee. I knew you had a house guest."

Turning to Nora, "Aydın here came to Laneia when he was a young boy. He grew up in a village northwest of Limassol.

Traditional villages in those days often had different names for each of the spoken languages. His village is called Çanakkale or Kantou. Not much left of it these days."

"Where are your family, your mom and dad?"

"It's complicated to explain. Maybe another time."

"I'm sorry, I didn't mean to pry," said Nora.

"No problem. I don't take it that way." Aydın pushed his chair back from the table and finished his Cypriot coffee. "How's the coffee? Do you like it?"

"It's strong but I'm getting used to it. You prepared it *metreo*. I do like it this way." Nora was famished and really dove into her breakfast. "This is so good Gavin. I'm not sure what I will do after you leave."

"You'll manage I am sure." Finishing up his eggs, Gavin stood and carried the dishes and glasses to the sink and began preparing a bin with dish soap and hot water.

"Gavin, please, I can do that when I get back from the airport. You're dressed so smart I wouldn't want you to get anything on your nice shirt. Really, I don't mind taking care of everything when I get back."

Gavin looked to Aydın, "Well young man, what will you be doing this day?"

"I have a few errands, but they can wait." Aydın turned and looked through the open doorway to the front garden where he focused on an ancient terra cotta vase. "Are you going to be told to return the artifacts?"

"I don't think so. I just want this business to be resolved. I find it hard to believe this has become such a big issue. I was saving these things from decay and preserving them better than any museum and now...." Gavin shook his head slowly. "Would you mind staying and holding down the fort here while Nora takes me to the airport? With so much attention on the items in the garden over the past couple of weeks, I don't think it would be a good idea to leave the place unattended just yet."

"No problem. I'll just be back up to the cafe and then return. When do you need to leave?"

Gavin looked at the ancient Bulova on his wrist. "My, it is that time. Nora, shall we?"

"I'm ready. I just need to grab my bag with the paperwork from the airline. Did they say where I needed to go to pick my bag up?"

"Yes, I'll show you when we get there. It shouldn't be difficult. Aydın, we are off. I will see you in a couple of weeks."

"*Malista, ghiasas.*"

"*Ghiasas.*"

Gavin grabbed the bag by the door and headed out with Nora catching up. He looked over his shoulder to her. "You're driving."

"OK, I think I know the way. I left the car just down the drive next to the stone wall."

"I'll just drop this in the boot." Gavin unlatched the trunk and dropped his roller bag in, then lowered himself into the passenger seat waiting for Nora to strap in.

It only took a couple of turns for Nora to find her way back to the road leading down the mountain. While they drove, Gavin Hart seemed lost in thought.

Breaking the silence Nora asked Gavin, "I noticed the antiquities in the gallery's front garden when I arrived. They are wonderful. What is the issue with them that you and Aydın were discussing just as we were leaving?"

"It is maybe more complicated than it needs to be, and honestly I don't understand any of it. One of the reasons for this trip is to revalidate my visa. The other is that I am working on obtaining my Cypriot citizenship and I need to return to the U.K. to retrieve some documents I left with a distant relative."

"You are going to become a Cypriot? Isn't that a lot of trouble?"

"No more trouble than the legal battle I have become embroiled in as a result of rescuing the artifacts."

"I don't understand."

"You saw the painting of the rocks…the one I showed you last evening when we were going over the gallery operation?"

"Yes, an unusual scene. I remember."

"Well my dear, that landscape is from a piece of property I own up on the Akamas peninsula. Shortly after I purchased it a few years back, I discovered several of the pieces that are now in the Laneia garden.

Those pieces were scattered about and deteriorating. I asked around and made the mistake of involving the Cypriot Museum Counsel and the Ministry of Antiquities. Nothing was being done to preserve any of the items. I found them scattered about and deteriorating, so I took matters into my own and rescued them."

"Why should that be such a problem?" Nora asked as she maneuvered the car onto the new highway bypass north of Limassol.

"Well first of all, I think I did the right thing. I was told that only a Cypriot citizen could possess historical artifacts. I offered to return the items to their original resting place but knew that wasn't the answer to resolving this issue and was later told that since they were already disturbed, returning them wasn't an option. So I find myself in this conundrum with one logical solution."

"I guess that makes sense. At least it explains your pursuit of citizenship."

"The change of citizenship will save me some money and trouble in the long run. You see, I have no ties to England and really have no intention of ever living there again. Cyprus has become my home."

"Aren't you concerned about the stability of the government

here?"

"Now why would you ask that? Look around you. Does the peace of this lovely island and the integrity of this highway give you any reason to suspect there is a stability problem with the government? I'm not at all worried."

"I guess I really don't know that much about it. Just some things I remembered from one of my journalism courses in school. The conflicts of the '70s and the complicated arrangement of government, plus the fact that there is a divided capitol come to mind. I'm not sure what that would mean to me if I were in your shoes contemplating living here."

"That is perfectly understandable. However, as an artist I'm focused on the beauty of the place. I get a strong sense of deep-rooted history that lives and breathes here. It inspires me. Perhaps you'll have similar experiences after you spend some time here."

Traffic was light on the highway for a Wednesday morning. Gavin pointed out several landmarks along the drive while passing north of Limassol, giving her a sense of orientation. The stretch leading to Larnaca passed through low open country.

"These large expensive looking villas next to the highway are all owned by Russians. They came here only recently in the last three or four years when the Cypriot government relaxed some of the trade policies. Lots of Russian money has come to the island recently."

"Why do they build these lovely homes right next to the freeway, if they could afford to build them where it is more quiet and peaceful?"

"Because they want everyone to see what they have."

Nora continued driving in silence, absorbing the contrast between the landscape and the ridiculous looking Russian properties they passed by.

Larnaca International Airport is on a flat strip of low rocky coastline surrounded by a marshy lagoon. The morning air was still and thick with humidity. The small airport parking area is conveniently close to the single level terminal. Nora parked a couple hundred meters from the front doors. Gavin grabbed his roller bag from the boot of the hire car and the two of them walked to the terminal. Inside, Gavin led Nora over to the Lufthansa counter.

After the attendant located her bag, Nora was able to quickly sort out the remaining paperwork. Satisfied that everything was going to be fine, Gavin turned to her and said, "Well my dear. That should do it then. I trust you'll be able to find your way back to the main road and return to Laneia without too much difficulty."

"Thanks Gavin, I'm already starting to feel pretty comfortable getting around. Don't worry about your gallery or your cat. By the way, what is his name?"

"*Kızıl Kaplan.* To match his markings. It means…"

"Yes, 'Red Tiger.' I know it. Why Turkish?"

"I didn't know it was Turkish. One of the villagers called him that when he was a kitten and it stuck. I just call him Kaplan."

"Well, you don't need to worry about him or anything else while you're away. I want to thank you for inviting me."

"Technically, I didn't invite you. Your brother did. But nonetheless, I am glad you'll be the one looking after the place. You have a enjoyable stay." Gavin then gave Nora a hug and an "air kiss" before turning to enter the airport security area.

Nora trundled her medium sized bag out of the terminal and to the rented Astra where she slung it into the back seat before driving back out to the main road and west toward Limassol. Even though she slept well the night before, it was only her second day on the island and the jet lag was really setting in. It was already late morning as she headed back on the road to Laneia.

From the main highway leading west to Limassol, she could see the Mediterranean coastline. There was an exit sign for Amathus Beach and a billboard for the Amathus Beach Hotel right next to it. The picture on the billboard showed a couple sitting at an umbrella table near the water having a meal. Nora decided to take a brief detour for a coffee and took the exit.

Nora was thinking to herself, either these sunglasses aren't strong enough, or it is really very bright, or I am really tired…and

I still need to be at Akrotiri for a silly cocktailé.

She finished the last of her *metreo* coffee feeling somewhat fortified, then got up to pay the tab, and drove the rest of the way back to the gallery in Laneia.

As she carried her single piece of luggage up the stone path to the main house, Nora noticed all the doors to the gallery were opened and the lights were on in the back rooms. Gavin's cat, Kaplan was sprawled out beneath the covered front porch basking in a ray of sunlight that angled its way beneath the roofline. Just at that moment, she remembered that Aydın had agreed to watch after the gallery while she was dropping Gavin off at the airport. Aydın emerged from the back rooms carrying a small bucket and some cleaning supplies suggesting that he had been cleaning the windows.

"When the windows are dusty, the natural light doesn't do justice to the art. I love Gavin's work. I find it inspiring, even though it isn't my style. Welcome back to your new home Nora. You must be feeling like you need a rest after all the trips to and from the airport. I'll just leave you to it."

She set her bag at the bottom of the stairs inside the main house and turned to Aydın who was beneath the threshold of the gallery doorway. "Thanks. It doesn't feel quite like home to me yet though. I will say though, that it is somewhat like a dream being here. I could get attached to this place."

Aydın bent down to give Kaplan a good belly scratch.

Afterward, the ginger colored cat rolled over twice, then got up and hopped onto a padded wooden chair next to the reception table just inside the door. "He's a good friend to everyone who comes here. He is never too far from people. When there is nobody here, he will go to the neighbors just to be near people. Don't be surprised if you find him sleeping on the bed with you at night." He approached Nora who was still standing in the doorway to the main house.

"I'll just put these back inside," he said lifting the cleaning supplies and bucket.

" Gosh, Aydın, excuse me, please go ahead." Realizing she was blocking the doorway, Nora stepped aside.

"I don't have a telephone. Most people in this village don't. You know where to find me if you need something?"

"Gavin showed me on our way out this morning. Thanks."

He emptied the bucket of water into the large utility sink in the kitchen and put the supplies back in a corner closet. He then wiped the dampness from his hands and turned to leave. "I'll drop by tomorrow afternoon sometime and see how you are doing. OK?"

"It's OK Aydın. You don't need…"

"No, really I don't mind, unless you prefer not to be bothered. I would understand."

"That would be fine Aydın. You don't impress me as the type to be a bother."

He seemed so easy going, relaxed and happy, smiling all the time. At least the brief times she'd been with him just this morning.

"Bye-bye for now my new friend. See you tomorrow."

"Oh, one last thing Aydın. I am heading out again late this afternoon. Gavin didn't really tell me anything about securing the gallery."

"I think he just wants you to treat the place like your own home. You go out, you close the door. No big thing." Laughing and shaking his head Aydın reminded her, "Things don't work that way here. Really you don't need to worry."

"But you stayed here all day because of the artifacts in the garden. I don't understand." She said.

"If they were going to come, they would have come right after Gavin left. Besides it is getting late. Those people he was worried about work on a government clock."

"Keys? He didn't explain anything about locking up."

"We don't lock our doors in this village. Everyone knows everyone. An art thief would have trouble getting very far stealing paintings from this village." He said this over his shoulder as he walked out the door.

Nora remained still and watched as he took up a casual pace striding along the stone path leading out of the garden. What a nice guy. Good looking in his jeans too, she thought. She picked up her bag and headed upstairs to arrange her things before laying down on the bed for a short rest.

Awhile later she awoke to a warm breeze rustling the sheer curtains as it blew through the partially opened double doors to the balcony.

"Shit, it must be late. I need to get myself together," she said to herself aloud. Noticing the time on her travel alarm clock next to the bed, she dashed across the hall to turn on the shower for a quick rinse. While drying off she drew out the only nice eveningwear she brought along and got herself ready for the evening with her brother.

Chapter 4

Akrotiri

Nora rarely caught herself rushing. Once she was set for the trip down the mountain to Akrotiri, she realized she had plenty of time. For a quiet stay on a Mediterranean island, she was beginning to realize that her first twenty-four hours had been mostly taken up by road trips in the car. "What the hell am I doing?" she thought to herself. "I've been here for just a little more than a day and I am going to have to 'play act' my way through a cocktail party...oh what fun. I sure hope Nils is in a better mood."

She saw the sign for Akrotiri SBA and took the exit from the main highway. The road to RAF Akrotiri took a stair step series of ninety-degree turns through grapefruit orchards. The afternoon winds were settling into a soft evening breeze out of the west and the low sun was casting long shadows.

Heading almost directly into the sun, she entered a long stretch of road bounded by eucalyptus and cypress trees creating a tunnel of vegetation. At the end of the tree tunnel, the road turned sharply to the left and the view opened wide to expose a massive field of radio antennas on either side of the road. To the left was a dry salt lake and to the right some low bondu scrub brush leading to a ridge of rock-strewn sand dunes creating a barrier that protected the low landscape from the wave action of the sea.

As promised her brother was waiting for her at the front gate of RAF Akrotiri. Nils opened the passenger side door and handed her the temporary vehicle pass he had prepared in advance.

"Nils, you look so, I don't know the words to describe…dashing?"

Nils was dressed in a lightweight grey suit, starched white shirt and a tie that subtly matched the seasonal colors and mood for such an evening.

"You like my monkey suit? It is part of the uniform for these kinds of occasions. Thanks for coming. It would have been really disappointing if you stood me up."

With no choices but to go straight ahead, Nora drove on past a set of low buildings on her left and in front of her was a display of a cold war era British "Lightning Jet" mounted on a pedestal. They continued on for about a half a kilometer before the road bent to the right.

"Just keep going. The mess will be up ahead on the right. Just to your left there are our blocks."

"Blocks?" replied Nora.

"Yeah, blocks. That is what they call the single level colonial style apartment buildings. I live half way down the one in the middle with the fence around it. It isn't much of a place. I can show you later."

As they pulled into the small parking area in front of the Officers' Mess, there were groups of smartly dressed couples walking up the paved path to the main door, a large heavy wood double wide opening, its exterior covered by extensive bougainvillea in full bloom. Nils led his sister through the main lobby area and through the bar to the back patio. The fading golden light of the evening made the back lawn look very inviting.

"I'll get us some drinks. What would you like?"

"An iced tea would be nice, thanks."

"Be right back." Nils headed over to the corner bar on the patio leaving Nora to take everything in. Strangely she didn't feel the least abandoned standing alone in the middle of the patio.

"I'll show you. Right here where this lovely young lady is standing. See. See how the marble tiles are a different shade than all the others?" An older British officer wearing the rank of Wing Commander and holding a slim glass of scotch was reminiscing to a younger RAF Flight Lieutenant about a wild night many years ago.

"Excuse me miss, but do you know that you are standing in a sacred spot?" The Wing Commander was on the verge of slurring his words.

"I'm sorry, no. I didn't know." Slightly perplexed, she stepped back and to the side looking at the marble patio tiles. Both of the officers looked at each other and gave a short belly laugh.

"Ah, a 'Yank.' We don't often have such lovely American women here with Olive Harvest."

"Olive Harvest? I don't know what that is. My brother invited me."

"Right. Your Yank brother is the spy from Olive Harvest then. I was just telling my mate here about the night my squadron mates got me drunk at a wedding and we burned the piano from the bar right here in this spot." He turned to the younger officer, "Brownie, can you picture it. A bunch of sloshed boys pouring glasses of perfectly good whisky all over the piano. I lost my favorite Zippo that night. Must of tossed it while lighting the liqueur. Well, that was a few years back anyway."

Nils approached the two officers from behind and eyed his sister, now looking a bit perplexed. He gave them a nod as he slipped around them. "These blokes don't have you taking the Mickey do they?" He asked her as he handed her the iced tea.

Nils took a sip of his gin and said, "Sir, this is my sis, Nora. Nora, this is Wing Commander Alastair Clark. We occasionally compare notes. The Wing Commander has pulled quite a few strings for us, so in spite of the fact that we are two countries separated by a common language, I believe we have a pretty good working relationship. Don't we sir?"

"Very pleased to meet you," said the Wing Commander as

he greeted Nora. "Did you know your brother is a wizard? I can't tell you more than that or I'd have to kill you, but I will say that he's managed to work his way to our good side." Turning to the younger officer, "Brownie here just got hired aboard the Red Arrows. Out here doing some reconnaissance for the air show this summer."

"Red Arrows?" asked Nora.

"Yes ma m. An air demonstration team." The younger officer reached for Nora's hand, gently lifted it to his lips and gave her hand a kiss. "A pleasure to meet you. Rodney Brown at your service. I take it you are familiar with aerobatic jets. We fly pretty close to each other and put on shows. A bit of a thrill actually. I'm the low man on the pole, which gives me the pleasure of traveling around before hand in order to meet engaging beauties like you. Perhaps you'd enjoy a flight with us. The Hawk is a two seater."

Nils gently took his sister by the elbow and excused them from the two drunken officers. "Gentlemen, Nora and I both thank you for the kind offer. However, at the moment, there is an important person who is leaving soon and I need Nora to meet him."

Nils often became uncomfortable socializing with military pilots in these settings. He spent his childhood yearning to fly jets like his father did. His dream was to attend the Air Force Academy, work his tail off and get his choice of assignments after pilot training. He instinctually knew it was his calling.

If his older sister hadn't interfered with his application package to the academy, he'd be wearing the wings of a USAF pilot right now, but instead he had to settle for an ROTC commission and a degree from the University of Nebraska. Even though he had a slot for pilot training, his entry into pilot training was delayed due to Air Force personnel reductions. Nils elected to pursue his only other military interest by joining the ranks of the national intelligence community.

The two RAF pilots liked Nils. The older of the two shouted toward him, "Right mate. Don't forget who's got your backside."

"You sir, always, and I don't forget much. I'll catch up with you later." Nils and Nora then headed straight for the only person in the vicinity wearing a uniform of the United States.

Colonel Jake Barrows, the US Defense Attaché to Cyprus, looked too young to be wearing eagles on the shoulders of his dark green US Army service dress uniform. The Colonel was shaking hands with the Group Captain in charge of RAF Akrotiri. He thanked the Group Captain's wife for the invitation to attend the cocktail event and made a move toward exiting through the Mess. Nils needed to get his attention.

"Sir! Excuse me, Sir?" The Colonel turned around recognizing Nils right away. Nils pulled Nora along with him as he made his way toward the Colonel, who was now standing in the hallway between the bar and the main door to the Officers' Mess.

"My boss told me you'd be here and that you wanted to meet my sister and me. We didn't want you to get away without the chance to say 'hi'."

"What a pleasant surprise. Well, I'll be, the son and daughter of Sven Johansson. I worked with your dad some years ago. Nils, I saw your name on the embassy list of US personnel assigned here so I called Lieutenant Colonel Spade and mentioned it would be nice to see you if there were an occasion for me to come down here to Akrotiri. I must say an added bonus that you are both here together." Looking to Nora he said, "Kiraz is it?"

"No sir, I go by Nora."

"Ah yes, thank you Nora. I only saw your names as they were posted from your passport information. Regrettably I am already late for another engagement. I was hoping we could chat a bit more. Nils has all my contact information, so perhaps you could arrange a visit to Nicosia and we could take in a meal. I would make the visit worth your while, maybe arrange for a 'Green Line' tour." Without looking to be in a rush, Colonel Barrows left the mess and climbed into the passenger side of the embassy car waiting just outside the door.

Nora turned to her brother and asked, "What is a 'Green Line' tour?"

"There is actually quite a bit of history behind giving your question a decent answer. I can explain all of it to you but not right now. Way too much to get into. The short answer is that the UN forces on the island conduct an orientation tour for diplomats and visiting dignitaries of the demilitarized zone that cuts through the heart of Nicosia and divides the entire island from one coast to the other."

"Sounds interesting. I want to learn everything there is to know about Cyprus."

"No you don't Nora. Not everything." Nils felt he was qualified to express his view. His official duties required him to learn the intimate details related to the origins of British Colonial rule on the island, the conditions in which it was turned over to the Cypriots in 1960 to be governed by representatives of both Greek and Turkish Cypriot officials. Nils learned of the external influences of the Greek National government and the seeds planted by Arch Bishop Makarios in the 1950s of *Enosis*, which was the notion that Greek Cypriots would be united under one single 'Hellenic' geographic region.

He thought he understood the Turkish Cypriot motivations for *Taxim*, the Turkish word for partition of the land and separate government administration that gave their minority population a voice and sense of safety. He was aware of how the Cypriot villagers resisted the oppressive British colonial rule resulting in periodic confrontations and bloodshed. He studied the roots of inter-communal struggles and atrocities suffered by both Greek and Turkish Cypriots.

Living, working, and spending his leisure time in the south of Cyprus however, only gave him a sense of the Greek Cypriot's ethnic interests regarding the future of the island. Furthermore, Nils spent only enough attention on the Cypriot government to maintain situational awareness within the context of the U.S. Department of Defense's larger regional interests. Nils Johansson wasn't interested in Cyprus or the people living there. His focus was to preserve a low profile for the U.S. mission that he was there to support. His instincts were also leading him to preserve his reputation as an officer so that he could finally get to undergraduate pilot training for his next assignment.

CHAPTER 5

Nils Johansson

High School Junior Year

"Did the mail come?" asked Nils as he entered the kitchen, his hair still wet from showering after working out with the track team.

"Sorry son, nothing for you today." Sven knew his son was on pins and needles waiting to hear back from the Air Force Academy with a letter of acceptance.

Sven was sitting at the head of the kitchen table with his dinner plate in front of him and a half glass of milk next to it. To Nils it looked like the meal was just about over with. His older sister Yasemin was seated next to her boyfriend Zach, who neither Nils nor his father liked. The three of them were just looking back and forth at one another when Nils walked in.

"Am I interrupting something? Where is Nora? I need to ask her something."

Yasemin chimed in, "She's out with Aunt Roni, and looking at fabric for the dress Aunt Roni promised she'd sew for the Junior Prom."

"That answers my question I guess. Sounds like she's going after all."

"Yep, she's going all right, with a group of her language club friends. Not a real date. Nobody asked her, poor girl." Yasemin seemed to be happy with the change of subject. Whatever she and Zach were discussing with her father ended when Nils walked in and Yasemin appeared relieved. She leaned in closer to Zach who was stabbing unconsciously at the remains of his meatloaf with his fork.

"Dad, I'm worried about not hearing back from the Academy. We're coming into the second week of May. I should be hearing by now. I made sure everything was in order. I've done everything. The grades, the appointment letters, I did everything. Even Major Harris said that my application package was the cleanest one he'd ever seen." Major Harris is the Air Force Academy's Regional Liaison Officer responsible for screening applicants and following up on their progress.

"You'll hear soon enough I'm sure." Sven sounded more detached and distant then ever. He never showed his children much in the way of emotion, but was always available for them. For some reason unknown to the twins, Sven had a special relationship with his older daughter, who seemed most able to get the lion's share of his attention.

"I just can't stand the waiting anymore is all. Jeff Martin heard back from West Point already. Most of the other guys are already having to make choices between the schools that accepted them."

"Your little goody two shoes war mongering brother isn't getting any love from his prized institution is he?" Taunted

Zach, whose longhair look and cloths were from a throwback era. Zach was never shy about sharing his opinion so long as it resulted in Yasemin continuing to hero worship his ideals.

"Zach, you don't have to rub it in. He's tense enough as it is," added Yasemin.

"Yeah, wound up tight as a top like all the other establishment types he longs to become." In most suburban households in the Midwest, Zach's habit of throwing around bold comments would have rendered him persona non grata.

"Yasemin, I can't believe you buy into this dumb ass loser's ideals. He's never been anywhere but Omaha. He's probably watched more than enough crappy movies about those crazy hippies who exist just to protest anything under the sun. He acts like someone who thinks he's God's gift to reinventing utopia."

"He's no loser Nils. He's a poet. He's even been published."

"Yeah right, published in the 'Great Plains Gazette' at Metropolitan Community College. I'm impressed."

"Now you're being a pig headed sarcastic jerk Nils."

Sven Johansson sat passively at the head of the kitchen table and said, "Nils come. Sit. Dinner is getting cold."

"Sorry dad, I can't sit and break bread with these narrow minds sitting around our family table."

"Narrow! You need to wake up flyboy. The only narrow mind I'm reading is the one standing there yelling at everyone."

Nils is not the type you would call a hot head. When he lost his temper it was usually on purpose. In an even tone looking straight at Zach, then his father he said, "I don't yell and haven't raised my voice since walking into this house, our house."

Nils calmly maneuvered over toward Zach. The contrast between the lithe athletic form of Nils standing beside the frail form of Zach who sat looking as if he'd avoided gym class his whole life was a melodramatic precursor to what happened next.

"Nils don't. He didn't mean anything by it. You don't need to do this!" Yasemin was shaking and nearly in tears. "Say you're sorry, Zach," she said.

It was too late. One swift move with his left arm and Nils pulled Zach's chair straight back from the table. Startled, Zach dropped the flatware onto his plate and nearly spilled the half empty glass of beer next to it. With his right hand twisted beneath the collar of Zach's worn military green fatigue shirt Nils lifted Zach completely out of the chair and led him to the front door, opened it and shoved him out and said with a calm voice, "What made you think your worthless hippy body is worthy of wearing a military uniform. For all you know this shirt belonged to a fallen warrior fighting for the freedoms you think it is OK to spit in the face of. Now get the hell out and don't come back here."

Nils's voice was calm and low, so Sven and Yasemin couldn't hear any of what he said. When he came back into the kitchen, Sven was still seated at the table and looked up at him turning his head slowly back and forth while maintaining eye contact. Yasemin had already left the room.

Moments later Yasemin returned still sobbing and holding something in her hand. She tossed the thick manila envelope on the kitchen table. The package slid over towards Nils who recognized immediately what it was.

"There, you silly ignorant boy. Don't say I never did anything for you. I've probably saved your life. You'd have gone to that school and gotten yourself killed flying planes."

"What? Yasemin, I can't believe you would do this to me. Who are you to...?" The package lying on the table was Nils's final application with the congressional appointment letters needed in order to admit him to the Air Force Academy for training in midsummer the following year.

Yasemin remained standing in front of Nils. Sven put his head in his hands and began rubbing his eyes thinking that things couldn't possibly be worse.

Nils took the few strides toward his older sister while grabbing the envelope from the table. He held it up to her. "You know how much this meant to me. I can't believe you'd do such a thing. I don't doubt that piece of shit boyfriend of yours took pleasure as your accomplice either. Both of you are going to get what is coming." He turned and walked out the front door and didn't return until late into the night when the house was dark.

The next morning, Nils awoke early to get his four-mile run in before heading off to school. The medicine cabinet of the hall bathroom, which he shared with his two sisters, had a shelf for each of them. Until the day his sister tampered with his mail and Nils decided to change things, the Johansson's had always respected one another's private belongings and spaces. What Nils had in mind that morning was in stark contrast to all the years of mutual respect among the Johansson siblings.

He found Yasemin's wheel shaped container holding her birth control pills and carefully replaced each of them with diet pills that he bought from the local Rite Aid the night before.

In late August 1993, Nils came home from an afternoon at his summer job as a lifeguard at the local YMCA. When he entered the living room, he was puzzled by what he saw. His dad was seated on the couch almost like a statue. His face was without any expression at all. On either side of him were his aunt Roni and his sister Nora. Both of them sharing a box of tissue, crying and talking in low comforting voices to each other.

"Yasemin is no longer with us," said Sven evenly without emotion as if he was reading a headline from the morning paper.

"What, what do you mean Dad?"

Nora got up from the couch and sprung at Nils grabbing on to him and hugging him. She looked up at him briefly and said, "On her way back from Zach's parents, she was in a car accident.

She died at the scene."

"Oh my God." Nils hugged Nora tightly and buried his face in her hair and began to sob himself.

The circumstances of that accident were never made clear to Nils or Nora. Nils learned the next morning from reading the paper that she hit a telephone pole while traveling at highway speed on State Route 4. The report didn't have much detail other than speculation that she may have swerved to avoid a dog or some other animal. There were no skid marks.

If the local media had not done such a thorough job of sensationalizing the accident, Nils would still have had some lingering doubts about Yasemin's state of mind and possible causes of the fateful crash. In an attempt to bring to light the consequences of pregnancy, birth out of wedlock, and suicide among young unmarried pregnant women, one of the local TV stations included additional information about Yasemin's tragic single vehicle accident.

When Nils learned that Yasemin was reported to have been pregnant, he was pretty certain that his actions of revenge a few months earlier could have been a contributing factor. The rest of the Johansson family wouldn't accept that Yasemin's death was a suicide. Nils knew he would bear the burden of his past and kept that secret to himself.

CHAPTER 6

Melanda Bay

Spring 2001

Even though it was only her second day on the island, the drive to Laneia village had become familiar enough that Nora was no longer concerned about driving back in the dark. She pulled into the village and down the familiar lane by the stone fence separating the Hart Gallery from the rest of the village interior. She was exhausted from all the driving and taking in all the new experiences.

She walked up the pathway to the lighted porch. She couldn't keep her mind from cataloguing the many things she wanted to do and see during her stay. She decided that she would need to make up a calendar in order to map out her time on Cyprus. The "Green Line" tour was definitely something she wanted to arrange right away, but top on her list was getting a good night sleep and spending a relaxing day getting familiar with the gallery.

She slipped off the practical sandals she was wearing and turned on the interior lights before heading straight for the upstairs room and the comfort of a bed and soft pillow. Kaplan was curled up at the head of the bed between the pillows with his head buried beneath a paw.

"Kaplan you sweet little guy. What sort of adventures have

you been up to today?" She moved him to the foot of the bed, stroked him until he curled up again. He stopped purring right away and was asleep again. Nora slipped out of her dress, pulled on a tee shirt, got into the bed, and switched off the lamp. She was asleep almost as soon as her head touched the pillow.

Nora spent the next couple of days in Laneia getting to know the village. There were a few lookers at the gallery, but as Gavin had warned her earlier, the season had not yet begun and she had yet to sell a painting. Even though Laneia had the feel of being off the beaten path, there were still some shops that catered to English speaking visitors. In one of them Nora found a book to read titled *The Aphrodite Plot* by Michael Jansen.

"I think you'll find that story is missing something."

Nora looked up and noticed Aydın standing just behind her, looking over her shoulder.

"I mean it is a good book, but there is more to learn about Cyprus then you'll get from reading that one." His comment sounded unconvincing and as always he was smiling. Then in a rapid but smooth Greek he asked his neighbor who runs the store if he could get a ride into Limassol later in the afternoon.

Out of the blue Nora looked up from the book and said, "I can drive you if you like."

"Just a few days and already you are understanding Greek. How is that?" Aydın asked, appearing unsurprised and almost laughing with joy that Nora was able to follow what he'd said.

"Call it a knack. I've always been fond of languages, but your body language provided lots of clues and I knew you didn't have a car."

"So this is not any trouble for you?"

"No not at all. It is such a beautiful day. Not too warm. I wanted to see if I could find Melanda Beach. I've heard it is a beautiful spot." She then set a large heavy box of clear water bottles on the counter and put the book on top, intending to pay for everything.

"What do you need these for?" said Aydın pointing to the box of bottled water. "There is a well at the Hart villa. In fact I bring water home from there all the time. You needn't worry. It is safe. These bottles…are for tourists." He grabbed the box and put it back on the shelf for her.

After paying for her new book, she turned to leave the shop. Aydın held the door for her and they walked out together.

"What was it you needed to go into Limassol for? Something special?"

"No, not really. I was going to pick up some new guitar strings. The 'E' broke last evening and I forgot I gave away my spare set to a friend. Anyway, Malanda isn't that easy to find. Other than my errand in Limassol, I had no plans for the rest of the day. I can show you the way to Malanda if you like."

"I was planning on hitting the road after picking up the water. Speaking of which, would you mind showing me this well?"

"Not a problem at all. I need to get something from home first. I'll catch up with you in the garden. After we draw some water we can maybe leave from there. Is that OK with you?"

"See you in a few then," said Nora, to nobody at all as Aydın had disappeared in a flash. He met up with her in the garden moments later brandishing a pair of wide mouth bottles to pump the well water into.

As they set off, Aydın turned to Nora, "I'm sorry, I forgot something else, but no worry, it is right on our way out. Could you just stop in front of the cafe while I run up to my place to get a few things?"

Nora stopped the car just a few meters down the road in front of the cafe as Aydın requested.

"Back in a flash," he said to her as he stepped out of the car.

Several minutes later he returned with a guitar in one hand and a small round wicker basket covered in a blue and white checked towel in the other. He put the guitar and basket in the backseat then joined Nora in the front.

"Ok, we can go."

Nora looked over at him, admiring his rugged good looks, loose black curly hair, and the color of his golden eyes, a hazel that changes with the surrounding light. She smiled to herself and turned again to concentrate on the road ahead, but not before Aydın noticed her looking at him.

"Is everything ok? You were looking at me funny."

She laughed, "Everything is fine Aydın. You are going to show me Melanda Beach. That is going to make my day."

They both smiled and drove off in silence for a while longer. Aydın reached for the radio knobs.

"You don't mind if I…"

"No please do."

"I'll see if I can find a station that plays some traditional folk music." The only stations coming were from two of the BFBS British Forces Broadcasting Stations. One of them played heavy metal music. Aydın chose the other one that played classic rock.

"I guess this is the best we can find for now. Next time we go someplace together I will bring some CDs. I think you'd like Cypriot music."

"Next time? How do you know there will be a next time?"

"Sorry, I didn't mean…"

Again Nora caught herself laughing aloud, "No really it's OK, I was kidding. I hope there will be a next time."

For what seemed like an eternity they drove on again with nothing but the sound of John Lennon's voice pouring out of the small speaker.

Then there was another voice joining in sounding much clearer, but soft enough not to drown out the instrumentals. It was Aydın's voice, singing the chorus from *Across the Universe*.

Nora looked over at him and saw that he was gazing out the

side window of the car as they rounded a bend in the road. Aydın's mind was a long way away as he continued to sing along looking out at the blue of the Mediterranean reflecting the morning light. Soon the song was over. Nora reached for the volume knob, turning it down to avoid having to listen to the DJ turn the station over to a commercial.

"Your voice is wonderful Aydın."

Embarrassed just a little, Aydın replied sheepishly, "I love that song. *Across the Universe*. It is a favorite. It makes me dream of possibilities."

"I could tell your mind was someplace else."

"No Nora, just here. I've only been here on Cyprus. To Turkey also, only because it is so close, but no place else."

"You say that like you have mixed feelings."

"I don't know really. This is my home."

"Where did you learn to speak such perfect English? I would have thought you studied abroad.   You hardly have an accent."

"You flatter me. I learned in school."

"Is it compulsory to learn English?"

"It depends. At the university where I studied, the courses were taught in English.

"Where was that?"

"Where was what?"

"The university you went to. Where?"

"Oh, sorry. The University of Nicosia. They have a campus in Limassol also."

"What did you study?"

"I wanted a degree in Fine Arts, but they only had two years of courses that focus on Music and Art. I had a scholarship for a business management degree. The school was very expensive and my uncle didn't leave enough to cover all the costs for the kind of program I would have liked. I would have had to go to Greece but I was afraid I couldn't afford it and...well, I didn't want to leave."

"So you got a Business Degree?"

"Oh, no. I didn't finish. The Management program was for Hotel and Restaurant Management. There is really no economy here in Cyprus that isn't connected to tourism. I lost interest and stopped going."

"I see. So what's next?"

Aydın looked at her with a grin. He shook his head slowly from side to side and gave her a nervous laugh then looked into her eyes with an easy smile and said, "Nora, there is no formula or path for these things. I live. I'm happy. It is simple."

Nora was puzzled. Not just about the handsome man sharing a ride in her car, but about the strange feelings stirring inside of her. As they approached the outskirts of Limassol she broke the silence that followed her attempts at getting to know Aydın.

"You're going to tell me where to go right?"

"Yes of course. I should have said something. The shop I like is on one of the side streets near the water. Turn right here. Go straight and I will tell you when you'll need to turn again. This road winds through the old Turkish industrial area, so just follow the traffic around. When you see the palms and the car parks across from the city beach you'll know we are close."

A little while later they parked in a spot under the trees along the waterfront. The late morning was wearing into midday but the air was still cool. Aydın took a jaunt up the side road toward the music shop and left Nora to wander the water front promenade until he completed his chore at the music shop. When Aydın returned he found Nora sitting in the shade of a palm atop the stone sea wall gazing out at the ships anchored outside of the harbor jetty.

"The scents of salt and oleander are winning you over I see." Aydın said this casually without drawing any attention from the other people enjoying the waterfront. There were all kinds of people on the promenade. Some in beach wear, some walking dogs, and some dressed in business attire taking a break from their offices.

Nora turned toward his voice. Anyone watching them would have thought they'd known each other for a very long time. They appeared to be comfortable together. "Hey, you're back. That was quick." He held up a small package in his left hand.

"Two sets of strings. That way I'll always have extras in case one of my friends breaks a string when we're playing together."

Nora hopped from the wall keeping her eyes on Aydın. "Shall we?"

"Yes, Melanda Beach. I will show you the way there. It isn't far." They got back into the car and headed out of the car park and away from Limassol.

"Take this exit here," said Aydın. Nora moved into left lane of the brand new highway and took the exit as instructed. The sign was a standard European variety with the names of the destinations that could be accessed from taking the exit. One of the village names was Paramali and another Avdimou. Melanda was not on the sign.

"This mosque is the only reminder that Turkish Cypriots ever lived in this area. Until a few years ago all these buildings and houses had chains and locks on the doors like the ones on the doors of the mosque." Aydın was beginning to sound like a well-informed tour guide.

The road through this part of the village was sandy and dusty with dry patches of weeds growing from the cracks in the asphalt. Many of the homes looked like they were under renovation. There were stacks of bricks and mounds of masonry sand in front of some of the stone structures.

"What became of the Turkish Cypriots?" asked Nora

innocently or perhaps ignorantly.

"A long story. I think it might be too complicated to explain right now. We still have a bit of a slow drive ahead on a bad road. You'll want to concentrate. Turn left at the next corner." Nora noticed that there was nothing ahead or beyond except a newly paved road with bright concrete curbs leading over a rise to an area that looked like it was being developed as a holiday villa. When she turned she saw a weathered billboard with an arrow pointing down a potholed dirt track. The sign said Kyrenia Beach Restaurant 6 Km.

"Aydın, you know I'm going to want to hear more about the Turkish Cypriots and the mosque." As she said this the right front tire of the Astra banged into a deep hole and the car lurched to the right. Nora compensated and slowed down then refocused her concentration on driving.

"Sorry about that."

"It is OK. We don't need to hurry. Just take it easy and everything will be fine."

"You've been on this road before, right?"

"Yes of course, lots of people come here."

"On tractors and four by fours?"

Laughing and shaking his head with a cool expression on his face, Aydın replied, "No Nora, tourists just like us with rental cars drive this road. You shall see." A bit further along, after they passed by a low field of melons that looked ready for harvest, there were several stretches with sand drifts and a few more tricky potholes. Then Aydın pointed to a fork on the right.

"Turn here."

"Really? Here?"

"Yes here! Nora, you need to trust people more. You shall see, I know the way and I assure you that you will not be disappointed when we get there."

Nora couldn't comprehend how this turn in the road would take her closer to the shore until they reached a grove of orange trees where the road again veered to the south, with a small rise on the right. They crested the rise, then the rutted road turned into a chalky white sand stone track that led to a small car park behind a modest concrete building. The place had a trellis and patio just five to ten feet above the rock strewn and sandy beach of Melanda Bay.

"Aydın. It is breath taking. What a lovely peaceful spot." Nora parked the car and grabbed her beach bag from the back seat. Aydın opened the back door and removed his guitar and the basket covered with the checkered cloth.

"This way. Come with me Nora. I want to show where you must be standing to really see this place for the first time." Aydın was smiling from ear to ear. His energy was infectious. He didn't lead her down the path to the beach right away. Instead he took her along a patio in front of the covered beach cafe.

Nora was surprised that the place appeared to be open and operating. There was a man preparing a tray behind the counter. There was an older couple sitting at a table closest to the pathway where Aydın and Nora passed.

"*Kalimera* Makis!" Aydın waved at the man in the restaurant.

"*Kalimera paliós fílos* Aydın. Please stop by later. I will make you a coffee."

"An old family friend." Aydın said to her.

"Now don't look back at the shore until I tell you, OK? Look down at the path as we walk. You should see the view from a special spot first. Then we can go down to the beach." They continued walking on a narrow dirt path above a low sandstone bluff just above the water. Nora could hear the lapping of the waves against the rock. On top of the bluff she felt the cool sea breeze and inhaled the aroma of dry grass and the scent of olive groves. The air was thick with a salty humidity but the sun still burned bright through the deep blue of the sky.

At the edge of the olive grove and just a few meters from the bluff, Aydın reached for her shoulders and turned her so that she was facing the bay.

"You can look now," he said.

Nora's jaw dropped. She raised both her hands to her cheeks and gaped at the scene.

"How…I mean did you…?" Tears pooled in Nora's eyes as she took in the view. The cool breezes coming in from the west textured the electric blue color of the water's surface. From the open field where she and Aydın stood, there were olive trees and low shrubs framing the scene of the white chalky cliffs overlooking the rocky beach beyond. In the distance the terraced foothills of Mount Olympus gave way to the darker green of Cyprus cedar conifers that reached up to the deep blue of the sky above.

Nora turned and looked up into Aydın's eyes and said, "When I was very young, there was a painting hanging on the wall of our dining room. It is identical to this view, colors and all. Did you know anything about the painting?"

"Honestly Nora, I didn't know. This was a favorite place of my uncle's. When I first met Gavin, I saw similar scenes hanging on the wall of the gallery. It turns out we had a mutual interest in this place, but for different reasons. It is beautiful though."

"Yes it is. I love it. I could stand here all day."

"Come this way. There is a nice place nearby where we can sit."

Aydın didn't even think about what he was doing when he gently reached for Nora's hand to guide her to the spot. It seemed to him the natural thing to do. With his guitar slung over his left shoulder and the basket in one hand and Nora's in his other hand, the two looked like a couple in love as they walked toward the edge of the bay.

Beneath a low golden oak up on the shallow bluff was a

group of smooth white rocks shaded by the tree.

"This is wonderful Aydın. I would love to stay here all afternoon."

"You are hungry I suppose?"

"Famished and thirsty. Yes."

"Here" Aydın handed her one of the water bottles they filled from the well, which Nora didn't hesitate to gulp from.

"I made some sandwiches. Halloumi cheese on fresh bread rolls from the village bakery." He spread the blue and white-checkered cloth over one of the rocks and transformed it into a small table. From the basket he pulled out a pair of clear plastic tumblers and a bottle of red Cypriot wine. Then he got out the sandwich rolls wrapped in white wax paper and set them on the cloth.

As he pulled the cork from the wine bottle, Nora noticed the label read, *"Mount Olympus Red."* There was nothing else printed on the label except *Etko - Omodos.*

"You've outdone yourself Aydın. I didn't expect anything quite so intimate."

"Really? It is just a snack at a beautiful spot. Don't you think?"

"You won't get any argument from me about this being a beautiful spot, but a snack? If I were to go on a lunch date in the U.S. with a bottle of red wine suddenly appearing from no-where, I'd begin to think I was on a date."

"It's just wine Nora. Not even a good wine but it goes with the sandwiches."

When they finished the sandwiches, Nora was sipping the last of her wine. Aydın was tuning his guitar after replacing the strings with the ones he'd picked up in town. He began to play in a modern picking style with a few folky minor chords bridging the instrumental rhythm. He hummed along and then began a soft lyric in Greek, testing to see how it sounded.

He played a few more bars before resting the guitar in his lap staring out over the water.

"You shouldn't stop. It is so beautiful."

"Thanks. The lyrics are from a poem I learned from my uncle before he passed. I've been struggling to find a melody that fits the words. I think of this poem when I come here."

"It sounds wonderful, but I wasn't able to understand much of it. Can you translate it?"

"I will play it again and try to sing it in English." He began picking at an intro and with the strumming rhythm before starting to hum and then sang.

He continued picking, and then began strumming and humming, and finally added words.

"It is so beautiful. Where did the poem come from originally?"

"I don't know. My uncle told me this poem when I was younger. He said it was 'engraved in stone long ago, lost in the shifting sand, in the midst of a crumbling world, the vision of one flower.'"

"It is lovely."

"Thank you. It is how I feel about Cyprus. My home." As he said this he continued to look out to the north and east, past the slopes of Troodos and to the far side of the mountains where it was impossible to see what was beyond.

Nora didn't want to spoil the moment but sensed somberness. As the sun moved across the sky, the oak no longer provided shade over the spot they were sitting.

"How about we walk back to the beach cafe. I could use a pick me up," suggested Nora.

"Pick me up?"

"Sorry, an American expression. A cup of coffee for some energy to face the late afternoon."

"Of course. We can do that but I must tell you that in Cyprus we rest during these hours. We rest and visit. There is no reason to rush back to anywhere." He put his guitar back into the cloth case he made for it, then collected the sandwich wrappers, empty wine bottle, the glasses, and put them into the basket. Nora shook the checkered cloth, folded it and laid it atop the basket.

"I'll carry the basket," she said as she stood. Nora watched Aydın as he got up and slung the guitar over his shoulder. She admired him and without thinking twice moved closer to him and slipped her arm around his waist pulling him toward her as they walked back on the path to the cafe. At that moment she knew she wanted to learn everything there was to know this man.

Aydın glanced down into her eyes and walked on slowly, enjoying the warmth and soft caress from Nora's hold on him. Before they knew it they were on the patio of the cafe. The tables were mostly empty. The few beach goers had likely returned home and it was still early for those who normally came for a dinner by the sea.

Dashing out from behind the counter at the back of the cafe Aydın heard his friend calling "*Kalispera Filos*"

"*Kalispera* Makis. We're just going to take this table and two coffees.

Makis turned to Nora. "*Posselene?*"

Nora had no idea what Makis was asking so she replied with one of the few Greek expressions she'd learned, "*Then katalaveno,*" saying she didn't understand.

Aydın smiled and looked at her. "He wants to know your name."

She smiled back at Aydın and turned to Makis and introduced herself in English.

"Nora, a lovely name. I bring your coffee, how do you like?"

"*Metreo. Parakalo,*" said Nora.

"*To ídio gia ména,*" Aydın added.

"I can see you will learn to speak Greek quickly. You have

a good teacher," said Makis in his best English. Makis left them to prepare the coffee.

Nora wanted to learn more about Aydın but was leery of jumping right in and grilling him with personal questions, so she switched to a different topic, one she was curious about since she dropped Gavin at the airport.

"Aydın, what is going on with Gavin? I mean, all that talk about the antiquities in the garden of the gallery. Is there something I should know about?"

Surprised at her question Aydın replied, "Why such interest? I really like Mr. Hart and I've known him for some time. We've developed a kind of partnership. We look after each other, but…"

"But?"

"You first, why the interest?"

"I don't know. He's a family friend. Seems like such a kind man. I wouldn't want anything to happen to him."

"Nora, he's already been in trouble. He was in jail up in Nicosia because of those artifacts. He disappeared for a while so I asked around and some of us from the village gathered the money to get him from the jail. He paid us all back, but still we didn't know the real reason he was detained with the police.

"Ok, why then?"

"I must warn you that when you ask a Cypriot to explain Cyprus history, you run up against different points of view. I try to be objective. What we were taught in school always seemed one sided to me. My uncle taught me to know better and to always realize that there is more than one side to any story. He survived all the troubles on Cyprus from the 1950s and beyond the war in '74. The best I can tell you about Mr. Hart is that he is naive and ignorant about some of the history he is brushing up against."

"I'm not sure I know what you are getting at Aydın, but I'm all ears."

"You see Nora, back in the 1950s Cypriots, both Greek and Turkish Cypriots alike, lived peacefully together in villages all over the island. My uncle's village, Kantou was one of these inter-communal villages. The Turkish Cypriots who lived there called the place Çanakkale. In those days, Cyprus was a British Colony, annexed in 1925 as a spoil of war. When Bishop Makarios introduced the notion of ENOSIS in the early '50s, turmoil sprang up everywhere on the island."

"I've heard of ENOSIS but it is escaping me at the moment. My school history is a bit rusty."

"It's OK, most foreigners I meet have no knowledge of our history. ENOSIS is not a complicated idea. It means that the people of Greece believe Cyprus should be included as part of one "Hellenistic Region" in the Mediterranean and united with Greece under one flag. It was or still is a movement misperceived by many Cypriots as a nationalist movement toward a free and independent Cyprus."

"What is wrong with that? It has to be better than partition."

"Ah, you see one side, yet there are two, maybe more. The Turkish Cypriots during that time were aware of this idea of ENOSIS but were still comfortable in their villages living together with Greek Cypriots. However, the ENOSIS movement was a burden to the British Colonial government. Most of this part of Cyprus's history is well known in the textbooks on both sides of the divide. In other words there is no argument that during the 1950s, Cypriot nationalists, mostly Greek Cypriots, formed an underground group of activists known as EOKA, who on occasion set off a stray bomb or two in an effort to encourage the British to leave Cyprus. As these events became more and more violent, the British exercised their colonial form of divide and rule by employing Turkish Cypriots in the local police forces. Can you imagine the distrust that developed in the villages between Greek and Turkish Cypriots?"

"Aydın, it sounds like you are saying that you believe that the British were the instigators of the violence in the villages during the 1950s. It also sounds like you've studied this subject in depth. Why?"

"Nora, I'm Cypriot, not Greek Cypriot, or Turkish Cypriot, but maybe both. I never knew my parents. I learned a lot from my uncle. His name was Xever Kostas and he lived the life of a kind and caring villager. Everyone just called him Kostas. I was told he was my father's brother and a village elder. He took me in, and together with his neighbors Andros and Kalista Elias, raised me. All of them saw what happened in Kantou - Çanakkale village in the mid 60s. They saw their dearest friends flee from people they thought they knew all their lives. They began to distrust them and had no trouble imagining the violence that happened in Balıkeşir village where I was born."

Nora reached across the table for Aydın's hand. It felt good to her. She looked into his eyes. "Not only are you the most handsome man I have ever kissed Aydın Kostas, but you are artistic, and worldly."

"Worldly? I've never been called that. Is this good?"

"Oh, very. It means you are smart, very perceptive, and did I already say good looking?" Nora was beginning to surprise herself with the mush that was oozing from her mind and out of her mouth. She couldn't contain the unexplainable emotion she felt when she was around this man.

As they both finished their coffee, Aydın had a wonderful thought. "Nora, let's go, I have another place I want to show you before we go back to Laneia." He then reached into his pocket and pulled out three large heavy coins, each worth a Cypriot pound, and left them on the table. He waved a goodbye to Makis who was serving another patron, reached for Nora's hand, and together they walked toward the car.

"Wanna drive?" asked Nora. "You know where we are going, and I don't."

"That's OK, I'll show you the way. I like watching you drive. You are beautiful when you concentrate on the road."

They drove back the way they came along the sandy single track through the low scrub and orchard and back through the remnant of the village where the small decaying mosque still stood. They rejoined the main highway toward Paphos.

"It is coming up shortly, just keep your eyes on the road and I'll tell you when to get ready to exit." Aydın said in a calm and relaxed tone. He reached for the knob on the car stereo and searched for some mood music.

"Aydın, is this the place? I've seen pictures. Is this it?"

"Easy Nora. Not yet. There will be a sign with a sharp turn off to 'Petra tou Romiou,' you can turn off there. Trust me. You'll love this place."

She turned off as instructed and parked in a small car park on the north side of the highway. There were several other cars in the lot already and another entered right behind them. The sun was very low on the horizon. The sky to the east and north took on a deep indigo blue creating a sharp contrast to the neutral colors of the island landscape beyond. Aydın guided Nora through a small tunnel beneath the highway that connected to a footpath leading to a rocky beach. As they emerged from the tunnel and onto the path, the view of an amazing scene was before them. Washed clean by the waves, were two sandstone rocks the size of small buildings, perched on the edge of the shore. As they walked closer to the beach, they passed by what looked like a fig tree with pieces of women's undergarments tied to the branches.

"Aydın, this place is beautiful. That tree we just passed is…well different."

He gave her a brief laugh, smiled, and his eye twinkled when he looked at her and said, "It is called 'the wishing tree' where young couples come to make a wish for a baby."

Nora looked back toward the tree and saw another couple. They both looked several years older then she and Aydın. The woman pulled a pastel colored lacy garment from her coat pocket. The man with her stood close and hugged her as she pulled back a branch and tied the spare fabric to it. The branch sprung back to its original position with a new wish tied to it for a hopeful couple. Nora turned her attention back to Aydın and they continued the short walk to the beach.

Where the cobbled stones turned to sand, the foam lapped at the shore with each washing wave. The surface of the sea to the west took on a golden glow as the sun began to set. Nora looked in both directions along the shore and saw there were several couples of all ages cuddling and hugging each other as they watched the setting sun.

"Aydın, thank you. Thank you for sharing this with me. I'm

still not sure what it all means, but I'm glad your instincts brought us here."

"The sun will be setting in a few moments. The meaning of this spot is simple. Aphrodite the goddess of love was born of the sea foam right here in this place. These couples…they love each other. They have wishes and this is the place where they share them with each other in hope that those wishes will become real."

Nora didn't say anything. She sat close beside Aydın on the sand and nestled her head against his shoulder and held on to him. Together they watched as the sun slowly sank beneath the waves. As the sky turned from gold to purple, the air became cool and the couples on the beach got up to leave, one by one. Aydın and Nora were the last to leave.

CHAPTER 7

Dinner with Friends

The antiquated telephone that sat on the wooden counter just inside the door to the Hart gallery had a loud tinny ring to it. Nora was in the kitchen of the main house, so it rang several times before she was able to pick up.

"Good morning, Hart Gallery," said Nora into the phone's mouthpiece, suppressing a shortness of breath from rushing to pick it up. She was trying to sound cheerful when she answered the caller.

"Jeeze Nora, I was about to hang up. I must have let it ring at least twenty times. I've been calling for the past couple of days and you never seem to be around."

"Nils, so nice of you to call," Nora answered with a touch of sarcasm but didn't feel like snapping at her brother.

"Sorry sis, I know you've been busy, but one of my colleagues invited us to dinner at his mother-in-law's. I thought you'd be interested to meet his family."

"Of course I'm interested. It's just that, well…" She hesitated thinking of the short time that remained before having to head back home. She sensed Aydın would be eager to spend every moment with her, so she was coveting the remaining time she had on the island to be with him.

"It's just what Nora? It's a family dinner with friends. I

thought of you because my friend Brad's wife's mother is Cypriot. She was a refugee from a village near Kyrenia and can tell stories like you could never imagine. Really, she is a walking talking history book and I think you should meet her."

"Too good to pass up Nils. Thanks for thinking of me. Could I possibly bring a guest?"

"Seriously? You met someone? My self reliant and independent sister, who goes out but never dates anyone twice, has met a nan who has captured her heart?"

"It isn't quite like that Nils. Aydın is a neighbor and friend of Gavin's."

"Oh, I see. An older more refined gentleman."

"No, you have it all wrong. He's about our age. You'll like him. So, can I bring him along as my guest, or not?"

"I'm sure it will be fine. This family is known for opening their home to guests. I'll let them know you'll be bringing a friend. It should be an interesting evening bringing your Turkish Cypriot boyfriend to the home of a Greek Cypriot refugee. I'm anxious to discover what he's doing in Laneia."

Nora couldn't suppress snapping back at him, "He's a Greek Cypriot Nils and it shouldn't matter anyway. These people need to get over their past."

Nils remained calm and decided that stirring the pot wasn't worth spoiling the chance to remain on speaking terms with his twin sister. "Nora, I don't disagree with your last point. I've been here too long and this place can get to you after awhile. I just assumed since Aydın is a Turkish name that he was from the north. You might ask him about it sometime."

Thinking about what Nils just said, Nora noticed Aydın standing at the threshold of the gallery entrance holding and stroking Kaplan. "Nils, can you hang on just a sec?" She cupped the mouthpiece of the phone and turned toward the gallery entryway.

"How long have you been standing there?" Nora asked in a worried tone.

"Awhile. I think Kaplan is hungry." He lowered the cat to the floor and as he rose he added, "It isn't exactly what I had in mind for this evening and even though I don't know what I'm agreeing to, you can tell Nils we'll be coming along together."

Still somewhat worried, Nora beamed at Aydın with the briefest of smiles, uncovered the mouthpiece of the phone and told Nils, "I just spoke with Aydın and we will both be coming."

Nils gave her the directions and she wrote them down then hung up the phone. "We need to be at our hosts in Kolossi at six-thirty this evening for dinner. Some Cypriot friends of Nils invited us."

"It sounded like you needed to talk your brother into allowing me to join you. I'm looking forward to meeting him."

Nora wanted Aydın to like her brother, but wasn't sure how things would go since Nils had changed so much in recent years,

"He's really a great guy Aydın. It's just that he's had a rough time of it since we graduated from high school. He worked so hard his whole life and in recent years it seems like everything he tries to do is plagued with obstacles. Please for me, keep an open mind?"

"Anything for you. We'll make the best of the evening, but let's save your last two nights for just the two of us. I don't want to let you out of my sight until you must leave."

"Well, you certainly know how to make a girl feel special, but spending every moment together might be difficult since I'm heading for Nicosia tomorrow."

"What's in Nicosia? I know, what ever it is, you can just forget about it. I have another plan for us."

"Aydın, I'm so thrilled you feel that way, but this is something I have to do. I came here to learn about Cyprus and I'm meeting someone up at the UN Headquarters at Ledra Palace Hotel tomorrow morning. I'll be getting a first hand look at "the green zone.""

He became serious for a moment and understood why Nora needed to follow through with her plans. "Do you need me to ride along with you to Nicosia then? It is a long drive and I am good company."

"I'd love to have you come along, but I don't know how long I'm going to be. Besides, I might need a favor if you could help me. I've had no way of getting in touch with Gavin. He sent a post card to tell me his plans to call here tomorrow to arrange for his return. I feel kind of bad that I've been such a rotten custodian here at the gallery. I've been out and about so much that I've only sold two pieces since Gavin left."

With a chuckle and while still laughing a little he said, "Gavin will be thrilled that you sold the pieces, believe me. He doesn't need the money. He just needs to move the art so that there is more wall space for the newer pieces."

Nora began to feel torn. Her yearning to be with Aydın at every moment was a foreign emotion. In her entire life she never had such feelings for anyone. She stood waiting, hoping Aydın would break the silence, which he did moments later.

"I will look after the gallery for you tomorrow. When you return from Nicosia, I'll have a surprise for you." He wanted to return the discussion back to their evening plans. "Nora, if anyone asks, I don't know why I was named Aydın. It has been a mystery to me my whole life. My uncle never knew either."

"It means *light*," Nora declared. "Aydın is *light* and it is a beautiful and fitting name for you. I love the sound of it and when I look at you, I feel warm and safe."

Her words froze him in place and he gazed at every curve of her face and absorbed every feature. She pushed the phone back into its spot on the counter and moved toward him closing the distance between them without breaking eye contact. On the tips of her toes, with her hands on both his shoulders, she rose up to kiss him. The sensation was electrifying and at the same time euphoric. As she pulled away from him she said, "This moment is ours forever, sealed in history. Nobody will ever take this perfection away." Her words came out in almost a whisper.

"I love you Nora. Please stay…at least for the summer. I know the scholarship is important and something you must return to, but I cannot bear the thought of you leaving so soon."

Nora pushed away from him and eased herself through the door and into the gallery garden without looking back toward him. Standing in the bright light of the morning sun, she turned around to see him still standing at the threshold with one hand braced against the doorjamb. She swiveled her head from side to side, unable to constrain the mixed emotion of happy and sad, and smiled while crying at the same time.

"You just made this situation all the more complicated." The only man in her entire life she'd ever heard say those three words, "I love you," was her father. Until now she'd never given a guy the chance to get to know her well enough. She knew though that Aydın was genuine but didn't have any idea what to do next.

"Things don't have to become complicated unless you want them to Nora." He said it in his relaxed and matter of fact sort of way and she knew he was right.

Collecting herself, she said, "We should bring something for tonight. I've never been invited to a Cypriot home. Is there something suitable we should consider bringing our host?"

He realized she was trying to avoid getting too serious and went along. "We could never go wrong with flowers. I have a vase that is in need of a new home and my neighbors won't mind if we do a bit of pruning."

Nora understood the implication, so she grabbed a set of pruning clippers and together, they took a stroll through the side streets of Laneia clipping from the over abundance of begonias and a variety of flowering herbs. The fig trees were also in bloom and Aydın clipped from one of them a beautiful pink and rose colored flower then held it up to Nora for inspection before he tucked it behind her ear between a few locks of her hair.

"Thanks for driving Aydın. I was beginning to think you didn't know how or didn't have a license." They had both been rather quiet through most of the drive down the mountain to Kolossi.

"As I told you earlier, I enjoy watching you drive. Actually, I enjoy watching you do everything." He smiled as he said this looking in her direction for a reaction before turning his eyes back to the road.

Nora appeared to be lost in thought, so Aydın decided not to push beyond what little conversation they had shared since he'd expressed his feelings for her that morning. "We're nearly there," he said.

Nora read off the directions from the notes she'd taken from

Nils over the phone. They turned off the pavement to a smaller gravel drive arriving in a cul-de-sac shared by three other family homes nestled beneath stands of gum trees and a few date palms. Pink and white oleanders bound the gardens of each home. They knew they were in the right place because as they pulled up, Nils was getting out of his car. He stood waiting until Aydın and Nora were out of their car and approached them.

"Prompt as usual sis. It's always been so nice to have something to count on from you."

Aydın stood close to Nora, unruffled by Nils's acerbic comment. "Nils, this is Aydın."

Nils extended his right hand and even though he'd learned many polite Greek expressions, he confined himself to English and said, "Any friend of my sister is a friend of mine. I'm Nils."

"It is a pleasure to meet you as well." Aydın gave Nils a firm handshake and put on a broad toothy smile. Nils glanced over to Nora with a raised eyebrow of approval.

"Shall we?" Breaking from the handshake with Nora's new beau, Nils extended his arm toward the house indicating they should head up the path to give a tap on the Chandler's front door.

The lady who answered the door was Yolanda Mitchell, wife of Nils's colleague Brad, from Akrotiri. Yolanda was a striking beauty with naturally blond hair, tall with a slight build, the daughter of British expatriate Charles Chandler. The only physical feature Yolanda shared with her Greek Cypriot mother, Elaina Apostolos, were her facial features, which appeared to be Greek down to the smallest molecule.

"*Kalispera, peraste*. Please come in." Yolanda spoke with an unusual British accent, which carried with it a touch of deep Greek. She ushered them into her parents' home and everyone was introduced. The aroma of grilled meats and fresh chopped vegetables filled the home. Two young blond boys were racing up and down the hall with plastic dinosaurs in each hand.

The short dark haired woman sliding a tray with ceramic *moussaka* bowls into the oven was Yolanda's mother, Elaina. She was dressed in a dark but lightweight dress adorned with traditional jewelry. The white lace kitchen apron protecting her fine clothing from the chores of preparing dinner, looked out of place.

"You'll have to excuse me," she said wiping her hands on her apron before introducing herself to her guests. "Charles is out back. He's got everything ready for whatever sort of drink you prefer this evening. Now hurry on out, I'll be with all of you momentarily." As she was saying this in her cheerful motherly way, she shut the oven door and removed the oven mitts from both her hands.

Nora was eager to present her host with the arrangement of flowers she and Aydın collected earlier in the day. "Mrs. Chandler, thank you so much for inviting us into your home."

She held out the flowers to her hostess.

"Yolanda, those will look fabulous in the living room. Would you dear?" Yolanda accepted the vase, and added some water.

As her daughter left to place the flowers in the adjoining room, Elaina said, "Oh they are lovely. Thank you for such a thoughtful gift to warm up the room."

"Mrs. Chandler." Nils held out a bottle of French Burgundy. "I have been saving this for a special occasion. Perhaps you'll want it for another time when it is just you and Mr. Chandler on a quiet evening."

"Don't be silly Nilsson. We'll serve it with the *souvlaki* along with the *meze* that Charles and I have prepared. Now please, there are chairs out back."

Charles Chandler was removing the last of the cubes of cut lamb from the grill. There was a pile of lemon rind on a plate nearby as evidence that the meat had taken in all of the lemon juices it could absorb. Nora couldn't get over the sight of this older British man wearing a pressed shirt and sport coat and grilling souvlaki in Cyprus.

Charles turned toward his guests with a broad happy smile. Introductions were made all around as he showed everyone to bar and asked them what he could fix for them.

He picked up his own drink which was sweating beads of moisture on the outside of the tall clear glass filled with a light amber liquid and ice with a twist of lime. "Mine is a 'Pimms Number One' in case you're curious." He said this while holding up the glass as an exhibit to be admired.

After Brad settled his two young sons inside in front of the telly to watch a "Wallace and Gromit" video, he came out back and joined everyone for a cocktail. Elaina finished preparing the courses for the evening *meze* on the back terrace. and had them ready in sequence as the evening progressed. With her preparation chores complete, she and Yolanda came to the table where Charles pulled chairs out for them and set drinks before them on the table.

Throughout the early part of the evening everyone enjoyed the *meze*. Brad, Yolanda, and Charles rotated the duties of removing empty small plates and replacing them with different delectable small courses. Elaina remained at the table to visit with her guests.

With the meal and dinner wines mostly finished, everyone remained at the table in the shadows of the evening. The sun had set long ago and the sounds of the evening insects were all around. Charles furnished a bottle of *zivania*, which Aydın discreetly advised Nora to avoid if she planned on waking early tomorrow for the trip to Nicosia.

"You go ahead Aydın. I'll good drive us back to Laneia," Nora said. Aydın gave her a pleasing grin, winked and brushed his lips to her cheek, then reached for the beaker of Cypriot moonshine.

"Yamas!" Nils said raising his glass. "I have some news I'd like to share with everyone since we seem to be celebrating."

Everyone turned attentively toward him. "Go on then," said Charles.

"Well, I've been waiting for orders to enter undergraduate pilot training every year since I was commissioned. Lieutenant Colonel Spade called me into his office this afternoon to tell me he'd received notification that the Air Forces Rated Personnel office finally granted me a pilot training slot. He handed me a set of orders to Moody Air Force Base, Georgia."

Nora thought she noticed her brother's dark disposition had changed when they met in front of the Chandler house earlier in the evening, but passed it off as his attempt at politeness. She was excited for him knowing that his dream of becoming a pilot was finally going to happen. "Fantastic Nils, when do you have to be there?" She asked.

"I leave at the end of May and report in at Moody sometime during the first week of June. Well, that is all my news. I'm excited about the adventure ahead and wanted to share the news with all of you."

Everyone around the Chandler table offered words of congratulations and encouragement to Nils. The conversation shifted to an account of Charles's early days in the British Army.

Curious, Nora asked, "Mrs. Chandler, when did you meet

Mr. Chandler. Was it here on Cyprus?"

Elaina was very proud to tell the story of how she met the dashing British Army Captain based at Dehkelia in the early 1970s. Charles was beaming at the way that she embellished the story of their courtship.

"What she hasn't told you is the grief that our relationship caused in my career. Somehow I managed to hang on for the next promotion, but was later forced to retire."

"When was that?" asked Nora.

"Let me tell it dear." Elaina was sliding into her story telling rhythm and her mood and body language were becoming animated and thoughtful at the same time.

Charles was all too eager to hear the story as Elaina had so rarely told it, and only to those who asked. He took another sip of the *zivania*. "Absolutely my sweet," he said. Then Elaina began.

"It was in the summer of 1972." She looked at Yolanda. "You were not even a glimmer in our eyes yet." She then made eye contact with everyone sitting around the table and continued with the story of how she met Charles.

"I was taking a few days off from my summer job. I was working as a chambermaid at a resort hotel in Varosha. In those years, Varosha was a prosperous place and popular among European holiday travelers because it was relatively inexpensive and had wonderful beaches. Since my family lived in Karmi,' now called Karaman near Kyrenia, two of my girlfriends from university joined me to share a room for the summer on the outskirts of Varosha so that we could save money for school.

When my mother and father came to visit for a long weekend, I borrowed my father's car and drove to Aiya Napa with my two friends. Just to get away and do something different. The irony is that it wasn't all that different than Varosha, except for one thing. There were lots of British soldiers taking their weekend leave.

That first evening, after spending a day at the beach, my friends and I were sitting at an outdoor cafe in the main square. There were men and women sitting around every table nearby. Many of them were drinking and having a cheerful time. To this day, I'm not really sure what happened, but there was a scuffle and a young drunken British man with short-cropped hair landed on our table and crashed to the pavement. We were startled and our dinner was everywhere.

By the time we were up and standing well away from where the young man fell, the scuffle had ended. My dashing hero in bright shining armor had everything under control. Charles had two of his NCOs escort the offending soldiers away. He pulled out a wad of Cypriot Pounds from his pocket and offered to pay the parties at the other tables for any spillage. The maître d' arrived at that moment and Charles had him eating out of his hand. Apologies were made in both directions and Charles assured the maître d' that his men wouldn't be causing any further disturbances. He was such a gentleman."

Charles was in a mellow mood hearing his wife embellish upon the stories of his heyday in the British Forces and felt the need to add further clarification. "It wasn't exactly like that. I had certain obligations with the local authorities you see."

Having shared this story a few times before, Elaina knew each part where Charles would try to steer the conversation to his military career and how this part of the story was the moment that changed his future with the British Army. This time she wasn't having any of it.

"Charles honey, this is my tale. I'm sure Nilsson and his sister and her guest would be very interested in the internal politics of your old Army, but tonight we are talking about how we met and made our home here in Cyprus."

"Mr. Chandler, I'm curious about your Army duties on Cyprus, but I get the feeling there is much more…I mean, gosh you're married and live here. Did you ever return to England or have you been here ever since?" asked Nora.

"My dear, that is indeed another story all together, but no, I've… I mean we've lived on Cyprus ever since. I've gone back to the U.K. from time to time, but only for short visits and with a yearning to get back here to the warmth of Elaina and Cyprus as soon as possible." He paused and rose from the table.

"Now I think Nils and Brad and I will join Yolanda in

cleaning up the kitchen." Yolanda had quietly left the table
earlier to tuck her sons into bed and straighten things in the
kitchen.

"Gentlemen, shall we?" Nils had visited the Chandlers on
other occasions and knew of his hostess's life experiences on the
island but somehow never had a passion to embrace the
connection of her experiences to the modernity of the world he
was working in daily.

"Mrs. Chandler, please don't leave anything out. You'll
promise me you'll tell my sister everything you've told me, OK?"

"Oh Nilsson, you can be sure of that. On the kitchen
counter there is a pitcher of lemon water. By now the ice has
probably melted. There are more cubes in the icebox. If you
would, I'm sure Nora and Aydın wouldn't mind a glass, and I
could sure use some."

"It would be my pleasure." Nils was in an accommodating
mood, probably because he allowed himself to be mellowed by
the *zivania*. Nora was glad her brother wasn't an angry drunk. In
fact deep down his good nature wouldn't allow it. As Nils rose
from his seat, he leaned to whisper into his sister's ear, "See I
told you this woman has stories to share." Nora smiled at her
brother and squeezed his hand as he left the table.

"Please go on Mrs. Chandler. I'm really enjoying this story.
It makes me feel connected to a life and a time that I knew
nothing of," said Aydın. Nora was surprised that Aydın said

anything at all.

"Let me see, where were we? Oh, yes. Charles was making amends with the staff at the cafe." Elaina continued.

"When the maître d' left, Charles noticed the three of us standing behind what was once our dinner table. Seeing that the calamari and marinara were splattered over the three of us he strode over to apologize. He was so gentle and confident at the same time. I was standing in the middle between Damala and Cyprian. Both of them were whispering something to each other at the same time about what a 'dish' this man was.

Charles stood before us holding out both of his hands, palms up in a resignation of apology and looking back and forth between the three of us, his eyes finally resting on me. He said, "I'm very sorry. Is there anything I can do to make it up to you? Something for cleaning the mess my boys have made of your beautiful dresses?'

Really we were all still wearing beach attire, just cheap linen pullovers with our bathing suits on underneath. Damala and Cyprian were still jabbering between each other and giggling. I didn't know what to say. I was taken by him immediately, so I stood there speechless and dumbfounded for a moment, then replied, 'don't give it another thought. These things happen. We were done with our dinner anyway.'

Charles offered to buy us after dinner drinks at a more quiet and refined outdoor lounge around the corner from the main square, and we accepted. The lounge was nice and played traditional music. Damala and Cyprian got up to dance on the small floor in front of the musicians, giving Charles a chance to focus on wooing me with his charms.

We made arrangements to meet again the following week, only that time instead of meeting in Aiya Napa, Charles came to Varosha by himself. Since I only had the use of my father's car on the rare occasion when he and my mother visited Varosha, Charles came up regularly throughout the summer. We became very close. Best friends, sharing every detail of our lives, hopes and dreams."

"Mrs. Chandler, what were some of those hopes?"

"Oh, my dear. There were too many. Most of them remain hopes today."

Aydın keyed into the older woman's emotion and sat up in his chair, slipped his arm off Nora's shoulder and leaned toward the Greek Cypriot woman and said, "I was very young. My family lived in Balıkesir. I was born there but never knew it as home. As my uncle used to say, I was spirited away by good fortune."

"When were you born Aydın?" Elaina had some idea as to the answer but wanted to confirm her suspicions.

"The 23rd of July, 1974. I don't know any of the details of how I ended up in Kantou where my uncle lived. I remember some of that village. It was very near to here, I think. The

Turkish Cypriot name of the village was Çanakkale. When I was seven years old, my uncle and I moved to Laneia with our closest friends, the Elias's. Anyway, you were saying about you and your husband…when did you get married?"

"We all lived through troubled times Aydın. The memories will never leave us. Thankfully there are many good memories to stamp out the bad. When I met Charles my hope was that we would become married and have children."

Elaina continued, "When I returned to school in Kyrenia in September of 1972, I had three more years before I could earn my degree. I studied history and literature. I wanted to become a librarian and be near to all the books of history.

Charles and I made an agreement. He would get leave for Christmas and meet my parents and my brother at our home in Karmi. That Christmas he asked my father for his blessing and then proposed to me. It was a long engagement complicated by Charles's army duties and the politics that put walls in front of us when it came to planning an official wedding. In the end, he gave up his career with the army so we could be married. It worked out for the best.

We were married in the spring of 1974. The wedding was a traditional all day event. My parents arranged for us to be married at Bellapais Abbey. Afterward, all of my relatives, our friends and neighbors, and even some of Charles's army friends came to the reception party in the center of Karmi.

By the time the dancing started in the late of night, we were both exhausted from the festivities. I had been wearing my wedding dress all through the day. Charles's shirt collar couldn't hide the fact that the heat of the day hung long into the evening hours.

We danced through the crowds of our family and friends still celebrating with Cypriot wine knowing that the sunrise was only a few hours away. As we danced everyone pinned envelopes stuffed with money onto my wedding gown. At the end of the night, it was so heavy with paper...I don't know if we ever actually counted the money. We agreed to toss it into a drawer, take what we needed for a honeymoon and deposit the rest in the bank. I will never forget that day and that night."

Aydın was lost in thought. Nora nudged him worried that he might have fallen asleep from the late hour and too much wine and *zivania*. He looked up at her indicating he was still awake and attentive. Nora asked, "Where did you live after the wedding? Did you go to Dehkelia to live on the base?"

"Oh no dear, that would have been forbidden. One of the arrangements Charles made with his regiment was that he would serve out the remainder of his tour of duty before moving from Dehkelia. My Father and Charles were able to work out a deal with one of my father's oldest friends. Charles was set to work as a transport administrator at the port of Limassol once his commitment to the army had ended. So I stayed with my parents and we waited...."

Elaina's voice trailed off into thought and a long pause. She took a drink from the cool lemon water before going on.

"Yes, we waited and looked forward to moving into our own home. It was a fearful and uncertain time. You see the Colonel's Coup in Greece had changed things. All through those early years of the 1970s there was turmoil when Georgios Grivas rekindled *enosis* and formed EOKA-B stirring up an already thick mixture of trouble. The coup in Greece had come to Cyprus.

Our Makarios fled in the early part of the summer. We all thought he had been killed during the coup. Nicos Sampson took over after Makarios disappeared and soon there were Greek Cypriots fighting Greek Cypriots."

Nora interrupted, "Makarios?" she asked.

"Arch Bishop Makarios was the president of Greek Cyprus and was thought of by the people as a national hero," said Aydın, filling in the blanks for Nora.

"And Sampson?" she asked.

"He was not a nationalist like our Makarios. He was only in power for a couple of weeks before being arrested for abuse of power," Elaina added before continuing her story.

"Charles was caught up in the whole affair. Somehow the British managed to get Makarios off the island during the failed coup. Charles was up in Erenköy inspecting an equipment depot when all of this happened. He won't talk about it but I know it must have been terrible because he took a detour through Karmi on his way back to Dehkelia.

My mother and I had been listening to the radio all day long waiting and hoping for news from Erenköy. We were scared and I was so afraid for Charles. I had no idea where he was until he came to my mother's home. When I saw him I was relieved. We embraced for a long time. My father and brother returned from work in the early afternoon

They said that all work had stopped. Everyone was told to go home and the men in the National Guard were ordered to report to their units. In those days all able men were members of the Cypriot National Guard.

The three men were all heading in separate directions. My mother and I didn't know if we would see any of them ever again. Before they left, my grandfather showed up. He had an apartment down by the Kyrenia harbor. He wanted to make sure my mother and I would be safe and planned to stay with us until things settled down.

When Charles and I kissed we did not say goodbye. He held me for a long time and then I watched him drive off in the jeep he borrowed from his regiment. My father and brother rushed away taking what they thought they would need in case the armory was short of supplies.

There were rumors of Turkey becoming involved. The commentary we heard over the radio from BBC repeated there was justification for Turkish involvement under the provisions of a treaty signed at the time of our independence. For the next few days we waited to hear if the Turkish Army was going to invade.

I'll never forget the day 20 July 1974. I went to look for Damala at her parent's house. Nobody was home. Damala and I were supposed to see one of the professors about a research project we had been working on at the university.

I still remember what I was wearing that day. It seems so silly. I had on a suede brown skirt with a big belt buckle and a beige blouse. The boots I was wearing were impractical, but it was the fashion of those days, and like most young women fashion was important to my friends and me.

When I got home my mother and my grandfather were sitting at the kitchen table listening intently to the radio and the news that ships from Turkey were already on their way to Cyprus.

A little while later, my grandfather went out into the garden to fill up some barrels with water. Before he was finished, he stormed into the kitchen looking for us and shouting for us to come outside. When we ran out, we could see the soldiers falling from the sky underneath parachutes, landing in the fields below our village.

My grandfather then led us into the kitchen again. In the center of the floor underneath the table there was a pull up door with a ladder leading down to a small dark cellar. My grandfather quickly scooted the table out of the way, lifted up the door and ushered my mother and me down the ladder.

As I remember, it was dark and scary, but not nearly as scary as what happened a few moments later. We could feel the ground shake as the falling bombs exploded and the cannon fire from the ships erupted. We stayed there in the dark for I don't know how long. The floor of our cellar was just dirt. The space was very small. There was part of an old door lying on its side so I climbed up onto it and curled up to stay warm. The noise from the explosions was deafening. Later my mother told people that she was sure that we were there for three days. I stayed curled up on that door the whole time too frightened to sleep.

It must have been days later when the noise from the fighting stopped. My grandfather went up to see if it was safe. He called us up and the three of us went out to the front garden to look down over Kyrenia only to see plumes of dark smoke smoldering up from the remains of several buildings and homes. Just down the hill in our own village I could see the burning remains and rubble of a once luxurious home that overlooked a vast orchard.

We saw some of the villagers who were fortunate enough to have a car, drive away toward the south with all their worldly goods strapped to the roof. Those on foot carried whatever they could and jumped on the backs of passing lorries. Sometime during those first hours of silence, we joined the other refugees to head south over the mountains.

We had no place in mind to go but knew it would be in our best interest to stay away from Nicosia, where so much of the fighting continued for weeks and months past the initial invasion. Some of the other refugees had relatives in Paphos and convinced us that we'd be safe there and taken care of, so we went along. Mostly what I remember of those times were the early mornings of traveling long distances on foot. When it got hot in the afternoons, we looked for shade and water. I don't know how long it took, but we ended up in the outskirts of Paphos when it was all over.

It seemed like people were afraid for a very long time. We heard reports from all over the island that the Turkish Army was rounding up Greek Cypriot sympathizers and shooting them on the spot. We also heard stories of chaos in the northern towns and villages.

Less than a month later, we heard on the news that the American Ambassador, Rodger Davies, was killed by a stray bullet passing through the window of the U.S. Embassy in Nicosia. Nobody believed that story, but it served as an example that the violence would continue because it happened only days after the announcement was broadcast over the radio that a formal ceasefire agreement was signed in Genève.

I don't remember every detail from those first months

because along with most of the other refugees, we had our hands full rebuilding our lives."

Elaina took a deep breath and sat back in her chair gazing up at the stars. Nils and Charles had long since returned to the back garden and stood in the shadows while Elaina told her story. Charles stepped over behind Elaina and wrapped a shawl that he brought out from the house around the shoulders of his bride.

"Oh thank you Charles. I was beginning to feel the chill of the night." She turned to kiss his hand that still lingered on her shoulder.

"It is getting late dear. We should think of our guests needing to get back."

"Certainly. I didn't mean to ramble." Elaina said this as she tucked the shawl around her while making eye contact with everyone in turn.

Nils immediately felt the need to say something. The *zivania* had evidently taken its effect. "Mrs. Chandler, I wouldn't ever say you ramble. In fact, I've never heard you share this particular story before. It makes me sad for what you had to go through. You and every other Cypriot who had no choice in the matter."

Nora was suddenly awakened by her brother's comment. Something she hadn't heard from him in a very long time. In spite of his slightly slurred speech, the tone of his voice suggested a genuine compassion and reminded her of the conversations and arguments they had when Nils was in the

Balkans.

He went on briefly, "When I was in Kosovo not too long ago, I saw up close what happens to the innocent people caught in the middle of conflict. People with no choice in the directions their lives must take just to stay safe. It is something that Americans aren't familiar with."

"Thank you Nilsson. I don't know what got into me this evening, but we all have our past don't we? Well, it is late. Nilsson, you are going to stay in the guest room tonight. Not another word about it either. You can drive back to Akrotiri early tomorrow morning."

As she rose from the table, Charles put an arm around her and with his other hand, gestured to the others to make their way into the house and front foyer.

"Thank you for the lovely evening and wonderful *meze*, Mrs. Chandler." Aydın said a few other things to her in Greek and a tear welled in her eye as she gave him a hug. As Aydın was shaking hands with Mr. Chandler, Nora and Elaina hugged one another.

"You are always welcome here Nora. Please anytime, and I do approve of this young man of yours. Don't let him out of your sight."

"Thank you Mrs. Chandler. I will definitely take you up on that offer. I look forward to your sharing how you and Mr. Chandler found each other again. It sounded like quite a lot to go through in your first year of marriage."

Brad and Yolanda escorted Aydın and Nora to the car and said their good-byes.

CHAPTER 8

The Green Line

Nora rose early with a realization that she'd be leaving Cyprus in a matter of days. Aydın was up early standing in the kitchen barefoot and shirtless wearing a pair of faded jeans when Nora came down taking in the aroma of freshly prepared Cypriot coffee. She reached for the coffee and thanked him for preparing it by giving him a soft kiss on the ear. He noticed she was already made up and dressed for her day out.

"You should go. There will be traffic when you get to Nicosia." Aydın sounded genuinely excited for her. "You can tell me all about it when you get back this evening."

Nora sipped from her *metreo* coffee and looked up at him. She set the cup back in its small saucer when she finished. "I guess I should be off then." She gave him a hug. "Thanks for last night... and the coffee too Aydın. You are so thoughtful." She reached down and gave Kaplan a scratch. The big orange cat rolled over and began to purr. "I haven't been very good to you have I?" admitted Nora.

"He's fine Nora. He's a spoiled old cat just like his master. Don't think for a second he minds, as long as he stays well fed." Aydın said this while gathering up some kitchen scraps and putting them on a small plate only to spoil the cat even more.

Nora followed the instructions her brother gave her over the phone. The Tuesday morning traffic in Nicosia was light so she had no trouble arriving ahead of schedule in front of the Headquarters building. The UN Peace Keeping Forces in Cyprus were housed in the former Ledra Palace Hotel in the heart of the divided capitol. When she arrived at the UN compound there were other well-dressed foreign visitors being met by various embassy personnel. A slender athletic looking blond woman, wearing the camouflaged uniform of a British Army Captain and capped with the ubiquitous blue beret worn by soldiers of all nations supporting overseas UN missions, approached Nora.

"Nora Johansson?"

"Yes," replied Nora.

"Good morning, I'm Captain Julie Ralston. I've worked with your brother Nilsson."

Nora looked into the bright blue eyes of the woman in front of her and noticed her sun darkened complexion, a stark contrast to her sun bleached hair pulled back tightly behind her beret.

Nora stretched out her hand to the captain, "Pleased to meet you Captain."

"Likewise. Just call me Julie OK?" The captain looked to be in her late twenties. She spoke swiftly and confidently with the precise enunciation of a graduate from the Royal Military Academy of Sandhurst.

"You'll have to endure a rather boring history and briefing

before your tour," the captain said, pointing into the anteroom just inside a courtyard area. She continued with her instructions, "It will be held just there and takes about twenty minutes. I'm not sure who'll be assigned to escort you, but the walking tours are conducted in groups no larger than four guests.

There will be a UN soldier at the front and another at the rear of your group. Each group will depart at fifteen minute intervals. I've arranged for you to be with the first group, so when you go inside, take the vacant seat in the front row.

After the tour I'll meet you in the UN cafeteria where the tour ends. Your brother has pulled some strings and has arranged another outing for you, which I'll explain when I see you in a couple of hours."

"Thanks Julie, I'm looking forward to the whole day."

"Right then, see you in awhile." The captain spun on her heels and was gone before Nora was aware she was standing alone in the courtyard.

Nora found the historical background and briefing to be a rather abbreviated version of what she'd learned from talking with Aydın and some recent research she'd conducted on her own. The one exception was that the presentation at the UN compound seemed pretty objective because it provided a chronology of events and parties involved during the late 50s, and the 1963-64 period of inter-communal strife.

It seemed that every effort was made by the UN to present

the facts without placing blame on any particular party. The history lesson concluded with a factoid about the naming of "The Green Line" in 1964, when the UN Peace Forces Commander, Major General Peter Young drew a "cease fire" line with a dark green crayon across the map of Cyprus.

With the exception of Aydın, nearly every Greek Cypriot Nora met focused on the events that took place in the summer of 1974. Nora was not only told, but also read from several sources that the Turkish Military "invaded" Cyprus, justifying their actions under the terms of the Treaty of Guarantee signed in 1960 when the British turned over governmental control of her former colony to Cyprus.

Nora noticed that few Greek Cypriots ever mention much about the coup that lead up to the events in 1974. A theme was becoming clear to her that the situation on Cyprus is complex and the people most directly impacted have drastically different perspectives of how the current situation on the island evolved.

The walking tour took less time then she thought it would. The ghostly buildings and homes along the route between the two sides of the divide were eerie. Through the back of one building she could see what was left of a "W.H. Smith" variety store with brand items such as stationery, post cards, and pens etc. still on the shelves collecting dust. Everywhere along the route it appeared that time froze in July and August of 1974 and nothing had been touched since then.

The UN soldiers guiding the visitors on the walk between the barbed wire in the buffer zone that cut through the heart of Nicosia explained how they kept track of every stone and piece of rubbish within the zone. Anything out of place would be investigated.

One of the visitors asked why such attention to detail, and the guide explained that in some locations, booby traps had been placed so that an unsuspecting intruder would be met with a surprise. He also explained how in some of the abandoned villages it had taken UN Inspection Teams many years to be sure that none of the damaged buildings or homes contained dangerous hazards; such as, trip wire grenades and hastily placed crude bombs.

Shortly after the final cease-fire on 16 August 1974, UN forces established the new buffer zone. Barriers and barbed wire were erected on either side. Both Greek Cypriot and Turkish soldiers began manning outposts that remain in a standoff to this day.

When Nora arrived in the UN cafeteria, she was treated to a final piece of history. The cafeteria not only sold snacks, but also served as a makeshift museum to the UN Forces on Cyprus.

Sitting at the edge of the main room behind a cable was a gleaming dark metallic green 1974 "Datsun 1200." There was a placard next to the display that explained how the car was discovered on the ground floor of a collapsed car dealership, trapped among the rubble with several other damaged and undamaged cars. Some of the UN soldiers while stationed in Nicosia, took it upon themselves to dismantle the car so that it could be moved from the confines of its trap and reassembled where it now rests.

Nora looked up from reading the information about the Datsun and noticed Captain Ralston striding toward her.

"Ms. Johansson, I trust that you found the tour interesting?"

"Absolutely and thank you Julie for arranging it for me. Oh, and I'm sorry, I should have insisted earlier, please call me Nora."

"Alright then Nora, are you ready to see some more of the buffer zone?"

"There is more? I mean, more that I can see and visit?" Nora was well aware of the extent of the buffer zone having just been given a detailed explanation during her tour including numerous references to a map.

"Yes, I've been instructed to put you in the charge of an American colleague of mine from your Embassy." Captain Ralston then led Nora out of the UN compound to the street where a shinny black Volvo sedan with diplomatic plates was waiting.

Standing beside the car was a blond, bronzed man with a cut physique who looked to be in his late thirties but was probably in his 40s. With his hair cropped short, dressed in khaki and wearing aviator sunglasses, the man looked anything but a U.S. Military officer.

"Nora Johansson, meet Colonel Jake Barrows, the U.S. Defense Attaché."

Nora stretched out her hand, "pleased to see you again Colonel. I didn't recognize you without the official uniform."

"It's Jake, just call me Jake, and yes it is nice to see you again as well. Your brother Nils has done some excellent work for us these past months. It is the least I can do to show you around."

"Right then, if that will be all sir, I'll be off," said Captain Ralston as she gave Colonel Barrows a brisk salute and waved goodbye to Nora.

"Thanks again Julie. I hope to see you again." Nora waved back to the captain then turned back to Jake who was holding the door to the Volvo open for her.

Nora was surprised that someone like Colonel Barrows would be able to take the time to show her around. She turned to the Attaché, "I thought my brother was too junior to have any pull. I'll admit I don't know much about his work, and thought it was confined to operations intelligence with the Air Force."

"It's complicated. I owe him a favor and don't mind one bit. Let's just say he has a promising future with his service."

"I guess that's good news. This is quite the surprise. Where are we going?"

"You'll see. It isn't far. I'll bring you back to your car when we're done. If I am correct in my assumption that you are interested in learning about the recent conflicts of Cyprus, I'm sure you'll be plenty impressed with where we're going."

Colonel Barrows drove Nora west on the A-9 from central Nicosia. On the western outskirts of the divided city, the buffer zone becomes very wide. The view from the road was mostly of broad open fields of tall grasses turning to a dry golden color. On the north side of the highway there was an unmarked road that led to a stretch of barbed wire and a barrier gate. Jake stopped the Volvo in front of the unguarded entry and used a key he drew from his pocket to unlock the gate, then he drove through and stopped to lock the gate behind them.

"There used to be a UN encampment here. I should say, there still is a camp, but nobody is stationed here anymore. When the Canadian forces took one of their many turns on the Green Line they must have become bored and frustrated, because the abandoned their posts all together. It is still unclear and I guess it depends on whom you ask, but what resulted was a substantial draw down of UN forces on the island since the Canadians pulled out in June of '93.

Soldiers from several different countries supporting the UN peacekeeping mission once occupied this camp and many others throughout the length of the buffer zone. The place is pretty quiet now."

"It feels like a ghost town." Said Nora.

"You aren't the first to use those words." Jake drove on a little further as the road wound it's way past another open area. "Lakatamia Cemetery. It is right up there. Again, depending on who you ask, it is a mass grave of either Greek soldiers, Greek Cypriot women and children, or filled with Turkish Cypriots who were victims of ethnic cleansing."

After hearing Mrs. Chandler describe her flight from the north last evening Nora wasn't sure she wanted the full tour. "We don't really need to go up there," said Nora.

"I wasn't planning on it. I just thought you'd want to know what kinds of things get discussed and by whom in this setting. If you are interested and have time, I can arrange for you to visit the north. There is a place up there near Famagusta. In the village of Muratağa there is an undisputed mass grave on the grounds of what was once a school. Turkish Cypriots living in the three villages of Muratağa, Sandallar, and Atlılar were rounded up on 14 August 1974 and massacred."

"That sounds terrible! You'd never know by listening to only one side of the story."

"There is some debate as to whether those civilians were killed by EOKA fighters or Greek Cypriot soldiers backed by Greece."

"Does it matter? What happened was terrible."

"It matters to them. Anyway, the atrocities throughout the period were committed by both sides...all sides."

"The period?"

"Yes, from '63-74 the victims or refugees were mostly Turkish Cypriots. In '74 the Coup of Colonels in Greece and the Coup against the Greek Cypriot government were clouded by the Turkish invasion on 20 July that summer."

"You said all sides. What exactly did you mean?"

"During the Coup, Greeks and Greek Cypriots were apparently attacking each other. EOKA was divided into two factions: EOKA-A and EOKA-B. The history books are pretty clear on who was involved and what their goals were. All of it traces back to the agenda in Athens at that time. However, what actually happened in the villages is still unclear. Depends who you talk to."

They drove a little further and the track they were driving on merged onto an access road. Nora was aware they had arrived at the service area of the Nicosia International Airport.

"Now this is a ghost town," she whispered slowly to herself.

"I imagine there were people in a pretty big hurry to get out of here once the shooting started." Jake continued with the history lesson of the battle that ensued over twenty-five years earlier. He described the locations of downed Turkish military aircraft as they walked across the tarmac pointing to various corners of the airfield.

As they rounded the corner of a large hangar, they saw before them an abandoned Cypriot airliner. Apparently a maintenance malfunction kept it from departing. After all the years in the sun, the paint was flaked and faded and the tires had long since gone flat. One of the doors at the rear had been removed. They walked on and passed through the doors of the main terminal. The interior was even spookier than what they saw from the outside.

"This was a state of the art facility for its time." Jake explained to Nora how some of his predecessors had visited the inside of the terminal several years earlier. As they walked along the central lobby he explained further.

Nora looked around at the interior design and layout. "The architecture kind of reminds me of an old movie. What it must have been like back in the days when air travel was available only to the very rich and people dressed up in their finest for the adventure. I always wanted to experience what that era must have been like, but seeing this, I don't know what to think."

"One of the urban myths about this terminal is that there was still baggage waiting on the carousel to be picked up when the attacks began. There were probably Teletype machines with airline tickets in the process of being printed that stopped half way through when the gate attendants ran for cover. In the cafeteria short order food was left on the grill, probably to burn to a char with the fires still lit when the cooking staff rushed out of the building. At one time there were cans of Pepsi and Coke still lining the shelves behind the glass doors of the refrigerators."

Nora looked around to confirm that too many years had passed. Even with the small number of official visitors whose presence was tightly controlled, the likelihood was that anything of value would have been looted. Nora speculated to herself that things were probably taken as memorabilia by the bored soldiers who were required to stay in the encampment that was within easy walking distance of the terminal.

As the Colonel Barrows drove Nora back into central Nicosia where her rental car was still parked, he looked across to her and asked, "How old are you anyway?"

"Same age as my brother. We're twins. Why? I thought you knew about us because you were friends with our dad."

"To be honest, your dad and I weren't all that close. He did things for me and I reciprocated. We are almost from different generations. Back to your brother, that young man is very serious. He's a studious matter of fact sort of guy. Makes him seem older I guess. You, on the other hand have a completely different brand of curiosity."

"How do you mean?"

"I watched you at the airport. I watched you listen to the history and could tell your imagination was running in circles trying to piece everything together. I listened to the way you ask your questions and I just wanted to remind you that Cyprus isn't the only place with a history of tragedy."

"Please Colonel, I may be young, but you don't have to tell me what I already know. I spent some time in Azerbaijan teaching English to poor high school kids. My Azeri was never that good, but I could understand enough to know what those kids wanted to share about their fears while coming of age in a land of conflict."

"Hey, take it easy. I certainly didn't mean to diminish what you've experienced in your young life. Really. I'm impressed with your interest, and God knows most gals your age who come here are only interested in what can be had on a 'fun in the sun' holiday. You aren't like that."

"Sorry Jake, I didn't mean to react so strongly. Sometimes I think about how evolved we are as humans and yet we still aren't smart enough or sophisticated enough to avoid killing each other. I guess for me it is a source of frustration to see the results. It is such a tragic waste."

"What has happened here has played itself out through every age and on every continent. I witnessed some of the horrors of the Balkan conflicts and the ones who suffer are never the ones who invite violence. They are simply the people in between."

There was silence between them for several minutes as they stood outside of the terminal building gazing out to the distant hills to the north and west beyond the forlorn runway.

The Attaché looked at Nora and said, "You are wise beyond your years. Your mom and dad must be proud."

"Dad is. He's the one who wanted me to come here. He said if 'I could wrap my brain around Cyprus,' I would be able to come to grips with some of the causes of conflict. He said if you know the causes you could become part of the solutions rather than a contributor to future problems.

My mom died when Nils and I were born. She was a Turkish Cypriot refugee. I don't know any of the details of my mom's past. Dad never talked about her while we were growing up. The guy who owns the place where I am staying told me about how he met them and what they were like." A tear streamed down Nora's face as she turned away in silence.

"I'm sorry, I didn't know. I mean, I'm sorry about your mother."

"It's OK, I didn't know her, but I really want to know what she was like…what her life was like. It is one of the reasons I came to Cyprus."

"Well then, we most certainly need to get you up to visit the north."

"Mom never lived there. She stayed behind in her village near Limassol."

"I think you still need to stay longer, or come back. The north is something you shouldn't miss experiencing," said Jake in an effort to lighten the conversation. "Azerbaijan aye? *Acaba Türkçe biliyorsun.*" He said, taking the chance that Nora might know some Turkish.

"Azaerbaycanlı! zahir Türk vae Azeri eynicinsli diller." Nora
understood the question and responded by telling Jake that the
Azerbaijani people's Azeri language was almost the same as
Turkish.

"A visit to the north could be a lot of fun for you. The
Turkish spoken in Cyprus is a bit different, but then again, Azeri
isn't Turkish. I'm sure you'd get along just fine. I know you'd
find the people to be very warm."

"You sound like a man who has spent some time there. I'll
take your word for it and when I return to Cyprus, I'll take you
up on that trip too." She said as Jake pulled up along side her car
in the visitor lot at the UN Headquarters. As she got out, she
thanked the Attaché again for the tour and promised to call
again.

Nora drove straight back to Laneia in the heat of the late
afternoon. She managed to miss the traffic that normally
swarmed the outskirts of Limassol. She was looking forward to
spending the evening with Aydın but her emotions were in a
roar. Her trip back gave her a chance to reflect on the things
she'd seen and heard about Cyprus in the past forty-eight hours.
As she pulled onto the gravel section of road leading to the
gallery, she decided to focus all her attentions on the evening
ahead.

She thought about Aydın and how his life represented
another face of the human tragedy of the Cyprus conflict. She

was mystified by why he didn't seem to let the past bother him, as she knew it would bother her. She was also reflective of the glimmer of compassion she saw in her brother the evening before. "The Nils I always loved as my closest relative and best friend is still there," she thought to herself.

When Nora got out of the car and walked up the path through the gallery garden, she saw Kaplan rise from his napping spot in front of the main door and pulled himself into a long cat stretch. As she approached he rolled onto his side and back, an irresistible invitation for Nora to bend down and give him a good belly scratch.

"Hey Tiger, you missed me? I haven't been much of a companion lately. Don't worry though, your daddy will be back soon to spoil you." Nora never had a pet like Kaplan. The family cat the Johanssons kept in their yard while growing up in Nebraska was a necessity. Either you had a cat around or you had mice in your house. It was as simple as that.

As she entered the kitchen, the scene was only slightly different than the one she'd left earlier that day. Aydın was standing before the kitchen table with his back to the sink brandishing an enormous French Chef's knife. He was wearing the same faded pair of jeans, barefoot, but instead of shirtless, he was only slightly better attired with a white linen chef's apron hanging from his neck and tied at the waist.

He noticed the look on Nora's face and couldn't quite make

out the meaning and thought he must have looked ridiculous standing there dressed like a peasant with a pile of freshly harvested vegetables already chopped in the large bowl on the table next to the cutting board. "He is indeed a catch," she thought to herself. "…and I'd better watch out because I'm getting used to being spoiled."

"I've already started the grill out in the side yard. I'm preparing a traditional Cypriot dish. All fresh. Have you ever heard of *fassoulia yiahni*?"

Nora shrugged her shoulders. "I have no idea what that is, but I'm sure it will be delicious. It sure looks like it will be and this kitchen smells amazing." She said this noticing a large pot simmering on the stove.

"Sorry about the wine," he said nodding over to a bottle and a beaker sitting over on the counter opposite the kitchen sink. "The Elias's only stock Cypriot wine on their shelves."

She recognized the tan label with the words *Mount Olympus Red*, and remembered the harsh dryness that accompanied the rough flavors of the Mavro grapes so common to the island.

"There is nothing to be sorry about, I enjoy the charm of a local wine. Besides, this can be the liquid equivalent to 'our song'."

"Our song? I don't know what you mean. I just opened the wine. It should be OK." He reached for the bottle and began pouring some into a waiting glass and handed it to her.

She took the glass and raised it saying, *"Yamas!"*

"Yamas!" said Aydın. After they both took a sip, he leaned down brushing a lock of hair from Nora's eye and gave her a welcome kiss then casually asked, "How was the tour? I hope the drive back wasn't difficult for you?"

"Nicosia was getting pretty hot by the time I left. Except for the heat, the drive back wasn't bad at all. I'm starting to feel at home here, but I'm really exhausted."

"The heat of a Cypriot summer makes people want to relax. You are starting to feel this, I can see. If you think it is hot now, wait till July. Nicosia can be over 40C in the afternoon, and it doesn't cool down much at night."

"Well, the tour was interesting. Between last night and everything today, it's just a lot to think about in such a short span of time. Did Gavin call?"

"Oh yes. He returns to Larnaca tomorrow evening. He said he'd call again with the flight details and arrival times. I told him the place burned down while he was away and he laughed." He gave her shoulder a soft squeeze brushed his lips across her ear. "It is almost ready for cooking and grilling. Are you hungry?"

"Actually, yes, I'm famished."

"Good, because this meal is almost ready to serve." He removed the apron he was wearing and retrieved a white cotton shirt from a peg on the wall near the back of the kitchen and slipped it on. He turned to reach for a deep plate with deboned chicken breasts that had been marinating in a mixture of olive oil and spices.

"Please, grab the wine and come along while I grill these." They stepped outside and around the corner from the main courtyard to a small semi circular flagstone patio.

There was a pair of metal bistro chairs arranged beside a small table with a blue and white-checkered tablecloth. On it were place settings for two and a clear glass chimney with a scented candle ready to be lit.

"Please sit. I'll just put these on the grill and go get the rest of the meal." After he put the chicken pieces on the grill he headed back to the kitchen for the large bowl of village salad he'd been preparing in the kitchen when Nora arrived.

He returned laden with the salad bowl, dressing bottles of olive oil and another bowl with wedges of fresh pita and began serving. Just before taking a seat and joining Nora for the first course, he turned the chicken on the grill. As he sat down he lifted the glass globe over the candle and lit it. The candle began to burn bright when he slipped the glass globe back into place sheltering the flame from the warm evening breeze blowing down from the mountain.

"I wanted the evening to be memorable since tomorrow is your last day. Is there a special way you'd like to spend the day? Somewhere you'd like to go?"

Nora looked over the rim of her wine glass admiring him. "I

wouldn't mind a tour of the Akamas. Maybe we can find those rocks of Gavin's, like the ones he painted that are hanging in the upper gallery." She paused and set her wine glass down before continuing. "Aydın, on the drive back from Nicosia, I did some thinking about your suggestion."

"Which is? I'm not following you?"

"About staying for the summer. There is still so much to see. I want to go to the north. I want to spend more time with you."

His smile broadened as he leaned forward reaching for both of her hands across the small table. He looked into the depths of her bright hazel colored eyes. "This makes me very happy Nora." There was no need to say more. He just kept smiling for a bit before breaking the spell. "It looks like you'll be learning the way Cypriots relax in the summer then. This news is really good. You will see."

Aydın rose from the table. "I'll just be a moment. The meat is ready and I will go in to bring the *fassoulia* out to the table."

Nora watched as he removed the slices of chicken from the grill and put them on a plate and set it on a tray beside the table. She blew him a kiss as he set off for the kitchen and he winked at her over his shoulder.

Leaving the kitchen with a large serving bowl filled with *fassoulia,* Aydın heard the phone ring and rattle from inside the main gallery. "Ah, that must be Gavin," he thought to himself.

149

"I'd better sneak in and answer it."

"*Kalispera*, Hart Gallery. This is Aydın may I help you?" He wanted to sound professional when he answered so Gavin would know the gallery was in good hands while he was away.

"It's Nils. Is my sister there?"

"Yes she just returned from Nicosia. You sound troubled Nils. Is everything alright?"

"Actually no. I received a call from the states about my dad. I really need to talk to Nora."

Aydın's heart sank knowing Nora probably wouldn't be staying the summer. "Of course, I'll put her on right away. Nils, whatever it is, let me know if there is something I can do to help."

"I just need to talk to her." Nils's normally confident voice sounded weak and shaken.

When Aydın returned to the table where Nora was sitting, she was looking beautiful in the glow of the candle light, happy and smiling from head to toe until she saw him approach.

"I thought you were going to bring the *fassoulia*. Did it burn or something?"

He left it on the small table in the gallery next to the phone. "No, nothing like that. The phone rang. I thought it was Gavin so I answered. It was your brother. He needs to talk to you right away."

Nora got up from her chair, setting her wine glass on the

table and gave Aydın a kiss on the cheek before going into the gallery to pick up the phone.

"I'll be right back. I love you Aydın."

He followed her into the gallery and watched and listened from the doorway. Nora's body language and muffled sobs were enough to tell him that the situation with her father wasn't good. The conversation was brief. Aydın saw her nod her head up and down several times before she set the handset back in its cradle. There were tears streaming from both eyes when she turned toward the door and noticed Aydın waiting for the news.

"My dad..." she said between quiet sobs. "He has been fighting skin cancer for several years. We thought he had more time since his treatments had him in remission. He just learned it spread into his lymphatic system. He's in the hospital for immediate treatment. Chemo, again."

Aydın took her gently by both shoulders and wrapped her in his arms. He kissed the top of her head and held her. "I'm sorry. I don't know him, but I can tell how you feel about him."

"We're leaving tonight. I've got to pack my things and meet Nils in Limassol." She pushed away from him and the tears flowed as she shook her head from side to side.

"I can take you. You're exhausted."

"Are you sure, how will you get back?"

"Nora, Nora, you worry about things that don't matter. Go get your things. I'll take you to meet Nils and we'll get you to the airport."

"What about us? Will you be here? I don't know when I'll make it back to Cyprus."

"I'll be here Nora. For you, whenever you get back...and if you don't return, I'll come find you. I love you."

A short while later, they were in the car park of the Orphanides store in Limassol where Nils was waiting with one of his fellow officers from Akrotiri. He shook hands with his colleague and hefted his small duffle into the boot of Nora's rental car.

"Hey sis." Nils gave her a hug.

"Hey." She just looked at him as he lowered himself into the back seat.

"Thank you Aydın." Nils said as the car pulled onto the main road leading to the highway.

Two hours later, Nils and Nora were on a plane to Frankfurt connecting to a direct flight to Dulles. They'd be in Bethesda, Maryland by noon the following day.

CHAPTER 9

Washington D.C.

At Dulles they picked up a rental car and drove to Nora's apartment in Arlington where they would freshen up with a shower and change of clothes before heading over to the hospital in Bethesda. They were both tired and jet lagged, but Nils had no trouble sleeping on the flight over the Atlantic, so he did the driving through the late morning Washington D.C. traffic while Nora dozed in the seat next to him. The stifling heat and humidity of the summer air in the D.C. area added to their exhaustion from traveling.

When Nils and Nora entered the private room on the comfortably air-conditioned 5th floor of Bethesda's Naval Hospital, they saw their dad sitting up in the bed. Sitting in a chair next to the bed was Sven's younger sister Ronella Stone.

"Hi Dad," said his twins simultaneously. Nora strode over to the bed to give her father a hug. Nils followed suite and gave his dad's shoulder a squeeze and shook hands with his father, "Nice to see you Dad. You don't look much worse for wear," said Nils.

"Hi Aunt Roni." Nora gave her aunt a hug also. "It has been awhile. You look well."

"It's also good to see you young lady. I hear you've been traveling." Roni then turned to her nephew, "Nilsson, your father tells me you are making a reputation for yourself. I wish the best for you."

"Oh Aunt Roni, haven't you learned by now that flattery will get you nowhere?" asked Nils.

"Well, I'll leave you two to chat with your old dad. I'll be back in awhile."

Ronella grabbed her handbag as she left the room.

"There is another chair over by the closet Nils. Bring it over and have a seat next to your sister." He enjoyed the first few moments of reuniting with both his children before his mood became somber. He wanted the happiness to last just a bit longer before breaking the latest news about his condition, so he tested the waters first and said, "It has been such a long time for me. I want to hear about Cyprus."

The twins did as they were directed slipping into their familiar roles as children of their single parent father. Both noticed right away that it was almost out of character for Sven to express interest in conversation. Conversation and interaction with them had all but disappeared following the death of their older sister several years earlier.

"What in particular do you want to hear about?" asked Nils.

"How about ladies first. Nora, how is Gavin? What were your first impressions of Cyprus?"

"He seemed fine Dad. I only got to see him just after I arrived. He helped me get settled at his gallery, then I took him to the airport. He wasn't planning to return until today, so I didn't really get to say goodbye."

"Well, he's quite a friend. We go back a ways. I'd sure like to see him again."

"He told me about when you met Mom. I saw the paintings and even visited Melanda Bay."

"So, you visited it then. What did you think of the place?"

"Magical, picturesque warm, and beautiful. I'm not sure I have enough words to describe the feeling of being there."

"I'll bet it is overrun by tourists these days." He said this with a tone of pessimism.

"Oh no Dad, not at all. The road leading down is still a dirt track with patches of sand and deep ruts. There aren't any signs. There was just the one cafe on the low cliff above the beach. It looked old enough to have been there in your day."

"Yes, I know the place. It was new and bright when I was there. It sounds like the road to the bay is just the same." Sven Johansson looked out through the window of the hospital room. His mind was six thousand miles and twenty-six years away.

Nils chimed into the conversation. "Dad, I got the news I've been waiting for all this time."

"UPT?" asked Sven.

Beaming from his recent selection to Undergraduate Pilot Training, Nils replied, "Yes, I report to Moody in three weeks. I'm not sure if I will go back to Akrotiri. When I left, Lieutenant

155

Colonel Spade said he'd have someone pack up my things and ship them back if I wanted."

"Moody? I thought that place closed a long time ago?"

"Nope, it's been open in a caretaker status for several years. A joint program introducing the new T-6 trainer has been set up there. My class will be the third to go through. T-38s and the Lead-In Fighter Training program are all right there."

"Well, congratulations Son. I'm certain you'll do fine with the flying." Sven seemed genuinely happy for his only son.

Nora could tell her dad enjoyed hearing about Cyprus so she continued sharing her experiences with him.

"When I first arrived on the island, Nils had me meet him at Chris's Blue Beach Tavern. It was sunny but not too warm and the winds from the west were just starting to blow." She went on to describe lunch and coffee. "Did you and Mom ever go there?"

"Oh boy, that does bring me back." Daydreaming again Sven struggled to reply to his daughter's question. "I think Hanife and I may have spent an afternoon or two on Curium's beach. Your mom lived in a village just up the road near Paramali. We spent most of our limited time together up that way. You saw Melanda Bay. That was our spot."

It was the first time Nora and Nils could recall their father ever speaking of their mother. It was a subject that never came up. Nils got up, found a pitcher of water and poured some into small cups before handing first one to his father, and then another for Nora, before taking one for himself.

As Nils returned to his chair beside the bed, his dad asked another question. "I wonder what you all think of the situation on Cyprus. The system of government there and the recent history of conflict. Nils, I know in your business you are getting the most up to date information. I'm curious to get your impressions."

"The place is complicated. Complicated beyond the concept of 're-unification' and getting over the past," began Nils. Sven adjusted his position on the bed and seemed to be taken by the discovery that Nils had become intimately familiar with what has become known as "The Cyprus Problem."

Sven probed for more from Nils, "I'm not sure what you mean. I don't see how things could be more convoluted than a government with a divided capitol and the influence of two major European powers working to keep it that way. Then you throw in the SBAs and…"

"You're right about all of that, but there have been some developments."

"Do share them. I'm really curious. Part of me…part of all of us is rolled up in the history of that island."

"There have been talks between Glafkos Klerides and Rauf Denktaş. There is some hope that things will change because of the potential for Cyprus to gain membership into the EU. It makes the "Olive Harvest" mission a touchy subject.

I've been to Nicosia with Lieutenant Colonel Spade several times and even met with Ambassador Bandler. He pretty much told us to watch our step. He said that the U.S. can't afford to bare an accusation of disrupting progress between the two sides now that they are finally talking. It means the unit's profile has to be very, very low."

Sven was truly interested in how his son had grasped the complexities of Cyprus. "You seem pessimistic about any positive outcome. These things take time. Maybe even lifetimes."

"Yes, but there is more, and I'm not sure how or where it is going to steer the future of Cyprus."

Even though Nils got his Bachelor of Science degree in applied mathematics, Nora knew her brother was astute and knowledgeable of history. She remembered how focused his self-study became during his time in the Balkans, but this was even more impressive. His confidence and ability to present the level of detail and understanding he'd attained during his short time in Cyprus was indication that her brother paid close attention to everyone and everything he came in contact with during his stay on the island. More astonishing to her was that he appeared to have genuine concern for the future of Cyprus. That was something that was lost on her when they were there together just a short time ago.

"Nils, when we were there together you seemed detached and appeared not to care about the future of Cyprus."

"It may have seemed that way Sis, but I've been struggling with making sense of the things I've learned."

Sven was now very attentive. "Go on then Nils, give us some idea of what you mean."

Nils went on to explain about how the Russian influence was everywhere. It was disturbing. "Lieutenant Colonel Spade shared with me some of his impressions about what happened after the Berlin Wall came down. He's done three tours of duty at RAF Akrotiri over the course of ten years and said the place had changed significantly since his first visit in 1989. He said the biggest change happened sometime shortly after the Berlin Wall came down. The Russians began to show up there in large numbers.

From my own experience, one could be in the car park of a historical archaeological site or at a beautiful remote beach, then, out of nowhere, a big fifteen-passenger tourist van would pull up. Usually, a huge Eastern European looking guy would step out from the front passenger side. Dressed smartly and moving almost in a gentleman like way, he would maneuver around and open the sliding passenger door and lend a hand to the ladies one at a time as they emerged from the van. The scene would always seem completely out of place to me.

These girls ranged in age from who knows how young up to

maybe 26 or 27 years old. It's hard to tell. They are always in heels, short skirts, or skimpy dresses and they always look like they are ready for a nightclub rather than a walk on the beach or stroll through an archaeological dig. The human trafficking trade now seems to have taken a firm hold on the southern part of the island. My sources advised that it is probably a good idea not to pry too deeply and learn too much about the ugliness of the growing prostitution economy. It could be a ticket to swim with the fishes."

Sven was reading the situation as Nils laid it out. "I take it you think these things will prevent further progress toward re-unification."

"I don't know what I think other than the place is becoming much more complicated. I don't see how an international plan can come together if there are powerful elements that want things to remain as they are. You should see some of the houses the Russians have built in recent years. They are huge and elaborate, built right beside the main highways where everyone can see them, to say, 'look at us, we are successful and prosperous.' Filthy thieves the lot of them."

Nora was vaguely aware of the things Nils was sharing with their father. She wasn't paying that much attention to the external forces at work on Cyprus, but was beginning to understand why her brother was able to maintain his distance from the personal struggles experienced by people like Elaina

Chandler.

"Well Nora, now you have some idea about your mother's home and the place where we met."

"I do. I have so much more to learn. I need to go back. I met someone."

Nora was surprised that her last comment seemed to sail right over her father's head. Sven didn't want to change the subject. He really was interested in hearing all about his daughter's relationship, but he needed to cut to the chase with respect to his health situation. Nora noticed his change in demeanor, "Aren't you going to ask me about him?"

"Sweetheart, I'm sorry, I am very interested. It's just that there is something very urgent that I need to share with the two of you before I can give you my full attention."

Nils didn't want his dad to beat around the bush any longer. "Go on Dad. Spill it."

"The cancer has spread."

"We heard that Dad. That's why we're here. We came to be with you. Support you during the treatments. Anything," said Nora.

Nils nodded his head in agreement. Sven looked back and forth between the two of them and slowly shook his head from side to side while casting his eyes toward the wad of bedding in his lap. Then he spoke softly.

"That is what I needed to tell both of you. I'm not going

ahead with the treatments. It is too late. The cancer is in my lymphatic system. Untreatable."

"But this is the 21st century. Modern medicine has worked miracles," protested Nils. Nora began to quietly sob as Nils asked his father, "Are the doctors saying anything about how long you have?"

"They don't have a good feel for that. Six months, a year maybe."

"You're not in pain are you? What happened that brought you here to the hospital?" Nora asked between sobs. She thought that her dad was done with the cancer. Especially after her last visit with him just a few weeks back before heading over to Cyprus.

"I'm actually feeling pretty good. A small mark showed up again on my left shoulder and I didn't feel like taking any chances. After the cancer went into remission the last time, they told me to come in every six months unless something showed up, and it did. They've got me in this bed because I've been shot up with some special radiologic fluids so they could conduct more tests. The stuff was pretty uncomfortable going in. I should be OK in a little while. I'm sorry to have to tell you this."

"It's OK Dad. You don't need to be sorry." Nils tried to sound genuine but couldn't shake the thought of all the lost years. Closing the gap on the emotional distance between them wasn't something he could easily fake. Furthermore, having grown up without a mother made it difficult for him to show compassion when it came to personal relationships.

"Well, I am sorry because there are a couple of things I've been thinking about. Like the baggage I have been carrying around for years. I never wanted to unload it on either of you, but your Aunt Ronnie convinced me last night that there may be some inner peace to be had if I told you both about some family matters."

Nora and Nils were more than intrigued by how forthcoming their father had suddenly become after so many years of being private. Nora was anxious to hear anything new about the life of the mother she never knew, and Nils was worried that the secret of his sister Yasemin's untimely death might be revealed. He knew he couldn't bear the thought of his father discovering that he might have played a role in her death. Not now, not when his father was on the road to his deathbed and not at a time when he needed the respect of the great Sven Kjell Johansson.

"The first order of business is to clear the air about your sister Yasemin." As he said this Nils became very uncomfortable. Sven went on confidently so as not to allow interruption while the twins sat and listened. "Nils, I know you will probably remember that evening when you came home from track workouts and Yasemin and Zach were sitting at the dinner table with me. You made quite a scene with Zach that night, if I remember correctly."

Nils was very agitated, but knew he needed his father to continue. "Yes I remember," he said.

"Well you probably have no idea what we were discussing before you walked in.

Nora had a vague recollection of the time period. She remembered that while she was preparing for the Junior Prom, there was some sort of falling out between Nils and Yasemin. She knew it had to do with Nils's academy application and Yasemine's interference. She'd sided with Nils on the issue, but didn't allow any of it to affect her loose relationship with her older sister.

Sven continued with his monologue about his older daughter. "That evening, Zach and Yasemin came to tell me that Yasemin was pregnant. I was hoping to hear from them that they had plans to get married and hoped that they had a game plan for completing school. Neither of those two things came up in the conversation. I was pretty disappointed in Yasemin. I thought that by being supportive and not saying anything about marriage or school that she'd feel safe coming to me for advice. I guess I was wrong about that." Sven turned his head away from the twins and misted up.

Nora rose from where she was sitting and leaned across the bed to give her dad a big hug. "It wasn't your fault. You were the most awesome dad to all of us. Yasemin knew that."

Nils was astonished. He hadn't noticed how tense he'd been, sitting there listening to his father dredge up the past. It took him awhile to process what he'd just heard. In his mind he recycled what his father had said and reconstructed his recollection of that evening and every detail of what he'd decided to do about his sister Yasemin's reckless move to hide his application to the Air Force Academy.

He felt a tremendous weight being lifted from him, mainly from the heavy guilt he'd been carrying around for the past eight years. At that moment he realized he couldn't possibly have had any hand in his sister's tragic death. No matter what their differences, Yasemin was still his sister and Nils had suffered so much unhappiness for believing she'd committed suicide over a pregnancy he thought he had a hand in.

Snapping back to the present, Nils got out of his chair and came around to the opposite side of the bed from his sister so he could look into his father's eyes. "Dad, it was an accident." He said this with confidence. She knew you cared about her. It didn't matter that Nora and I were in the dark about her being pregnant. We were all there for her and she knew we always would be. Those rumors were all lies and we can't let stuff like that ruin us or change us into people we don't want to be."

"Thanks Son. Thanks for that." Sven collected himself, grasped Nils firmly by the shoulder. "You're going to be a great pilot Son. I know this. It is in our blood." It was all old Sven could come up with having no real "man to man" experience with his only son.

Nils strode back around to the other side of the bed and leaned his hand on his sister's shoulder, a signal to give her dad some breathing room. As Sven turned back toward them, they sat back down in the chairs beside the bed.

Sven then realized it was a good time to stick to the mental script he'd prepared in advance of this visit. "The other matter I so unfairly kept from you had to do with your mother." He was still choked up, but not so much about his deceased wife Hanife as realizing how her children grew up knowing nothing about her. Sven had his times of grief and although he never got over his wife, he learned to live with losing her and focused his attention to the best of his ability on raising his three children.

As he continued, his sister Ronella quietly entered Sven's hospital room. She was glad to see that her brother was following her advice, by sharing things he knew that might bring his family closer together when they needed it the most. She had with her a small vase of bright summer flowers and without interrupting Sven's monologue put them on the windowsill.

Sven went on. "I met your mother in the fall of 1970. I had just been assigned to the U-2 unit at Davis Monthan Air Force Base and hadn't been home from Vietnam very long when we were deployed to monitor the conflict between Israel and Egypt." He noticed his sister Roni was wrestling with her own emotions recalling those days having just been informed that her husband was listed as MIA.

"Roni, please sit down," he motioned to the corner of the bed across from the twins. "Those were difficult times for all of us." He continued. "The only location we had access to was RAF Akrotiri, which took some diplomacy to get us there. The Department of Defense and the U.S. State Department were able to easily sway the Brits into an agreement when they were reminded about the last major conflict in the region.

In 1967 Israeli jets attacked the U.S.S. Liberty, which was rumored to be spying off the coast of Egypt. Though it would have been a stretch, the British weren't willing to take the chance that one or the other combatants would do something unpredictable against friendly forces in the East Mediterranean. So, we were there and we flew reconnaissance missions that we hoped would garner information useful in shaping a more stable future for the region."

He took a long drink of the water before continuing. "I knew nothing about Cyprus until I met your mother. It was a chance meeting. A colleague of mine was invited to a Greek Cypriot wedding in a village near Evdimou.

I don't remember much about the wedding; just that it took place on a warm evening in late September and that it seemed like everyone in the village turned out for it. I noticed Hanife when she arrived at the top of the lane leading into the village center. She was with a small group of people who looked to be family. Two young men escorting an older woman on one end, and an older gentleman walking beside this gorgeous beauty who'd caught my eye. She was holding the hand of a much younger girl of maybe ten years old. All of them were dressed in their finest for the event.

There were all kinds of foods. All of it was local and fresh, including six lambs that had been rotating on spits over open coals throughout the day. The local butcher was attending to each of them in turn as the guests loaded their plates with the delectable flavors of the Mediterranean.

I wasn't hungry at all. Once I'd spotted Hanife, I wanted to know everything about her. She was wearing a dark short-sleeved summer dress with white dots individually sewn into the fabric. She had a lace wrap over her shoulders and wore low heels and her dark hair had the silkiest shine. I watched as she and her family proceeded toward a table where a group of friends were saving them seats. When she left her shawl and hand bag at the table with the others so she could assist the younger girl with the buffet, I made my move."

Nora was really getting into the story. Having just returned from Cyprus she didn't have any difficulty picturing the village celebration. "Dad, were you stalking her?"

The light moment made Nils laugh. "I'm trying to picture Dad 'stalking' our mom. Really Nora, you come up with the funniest stuff."

Even Roni took notice of Nora's humorous comment. Sven paused during all of the lighthearted banter before adding his own bit to it. "Yeah, if that is what it is called these days, I guess I was stalking your mother." All of them broke out in laughter at once.

When the ruckus in the small room calmed, Nils asked his dad, "How long do you have to stay here anyway?"

"Actually I should hear soon. I'm really feeling fine. In fact, I feel great now that all of you are here. There are still some test results to wait on before they release me. Just in case."

"In case what?" asked Nora.

"In case there is something that could change my decision to forego further treatment. I don't suspect they will find anything, but you never know."

By coincidence, a doctor wearing a typical white coat and sporting designer eyeglasses stepped into the room holding a patient file. Everyone turned as Sven said, "Good timing doctor. This is my family. All of it."

"Your entire family."

"Yep. All of it right here in this room. Everything in the world that matters to me is right here in my immediate field of view."

"Well I have the test results." The doctor looked around at everyone and back at Sven, anticipating his permission to share the information while everyone remained in the room.

"Spit it out then. They can all stay and hear it. I've nothing to keep secret." It was an ironic statement given the previous conversation with his family members and it caused Sven to laugh within as he said it.

The doctor opened the folder and glanced through a couple of the pages, not because he needed to verify what he already knew, but rather out of habit. "According to these test results Mr. Johansson, there are no additional treatment options that will improve your condition. I wish I had better news," the doctor said as he closed the folder, removed his glasses and put them in the breast pocket of his lab coat.

"I guess this means I can check out then?" Sven was ready to go home and spend some more time with his family right away.

The doctor replied, "The out-processing paperwork is already being prepared. You can retrieve your clothes from the closet and by the time you are dressed, the papers will be ready to be signed at the reception counter on your way out.

The doctor extended his hand and the two men shook. "I wish you the best," said the doctor.

"Thanks," said Sven as the doctor departed.

"Now what?" asked Nora.

"Now we get out of here and plan an evening together to celebrate."

"Celebrate? Are you kidding?" Ronella piped in.

"No, Sis, I'm serious. My only son just informed me that he's going to be a United States Air Force Pilot and that is something we can all celebrate." Roni just shook her head from side to side. Nils and Nora looked at each other and smiled.

"Some privacy while I change?" Sven was eager to get out of the hospital garb and on to better things.

"We'll wait for you at the reception desk," said Roni, and they all left the room closing the door behind them.

Sven Johansson's small Georgetown apartment wasn't the best for hosting guests, but cozy enough for his son and daughter to stay a night or two camping in the small living room. Nils was up early in spite of their celebrating the night before. He never was much of a party animal, so a big night out for him amounted to maybe three drinks. The evening with the Chandlers just a few days earlier further weakened his constitution for alcohol, so he didn't allow himself to over indulge.

He set about making coffee even though the radio weather report forecast another blistering day for the nation's capitol. Hot coffee on a hot day normally didn't seem very appealing to him but he thought his dad and sister might enjoy waking to the aroma and a little something to get their day started.

"Good morning Nils," said Nora emerging from the small bathroom. She had always been an early riser.

"Same to you. You look no worse off for wear. Coffee is on the counter if you're interested." Nils noticed that she was already dressed to meet the day.

Nils thought about how different his sister was from Josette. Waking early wasn't a trait the mother of his son had in common with his sister. Regardless, Nils had no difficulty adjusting to Josette in her role as a loving mother to his son, even if she was slow to get out of bed in the morning.

Nils imagined how things might be if he were still together with her. He could have Martin all to himself in those early hours before work. Before leaving the house he'd bring Martin into the bedroom where Josette would hold out both her arms while still in the bed. Bleary eyed, she'd call for him to help her wake up and start their day together. He yearned for a chance to experience being a father to his son and was determined to find a way to reconcile with Josette.

"I take it you don't have anything going on today. Is that a safe bet Nils?"

"Not yet, I thought I'd wait and see what Dad might be up to. I have a few things I need to sort out. I still can't get over how he's taking the news about the cancer so casually. God damn it the man is terminally ill."

"That thought has been nagging at me too. Pretty soon we're both going to be orphans."

"Don't joke about stuff like that Nora," he said firmly.

"I didn't mean it to come out that way. Maybe he's just a little bit in denial or he's trying to put it out of his mind because we're here. Anyway, don't get your hopes up that he's going to go out and do guy stuff with you all day. He still owes me, or us if you're interested, the rest of his courtship story about getting married to Mom."

"Oh I'm interested all right. Let's wait to see what kind of mood he's in and if necessary we'll tag team or play good cop-bad cop to get him back on topic. Deal?"

"Deal."

While the twins were having their coffee and plotting their day, Sven was drying off from a cool shower. The lease on his Georgetown flat was going to be up for renewal at the end of the month. When he looked out through the bathroom window at the morning haze and the beginnings of another stifling dog day afternoon, he decided there was no longer a compelling reason to stay in the capitol region.

In the spirit of the season he pulled on a pair of khaki shorts and threw on a floral tropical shirt complete with permanent wrinkles and smudges from coconut oil. He smelled the fresh coffee pouring from the small spaces of the kitchen and adjoining living area. He slipped on a worn out looking pair of Birkenstocks before joining his son and daughter.

"Hey Dad. Good morning," said his twins in unison.

"*Kalimera, Güneydin.* The coffee smells delicious." Sven

headed straight for the cabinet above the counter and pulled down a mug then poured a cup from the pot Nils brewed for them.

"Good morning to you too. So you remember some Greek and Turkish words. I'm impressed. Did you sleep well Dad?" asked Nora.

"Better than I have in a very long time. Thanks. How about you two? The couch and futon don't amount to much for guest beds."

"I don't know about Nils, but the futon was plenty comfortable for me. Thanks for last night and the idea of coming back here together. I wasn't looking forward to returning to my place late at night after being away so long." Nora's Arlington apartment was up the Lee Highway from the Rosslyn neighborhood. The small studio was all that she could afford and still be within walking distance of the bus and the Metro. She'd never owned a car.

Feeling slightly disoriented from the long trip plus the realization that his past actions didn't contribute to Yasemin's death, Nils' emotions rose to the surface. "Dad, what the hell man? How can you be so chipper when you're, well...ahhh?" Nils wasn't even sure how to address his father's terminal illness.

"I think I know what you're worried about and you need to let it go. I haven't felt so liberated in years. I've got you both back in my life, which is just what I need right now. By the way, who taught you to brew such a strong coffee?" He looked up at Nils and took another sip. "It's just the way I like it."

"Must be from having spent so much time with Cypriots. There's a small snack shack across the ramp from O.H." O.H. was shorthand for the American "Olive Harvest" operation on RAF Akrotiri. Nils continued, "It's a corrugated roofed place where an older Cypriot couple makes breakfast sandwiches and the best coffee on the peninsula. Anyway, when I make coffee, even though it isn't Cypriot coffee, I like it to be strong."

Sven looked at his son and asked, "How old did the woman look, the one that brewed the coffee in the snack shack? Was she still using the metal box full of hot sand?"

"No telling her age. She looked to be eighty years old but could have as easily been in her fifties. She's got that hard working native type look, like the gentleman who makes the grilled halloumi sandwiches. A pound twenty is enough for both a *metreo* and a sandwich roll."

"It sounds like the only thing that's changed is the price! I used to go to that same little shack. Only in my day one of those sandwiches was about twenty-five cents. I think the woman's name was Kristalla."

"Wow! That has to be her then. Everyone calls her Ms. Kriss." Nils was smiling and wagging his head back and forth adding under his breath, "They are living relics I suppose."

"On the topic of Cyprus, I've been doing some

thinking…I'd like to go back for a visit, a nostalgia trip. Just for a week or two. What do you guys think?"

"Dad that's a fantastic idea. When?" Nora asked.

"Sooner than later. When I made the decision to forego treatment, the doctor couldn't tell me how or exactly when a change in my physical condition would hit me, but I'm feeling pretty good right now."

Nils was happy for his dad but wasn't eager to reverse course and return to Cyprus so soon. When he left, he had some leave saved up and wanted to use it to visit his own son Martin and see where he stood with Josette. It would mean a trip to France before reporting onto Moody AFB to start his Joint Specialized Undergraduate Pilot Training.

Nora was bursting with excitement and turned to Nils. "Nils, you can come with us. I still have some money saved and I've got a promise to keep with a certain someone. What do you say? You can stop and see Josette and Martin, either on the way there or on the way back."

"Dad, I'm really sorry. I have some things I need to take care of in France. Things I should have been working on all along. I need to get back there before my training starts. I don't think I can join you on Cyprus. Maybe we could all go to France together as a stop over on your way to Cyprus. You understand don't you?"

Sven set his coffee cup down and rested his hand on his

son's shoulder. "I'm proud of you Son. You do what you need to do. If they still have Family Day while you're in training, I'll come visit you in Georgia." He gave his son's shoulder a firm squeeze.

Nora protested. "Dad, let's do it. Let's go to Istres on the way. We can stay a couple of days. You can meet your grandson Martin. I want to meet him too." She twisted around toward Nils. "Show him the picture of Martin."

Nils grabbed his wallet from the coffee table and pulled out the picture of Josette and his son to show is dad.

"That settles it then. France, and then on to Cyprus. We can make the arrangements later this afternoon. I'm starving and the cupboards are bare. Your Aunt Roni is staying over at the Key Bridge Marriot. They put on a breakfast spread on the top floor that is fantastic. How about I give her a ring and we can all join up for some sustenance?"

The twins nodded their approval of the breakfast idea. When Sven got off the phone, he looked at Nora as if he was trying to recall something he wanted to say to her.

She looked back at him waiting and just as she shrugged her shoulders and started to gather her handbag from the kitchen, Sven asked after her, "Didn't you say something yesterday when we were talking about Cyprus about meeting someone while you were there?"

"Dad, there's been so much going on in such a short span of

time, I'm surprised you remembered! I'll tell you all about him when you finish telling us the rest of the story about falling in love and marrying Mom."

Caught off guard, Sven wasn't quite ready to dive that far back into the past again. "How about we eat first. There's so much I want to tell you and show you. We'll have all afternoon and a lot of time on airplanes and trains in the next few days for that conversation."

"Fair enough," she said as she walked through the front door that Nils was holding open for everyone signaling it was time to go.

During their short walk to the hotel where Ronella was staying, they took a steep long staircase leading from Prospect Street down to M. Street. Following behind their father, Nora leaned over to her brother.

"Did you know we are walking down 'the Exorcist Stairs'?"

"What? Huh?"

"You've never heard of the movie 'The Exorcist?'"

"It was before my time. Yours too." Nils just shook his head and continued down.

They crossed M Street and then over the Key Bridge. Already there were boaters enjoying the sun on the Potomac. Crossing in both directions, there was the usual combination of runners and bikers on the bridge getting in their workout before the heat of the day became too crushing.

Ronella met them on the top floor of the hotel where together they took up window seats with a commanding view of Washington D.C., the monuments, and the seat of American government.

"This was a lovely idea Aunt Roni," said Nora.

"I heard the view from here is one of the best. I'm going to be heading back to Nebraska this afternoon." She said this looking at her brother. "Are you going to be alright Sven?"

"Absolutely. We're leaving town as well, all of us. We're going to France where I can meet my one and only grandchild for the first time. Then Nora and I are going to return to Cyprus."

"That sounds like a long trip. You think you can handle it? I mean, in your condition?" Ronella sounded doubtful.

"Never felt better. Really. I need to do these things while I still can. The twins and I will be making our travel arrangements later this afternoon and we'll be leaving as soon as possible."

His sister smiled at him. "Well, I'm glad. Come back to Omaha when you return. My place is plenty big. I'd like to spend some time with you too."

"I think I'd like that Roni. Thanks."

"Dad, I need to head over to my place. I've got some bills to pay and I'm expecting some follow up from Georgetown on my fall schedule of classes. Call me later?" Nora excused herself and gave her aunt a kiss goodbye thanking her for coming out to be with her dad.

"I'll call this afternoon and we can sort out our travel plans," replied Sven.

"Nils are you coming over later?" asked Nora.

"Yes, I'll bring your bag along. Does your building still have the same door code?"

"Yes, but give me a buzz when you get there. Just in case."

CHAPTER 10

France

Less than twenty-four hours later the three of them were enroute to Istres France via Paris and Marseille. All three of them were able to sleep through the night during the flight over the Atlantic. The warmth of the summer's morning sun spread across the interior of France as they boarded the fast train leaving from Paris's Gare du Lyon. Though weary from traveling, they were all wide awake.

"Well Dad, you did promise." Nora looked her father in the eye with longing anticipation.

"Promise?"

"Yes, if I remember right, when you were describing the time you first met Mom, you were stalking her at a Greek Cypriot wedding."

He looked at the faces of his two grown children noticing the anticipation and knew he wouldn't get out of telling his long tale. He adjusted himself to a more comfortable position inside the rail car's luxurious private compartment and peered at the countryside as it streaked past, then took a deep breath.

"She was so beautiful. Stunning actually. The navy blue of her dress she was offset by the white collar and sleeves accenting the deep olive of her smooth skin. Even in the faded light of the evening, her dark hazel colored eyes spoke to me across the distance. Nora, yours are very much like your mother's." He looked at his daughter's fine features. She seemed proud that her looks resembled the beautiful mother she never knew.

"While your mom was helping the young girl at the wedding buffet, I got up, grabbed a plate and timed my arrival at the opposite side of the buffet so I could introduce myself. There was a tray of tomatoes between us and I grabbed the only serving spoon just as she began to reach for it. I smiled at her and offered it to her pretending my rudeness was an accident. I told her I was sorry and she kept smiling while helping the little girl dish up some of the foods." Sven paused and seemed to be lost in thought for a long moment before going on.

"She said her name was Hanife and asked me where I was from. We chatted more as we went through the buffet. Later in the evening I maneuvered to the table where she was seated. You should have seen the looks from the villagers seated at her table when I asked her to dance."

Nils didn't want to break the momentum of the story but was curious. "Did you know at that time that mom was a Turkish Cypriot?"

"No, I only knew she was more exotic and beautiful than any woman I'd ever met. She didn't look anything like the people she came to the wedding with. I later learned why."

An announcement in French came over the intercom of the modern compartment to inform passengers that the dining cars were open for *petit déjeuner*. Sven suggested that they all get some coffee and something to eat. They still had a few hours to travel before arriving in Marseille where Josette would be picking them up.

The twins were burning with curiosity about their parents past all through the short breakfast. Between cups of coffee, Sven assured them that they were going to learn everything about their mother's life on Cyprus. At least to the extent of what he knew about it.

When they were all settled back in the compartment, Sven pulled down a ragged leather satchel that he'd grown accustomed to using whenever he traveled. "I brought along a few things to share with both of you. Things that belonged to your mother."

He sat across from the twins and opened a manila envelope that contained some black and white as well as a few color Polaroids. There were also some newspaper clippings mounted on card stock. One by one he handed the photographs across to the twins so that they could see them.

The first photograph he showed them was a black and white. The four edges were scalloped in a uniform fringe pattern dating it to the early 1960s. The main subjects were two young girls who appeared to be dressed in school uniforms. They were holding their books in their outer arms and clasping hands as they stood side by side in front of a low stonewall in front of a traditional village home with a tiled roof.

Nora handed the photo over to Nils who promptly turned it over. On the back there were two names, *Hanife ve Dedim*. Beneath the names there was something written in Turkish with the date. Nils passed the photo over to Nora.

"First day of school - Fall 1963." She read then looked across to Sven. "Who is this girl Dedim standing next to Mom?"

"Dedim was your mother's younger sister."

"Was? Did she die?" asked Nils.

"I don't know. Your mother didn't know either."

They continued looking at the other photos and items from the envelope while Sven explained much of what his wife had shared with him about her on Cyprus before they met.

He told them as much as he knew about Çanakkale village where the Yılmaz sisters lived with their parents before the inter-communal clash that forced them from their home and each other, leaving them without parents to raise them.

Sven pulled another of the old scallop fringed black and white photos from the small batch. In the picture there were three children, the Yılmaz sisters and a taller boy who didn't look like he was a relative. He handed the photo across to Nils who again flipped it over to read the names written in blue ink from a ball tipped pen. *"Dedim, Hanife, ve Hristos."*

"Who is this boy?" asked Nora.

Sven flipped through a couple of more pictures before finding the one he was looking for. He handed a color Polaroid to Nora and said, "Hristos Zavos was one of your mother's childhood friends. They grew up together in Çanakkale village. After clashes in their village, the Zavos family moved to a small plantation between Paramali and Evdimou just to the west of Limassol. The Zavos family took your mother in and raised her as one of their own."

Nora studied the picture. Her mother was sitting at a wooden table underneath a trellis on a patio filled with other tables. Behind the table was an older couple dressed as though they were going to be serving guests all afternoon. Hristos Zavos was standing beside Hanife dressed smartly in dark slacks and a white cotton shirt with sleeves rolled up, wearing an apron and holding a bottle and some wine glasses.

"The Zavos family built a small tavern on the southern edges of the plantation overlooking the sea. They made their living preparing and serving lunches and dinners to guests from Episkopi, Pissouri, and tourists from every place you could imagine."

"I wonder if Hristos Zavos has any idea what happened to our aunt?" Nils asked.

"The Zavos tavern is one of the first places I plan on visiting when we get to Cyprus," Sven offered.

"Dad, how come you never shared any of this with us?" Nora's tone didn't sound accusatory but she was having trouble understanding why he hadn't shared this information about their mother before.

"Those were difficult times for me. You were just newborns and I was shocked by the sudden responsibility of raising you. Yasemin was just a toddler. I went into myself and I guess I never really came out. I'm sorry."

Nils turned to Nora and tried to lighten the conversation, "Is it just me, or does it seem to you like Dad keeps finding ways to avoid telling us more about how he and mom ended up getting married?"

Nora didn't answer. She was doing her best to push down feelings of resentment for having been kept in the dark not having had the chance to know about her before now. She turned toward her father and gave him a look suggesting she wasn't going to let him off the hook on this one. Not now that Pandora's Box had finally been opened.

Sven took a deep breath. "You know, this could be a very long story."

"Dad, we still have over an hour before we arrive at St. Charles Station," said Nils.

"Alright then." Sven then turned to look directly at Nora searching for signs of forgiveness before continuing the story. "I arranged to meet your mother the next day after the village wedding. I had only been in Cyprus for about a month and hadn't seen much of the island. Hanife promised to give me a tour of her favorite places. Since I had access to a car I offered to drive. We saw most of the sights, Curium, Petra tou Romiou, Paphos, and at the end of that first day Melanda Bay. Your mom was a very delightful tour guide.

It was a quiet time of the year for Cyprus. Even back then there were throngs of tourists from the European countries during the summer season. By late September when I met your mother, most had already returned home. Your mother didn't know anything about what I was doing in Cyprus. The U-2 mission on Akrotiri was a well guarded secret in those days."

Nils couldn't keep from smirking and shaking his head back and forth. "That certainly isn't the case these days. The souvenir shops even sell trinkets with images of the U-2 flying from the peninsula. Officially the mission isn't a secret anymore, but Olive Harvest doesn't advertise American presence because the absence of a Status of Forces Agreement poses peculiar challenges for the commander."

"I guess maybe things were easier back in my day." Sven glanced over at Nils proud that his son was so engaged in his work in the same the unit he had been assigned to so many years before. "We had a pretty small foot-print. There were only three pilots and we flew maybe twice per week. The summer winds were so strong in the afternoon we had to cancel many of our missions." He looked again at Nils.

"We had no divert options for alternate landing bases. The Cold War was in full throw and diverting a U-2 to anywhere else in the region meant we'd never see the airplane again. None of us wanted to think about what it meant if we couldn't land back at Akrotiri. Anyway, I had a lot of time on my hands and made every effort to spend it with your mother. There weren't very many people in the unit and nobody had any idea what I was doing with my spare time."

"Kinda like 'it's easier to beg for forgiveness than to ask for permission,' " Nils interjected.

"Something along those lines. Sounds like you had to learn those lessons too."

"Sure did," said Nils.

Sven went on describing his outings with Hanife. Nora was particularly interested in her father's recollection of their first visit to Laneia Village and their chance meeting with Gavin Hart. Her father's description of that visit was nearly identical to the one Gavin had shared with her. His recollection turned to nostalgia when he told his twins that the wooing of their mother was cut short when the Israeli - Egyptian Cease Fire was stabilized.

When Sven got his redeployment instructions that first week of November 1970, he took Hanife to Melanda Bay to say goodbye. The sun set early in November and as they watched the pink hues of light on the chalky white bluff at the south end of the bay, the low grey clouds covering Mount Olympus throughout the day, became heavy and dark with rain.

Sven drove Hanife back to Evdimou before returning to his quarters on the RAF base. He departed the next morning from Akrotiri aboard an RAF VC-10. He wasn't sure if or how or when he would ever see Hanife again. When he shared this part of his past, his eyes became glassy and he apologized to Nora and Nils for having nothing left to share.

The years of living under the same roof with a father who had never shown them the closeness they experienced with him in recent days made their time on the train seem surreal. Both of them realized their lives were woven into a past with which neither of them had any connection.

"Dad, I know what you mean about Melanda Bay. I was there recently with a special friend. I want you to meet him. We'll all go there together and spend the day. It will be fun." As Nora earnestly declared this intention to her father, her mind drifted to thoughts of Aydın. She realized she hadn't had a chance to let him know she would be returning right away.

"But you eventually got married. Did mom come to the US?" Nils asked this question because he was curious whether the security requirements for reporting contact with foreign nationals had been as tightly controlled then as they are for current service members. As an intelligence officer, one of Nils's responsibilities was to act as the security officer for the unit and liaise with the Regional Security Officer or RSO at the U.S. Embassy in Nicosia.

"The complications with security clearances and reporting became an issue for me over the following years. It was torture for a while but eventually I just stopped thinking about it. I never gave Hanife any means of reaching me back in the states for fear of having my security clearance revoked. I never reported our contact. Frankly I never thought about it until it was time to leave Cyprus. When we debriefed the deployment back at Davis Monthan AFB, it was too late to bring it up."

Nora turned away and couldn't look at her father. It took her a few minutes to collect her thoughts. "You were willing to just let her go then?" She was afraid that all men dealt with their emotions in the same fashion and wondered if Aydın was just as willing to put her out of his mind.

"It wasn't like that," replied Sven. I wasn't really sure what I was going to do. I was reassigned to Offutt Air Force Base in Nebraska and was living in Omaha with your Aunt Ronella. She was struggling with her own demons during that time and I was wrestling with figuring a way to get back to Cyprus to be with Hanife and ask her to marry me."

Nora seemed relieved to hear that her dad was faithful to his feelings after he left Cyprus. "So you did go back?"

"I don't know where the time went during the interval before I returned. There weren't very many U-2 pilots back then. There was a brief conflict in Israel that ended in October 1973."

"The Yom Kippur War. I think the world paid attention to that one Dad," said Nils.

"Yes they did. I was immediately reassigned to Laughlin AFB in Texas to re-qualify in the U-2, then deployed to Cyprus again in the spring of 1974 to monitor the cease-fire between Israel, Egypt, and Syria. That region of the world was very unstable. When we started up flying again in April that year, it seemed like we were very busy. We still had the same problems with windy afternoons and no divert options, but it seemed like we flew anyway and often landed back at Akrotiri with the winds well beyond the limits of the aircraft. We believed the risks were worth taking since the stakes were so high."

"Didn't you try to find Mom?" Nora asked with a disbelieving tone as if Sven didn't take the first opportunity to look for her.

Sven looked into his daughter's eyes and swung his head slowly from side to side. "You have to believe me Nora I went to Evdimou at the first opportunity. I went to the Zavos's Tavern and asked about her and they told me she'd gone up to Nicosia to go back to the university. My unit was so busy that summer and travel was largely restricted so I became frustrated and concerned that I'd lost her forever."

"When I was in Cyprus a couple of weeks ago, Nils introduced me to some relatives of one of his colleagues." She turned to her brother, indicating to him she wanted him to explain the connection and a little about the evening at the Chandler's. Nils obliged and gave his dad a brief summary of Mrs. Chandler's recollections of those turbulent times in Cyprus.

"So you did learn a little bit about the Cypriot history while you were there. Lucky you," said Sven.

"Yes and there's still so much more I want to discover. Now I have a good reason to explore the northern part of Cyprus and maybe find out something about aunt Dedim."

"I hope you do see the rest of the island. Just promise me something."

"What's that Dad?" asked Nora.

Sven first looked at his daughter and then turned to Nils before looking into Nora's eyes again. "There may be a Green Line dividing the island but there is no 'right' side of the issue. Promise me you won't take sides."

Both twins nodded their understanding. They were all silent for what seemed an eternity. Nora was hoping her father would continue with the stories of those early days with their mother.

Nils saved Nora from having to coax the story along. "What were the circumstances of finding Mom again?"

"I suppose by now both of you are pretty well versed in what happened in Cyprus in late July 1974. Am I right?"

Both his children gave an affirmative nod. "Go on. Continue," urged Nils.

"Well, actually things got pretty heated before that. Are you familiar with the Colonel's Coup or Greek Junta?"

Again both of them nodded yes.

"Well, I'm impressed that you both have taken an interest in this bit of history. I won't expound on the details then. Just that when the coup attempt failed, the entire island began to fall apart and it seemed like there was nothing to stop the chaos. Remnants of the EOKA-B faction were responsible for violence in villages all over the island. The villages in the Paphos and Limassol areas experienced Greeks killing Greeks. When Turkey formally engaged with operation 'Attila,' it was a legal intervention under the Treaty of Guarantee."

"I'm familiar with the justifications for Turkish involvement but these days, 'Attila' is referred to as the Turkish Invasion. Don't get me wrong Dad. I'm not taking sides, but the research I've done this past year for my work points very clearly to the fact that the Turkish Cypriots today are unsupportive of the Turkish Army occupation and do not mingle well with Turkish settlers who have since come to Cyprus."

"Nils, that is very interesting. I really have no experience with what has happened to Cyprus since we left."

"Dad, you just said, 'when WE left.' I'm on pins and needles in anticipation of how you got back together with Mom!"

"Sorry Nora, I'm getting to that. I wanted you to have a feel for how complicated the political situation was, maybe because I was a little embarrassed that the U.S. was just standing by while all this violence was taking place and innocent lives were in the balance."

Nora and Nils could see that their father seemed to be struggling with getting on with the story. Nils interjected, "Dad, I know it must have been strange for you to stand by and see it all unfold. The politics of the Cold War seemed to tie everyone's hands. Even though both Greece and Turkey were NATO allies, resolving the problems between them with respect to Cyprus took a back seat to keeping tabs on the Soviet Union."

"You are right, but it seemed to me like we were picking and choosing. In the summer of 1964, President Johnson wrote a letter to Turkey's Prime Minister Inonu advising him that if the Turkish Army engaged in Cyprus that Turkey's position as part of NATO would be in jeopardy. Ten years later the attempted coup must have had an impact on U.S. foreign policy. Unfortunately the Cypriots got to suffer two major bouts of violence created by two NATO partners. The absurdity of it…." Sven trailed off in silence.

Hearing her father struggling to come to grips with the impact of historical events, something finally clicked in Nora's mind. "Dad, you've let Cyprus and everything that happened there become personal."

"For me it is. Maybe things would have been different for your mother if history had taken a different path."

"You could say that about anyone or any event," added Nils.

"True. I loved your mother though. More deeply than any person could love another, which is why it is personal for me. Maybe if everyone had personal connections throughout the world, we would be free from senseless violence."

Nils knew his dad was right about this, having seen what happened in the Balkans.

The train slowed, as they got closer to Marseilles. Nora wanted the momentum of the conversation to continue knowing that once they arrived, Nils and her father would be more interested in visiting with Martin and Josette. "When did you finally meet up with Mom then?" she asked.

"An acquaintance of mine at Episkopi Garrison called me and warned me that the RAF Air Vice Marshall wanted to see me and that I should expect a call. This was 18 August, and the dust from the initial violence had begun to settle. I remember the date, because our ambassador to Cyprus, Roger Davis was killed two days later."

"I read that Ambassador Davies was killed by a stray bullet, shot right through the window of the embassy in Nicosia," added Nils.

"That is the story anyway, but when you 'Monday Morning Quarterback' all the events, it starts to sound like the Kennedy assassination with its many theories. I don't buy any of the eyewash the media put out related to Davies's death either," said Sven.

Nora couldn't get over how her father seemed to seek every possible avenue to avoid finishing the story about how he ended up in a marriage with Hanife. "Dad, you're getting off topic again. You were telling us about the call from Episkopi...."

"Oh yes, where was I? In typical British fashion, as soon as I hung up the phone with my buddy, it rang again immediately. It was the AVM's executive. He said the AVM, the Air Vice Marshall, had urgent business he needed to discuss with me and wanted to know how soon I could be there. Since we weren't flying and it was still early in the morning, I told him I'd need an hour, which we agreed to.

I rushed back to my quarters put on my only suit, added a matching tie and made sure my shoes were shined before heading up to Episkopi Garrison and the SBA HQ office for this urgent meeting with the AVM. He was in charge of all RAF resources on the Sovereign Base Areas or SBAs and his land counterpart was a British Army Brigadier whom I'd had the pleasure of meeting only weeks before. The heat of the late summer morning hadn't set in by the time I pulled into the car park adjacent to the headquarters building. I was trying my best not to break a sweat before my meeting with the big man.

I reported to the AVM's front office and was surprised at how spartan everything was. An older looking staff sergeant greeted me and said the AVM was in a conference call and would be with me shortly. A couple minutes later, the door to his office cracked open and a tall and ancient looking gentleman presented himself. He was dressed in the dark gray blue uniform of his service. With one hand on the door and in the other waving a lit cigarette, he gestured for me to enter.

'I must apologize for keeping you waiting, but as you well know there are duties to attend to,' he said it in the gravelly voice of a chain smoker. He had a weathered and wrinkled face making it impossible to estimate his age. I followed his lead and took a seat in the chair he offered.

The entire visit was like a scene from a 1960s vintage British spy film or some sort of combination of a cold war KGB interrogation rolled up into a pep talk by the supreme allied commander from WWII times. I was seated in this low-slung fabric covered chair that had long since outlived the fashion of its day. In fact the AVM's office was a throwback to the late 1950s. The best I could say about it was there was a lot of hard wood around and his desk was enormous, noticeably clear of any clutter.

The office was in a corner section of the building with wrap around windows providing a magnificent view of Curium Bay stretching down the west coast of the Akrotiri peninsula. The chair I was seated in was positioned in a beam of morning sunlight, and its heat burned through the glass and made me hot and very uncomfortable.

I found myself on the receiving end of a one-way

conversation. The AVM sat across from me. His chair was in the darkest shadow of the room. He crossed his legs, one over the other and shook another Lucky Strike from the pack he pulled from his uniform shirt pocket. He tossed the pack onto the low coffee table that spanned the distance between us. He lit up the cigarette with an antique stainless steel Zippo lighter and mumbled, 'Nasty habit that...but I am too set in my ways to do otherwise.' I sat for what seemed like an interminable amount of time and I could feel beads of perspiration forming on my forehead.

The AVM got up from his chair and continued to lecture me on the history of MOD UK, US, and NATO relations. He elaborated on the role of the UN as it applied to the current situation on Cyprus. He never really made eye contact with me. He lectured to me as though I was his student.

I watched him as he moved from the window still holding the cigarette. He had only taken one drag from it. I thought it would be possible to estimate the amount of time that passed during this bizarre encounter by the length of ash burning down the paper of his cigarette. I couldn't take my eyes from his cigarette, because I was certain that the inch worth of ashes that hung on the end of it would suddenly drop to the floor and cause a break in the AVM's lecture.

He took a pace or two toward the chair he had been sitting in earlier and walked around the back of it. In the center of the coffee table was a heavy clear glass ashtray. He stepped from behind the chair and leaned across the table just in time for the cigarette ash to drop into the tray on the table without his having to flick or tap it from the cigarette. He stepped back and took another drag and continued his monologue on political military relations and a moment later he returned his cigarette to the ashtray, this time to snuff it out.

That is when the lecture changed from a history lesson to a warning. I still didn't know what was so urgent about my coming to see him, but what he told me next changed everything."

This last statement got the twins attention and they suddenly perked up and listened more intently.

"The reason I couldn't find your mother through the Zavos family was because she had taken up a position as a nanny and live-in house maid at Episkopi for a British officer and his family."

"Why wouldn't the Zavos's have known where she went?" asked Nora.

Sven pulled another item from the leather satchel. It was a small portfolio of photographs. He held it in both hands and didn't open it right away. "The urgency of the meeting I had with the AVM at Episkopi occurred because all foreign nationals working on the SBAs were asked to produce documentation showing their place of birth and nationality or they couldn't stay.

The AVM said to me, 'There is a Miss Hanife Yılmaz, a local

woman with her infant child who can no longer stay here. I'm sure you are aware of the refugee situation. I'm not sure things would go over well for you with respect to your American superiors should they know your involvement.' I stopped listening to him when I heard your mother's name. I completely froze up when it registered that she had an infant child."

Sven then took out the book of photographs and opened it. On the first page was a color photo of a beautiful young woman in cream-colored formal attire leaning down and holding hands with a small girl who appeared to be wearing her Sunday best. They must have been looking at the person taking the picture and laughing because both their faces were animated with big smiles and laughing eyes. The little girl was blond and blue eyed. "Two women who meant the world to me who I'll never see again." Sven gazed at the photo for a long beat before handing the booklet across to the twins.

Nora took the portfolio from her father and leafed through a collection of wedding photos. She recognized some of the faces. Hristos Zavos, the childhood friend of her mother was in one of the pictures along with a young dark haired woman standing beside his father Kostas. All of them were holding champagne glasses and all of them aged by some ten years.

"From the photos it looks like the wedding reception was on the back patio of the RAF Akrotiri Officer's Mess," said Nils.

"It sure was. In fact we did a quiet wedding ceremony at the chapel across the street. It took some doing for me to arrange for Mr. Zavos and his son to be there, but Hanife needed someone to give the bride away and Mr. Zavos was like a father to her. The reception party lasted nearly the entire night, or at least we were told. It was rumored that some of my RAF buddies even burned a piano that night right there on the patio." Sven noticed the grin on his daughter's face. "Did I say something you find amusing?" he asked Nora.

"No Dad, it's just that I heard about this legendary piano burning when Nils invited me to the Akrotiri Officers' Mess a couple of weeks ago. I even saw the spot on the patio that was damaged."

Sven smiled back at her before Nora and Nils leafed through the pictures. Sven continued his story of the bureaucratic red tape he went through in order to be able to marry Hanife before his unit was called back to the U.S. in mid- November.

When he returned to Offutt with his young family that winter, he was urged to separate from the Air Force and was offered a Civil Servant position with the Department of Defense, which allowed him to stay in Omaha. Old Sven welled up and said, "You know I loved your mom. I loved Yasemin so much, I just never showed her. She drifted and became rebellious and it was my fault. I was so much at a loss for what to do in those days."

Nora moved across the aisle in the compartment, sat down

beside her dad and hugged him. Nils searched for some words but they wouldn't come. Finally he offered, "You can't blame yourself Dad. You did the best you could. I can't speak for Nora, but I think we had it pretty good." Nobody spoke for what seemed like an eternity.

Nora made some space between her and Sven so that she could make eye contact and said, "Yasemin was so lucky. She might have still been pretty young, but she knew Mom. I think that is one of the reasons she was different. She was fun when we were little." Nils stayed quiet. One of the lessons he learned as a young officer was to keep silent when he had the urge to say something out of pure emotion that would likely ruin the moment.

Sven broke the silence as the train began to jostle from side to side passing over the switching tracks at the fringes of the station. "I see that we've arrived and I cannot wait to finally meet my grandson," he said proudly, beaming at his son. The twins were relieved for the shift in everyone's mood. Nils smiled at his dad and while nodding approval said, "Dad, thanks so much for sharing the past with us and filling in some of the blanks about Mom."

"I feel relieved and liberated. Thanks for listening to an old man's blubbering," said Sven.

CHAPTER 11

Nils and Josette

The Johanssons perfected the art of traveling light. When Josette saw them get off the train on the arrival platform she was prepared to wait with them while porters delivered their luggage and was glad she chose not to bring Martin along.

Nils saw her first and picked up the pace, leaving Nora and Sven to catch up.

"Oh mon petit amour, bonjour," he said as they greeted one another with *des bisous*.

"Nils it is so good to see you. Martin is so excited that you are here. He's missed you terribly."

"I've missed both of you as well." Nils loved the sound of Josette's accent when she spoke English. He gently guided her to meet Nora and Sven.

"Dad, this is Josette. Josette, my father Sven." Air kisses were exchanged, and then Nils repeated the introductions with Nora.

"Where is Martin?" Nils asked Josette.

"Home. He's eager to see you. I would have brought him along, but the car is maybe too small with the four of us and luggage." She shrugged and gave Nils a broad grin. She noticed something different about Nils, but couldn't put her finger on it. He seemed thoughtful to her.

She noticed everyone was ready to go. "You have everything?" she asked.

"Oui merci, c'est parfait." Sven said.

"Ah, vous aussi, vous parlez français?"

"Je me débrouille. It has been a long time. I picked up some from my days in Viet Nam."

Mystery solved, Nora and Nils stopped looking puzzled and gave a simultaneous giggle.

"I parked over near the *sortie.* If we don't leave right away, the commute trains will arrive. We won't like that much. Come." Josette tipped her head to the left and led the way to the car.

Nils just watched her, admiring what he'd come to love about her when they met two years ago. Her straight brunette hair was cropped short, emphasizing her fine facial features, long neck and jaw line. Even in her choice of bright but practical clothing and sensible shoes she managed to look classy and in Nils' eyes, French. Nora watched Josette throw open the trunk of the Peugeot and could easily see why Nils would be attracted to her.

Once their bags were loaded, they piled into the little French compact for the forty-minute drive to Josette's parents' villa. Sven sat up front with Josette, who provided commentary about the local area as they drove. As they approached the villa in Miramas, the landscape was typically Mediterranean with juniper and the occasional spire of Italian cypress clustered around the terraced homes.

It seemed all the homes had panoramic views of the Mediterranean all the way to the horizon to the south. The Neveu villa was a modest but practical residence, with a small semi circular gravel drive. The main structure was on a single level with sun bleached peach colored plaster and a terra cotta roof. Window boxes hung from every window with bright begonias blooming from each of them.

The early summer sun was directly overhead by the time they arrived. Josette led everyone through the open foyer to the back garden. On the lawn beside the small swimming pool, Nils spotted his tow headed son on hands and knees playing with a toy airplane while his grandparents watched nearby beneath the shade of an umbrella table.

A man about Sven's age rose from his chair to welcome his guests. As he did, Nils intercepted him and gave him a brief greeting saying something in French before heading directly for Martin. Josette introduced Sven and Nora to her father Alain. She then led Nora onto the patio to make the introduction with her mother. The two older men followed conversing in broken English and French.

As they walked around the edge of the pool, Josette said to Nora, "Look at my man and his son."

"Nils seems very happy," said Nora.

"Yes, but more than that. When he came home on leave for Martin's birthday just after Christmas, he was not so happy as he is now. Something is changed in him."

"You are probably right about that." Nora knew she was going to like Josette. The woman was overflowing with intuition and common sense.

"*Maman?* This is Nora Johansson and her father Sven." The older woman put down her iced tea and rose to greet them.

"*Ravie de vous rencontrer, je suis Claire.*" she said as she greeted both Nora and Sven. She then struggled through some of her rarely used English and said, "Welcome to our home." She gestured toward Nils and Martin. "As you can see, they are happy to see each other. We are so happy to have you come visit here in France."

"We are delighted, and thank you for having us." Sven replied to her in French, then switched to English and said, "I'm afraid my French is not very good. It has been a very long time."

Just then, Nils sprinted over to the group of adults standing at the edge of the pool. "Dad, Sis, this is Martin. Martin, *ton grandpère et ta tante Nora.*" Nils was holding Martin up on his shoulder. He passed his son across to Sven.

"Wow! What a stout young man." He looked at Nils and then Josette and said, "You've both done well. No granddad could be prouder."

After Sven passed young Martin off to Nora, Alain clapped

Sven on the shoulder and gave him a broad smile nodding his head up and down. "This calls for celebration." He turned to the covered area of the patio next to the house. While the Johanssons were getting acquainted with Martin, Claire slipped into the kitchen to retrieve a tray with champagne flutes. Josette followed closely with two bottles of champagne. They all took up chairs around an outdoor dining table nestled up close to the house under the shade of the vine-covered arbor.

They all enjoyed a toast.

"How long will you be staying in France?" asked Alain.

"My dad and I are heading to Cyprus the day after tomorrow," Nora replied.

"And Nils?" Claire asked then looked over at Nils.

"I'm not sure. Martin's grown so much since I last saw him. I don't want to miss anything."

Josette seemed happy that Nils appeared interested in staying. In the past he couldn't wait to get away from the Neveu family, which was something that had bothered her. Claire then asked Nora about Cyprus. Nils waited and listened to the conversation going around the table eager to get a moment or two alone with Josette. As she finished her champagne Nils got up and stood beside her chair, leaned down and gently rested his hand over hers while whispering something in her ear. The others could see the straight line of her lips rise into a delicate smile as she turned her head to look up at him nodding in the affirmative.

"While you are getting acquainted, Nils and I have some things to talk about. If you'll excuse us?" Josette announced to her parents and guests.

"Of course," said Alain as he rose from the table. Sven also got up from his seat briefly as Josette got up from her chair. Nils escorted her to the entryway and outside. He and Josette heard the others resume their conversation. Martin was in good hands as Nora and Sven were still doting on him.

They left the house to take an early evening walk. Nils turned to Josette and said, "Thank you Josette for not making this difficult."

"It is OK, you wanted to talk, so let's talk." She still couldn't put her finger on what she liked about this new version of Nils. She tried to convince herself that she hadn't seen this side of him since they met, but knew that wasn't entirely true. Ever since she'd known him, he seemed guarded, as if he were holding something back. But now, just in the brief time since his arrival in France, she felt as if an opening through the corridor of their rocky relationship was letting light in for the first time.

"Until very recently I've been carrying around some pretty heavy emotional baggage," Nils declared. Things have changed. I feel more at peace for the first time since high school.

"I sensed something. Maybe because you never said much about your father, and now, well...here he is with you on a family holiday of sorts. By the way, I really like Nora."

"You hardly know her. You just met."

"Yes, but she is just how you talked about her when we were together. She's really pretty. It is good she doesn't look like you." Josette was attempting some humor and Nils could tell she was trying to lighten the mood to get him to talk more.

"My dad is terminally ill. Cancer."

"And you don't seem sad."

"I am. I'm sad for what we missed. We never really talked about anything besides sports and the Air Force. It got to be a chore after so many years. Just last week he told Nora and me about his condition. Of course we both knew about the cancer, but it had been in remission for the past two years. I suppose when a man is facing his own mortality it changes him. My dad opened up to us the day we came to visit him in the hospital." Nils paused as they continued their stroll up a path toward the community park overlooking the village.

"What about this 'emotional baggage' then?" asked Josette.

"I was getting to that. It was like the flood gates had opened and Dad told us all kinds of things about our family history that Nora and I were never aware of. Most of it is still a mystery and a lot of it has to do with our mother."

Josette looked up at Nils to see if his expression changed at all when he brought up the subject of his mother. Shortly after they'd met, he and Josette shared all that they knew about their families. Josette remembered that whenever Nils spoke of his mother, there didn't seem to be any emotion. This was probably because he never knew her and didn't know anything about her. However, recently things had changed for Nils.

"So you've learned something about your mother. *C'est ça?*"

"She lived through a lot before she met my dad. I could tell from the pictures of the two of them and the way that my dad talks about her that she was a cheerful and wonderful strong woman. Imagine a Turkish Cypriot girl who lost everything, growing up in a Greek Cypriot village without her family. I would have loved to have known her, Josette." For the first time Josette noticed cracks in Nils's emotional armor.

"This doesn't sound like the baggage you mentioned. What about that?"

For Nils it was like standing at a precipice high above a cold pool, apprehensive about taking the plunge. As they approached a railing by an overlook along the footpath, Nils stopped walking. Josette came up short, turned and looked at him. He put both his hands on her shoulders and began.

"My older sister was pregnant when she was killed."

"Yes, you told me that already." Josette patiently waited for Nils to share more.

"There was much more to it. For years I thought I had a hand in her death." Nils then explained about the night he literally threw her boyfriend Zach out of their house and how

Yasemin had stolen his dream by snatching his application package to the U.S. Air Force Academy from the outgoing post and threw it at him in retaliation for the way he had treated Zach.

"Josette, please don't judge me for what I need to tell you. Promise?"

Josette was taken by the changes she was seeing in the father of her son. Deep down she knew she must have loved him at one time and realized now she still did. Regardless of the battles in their relationship, she'd always known Nils to be courageous and to the point. She was perplexed by his apprehension and caution, as he told this story.

"Nils, you know you can tell me anything. There can never be anything too horrible that we can't work out together. No matter, it is important for Martin's sake. I promise no judgments."

Nils took a deep breath before continuing. "What I'm about to say, I've never told anyone," he said before going on. "That night after Yasemin threw the unsent application package at me, I did something rash. I woke early the next morning and replaced all of her birth control pills with diet pills. I wanted to get back at her. I didn't know what I could have been thinking or how it would have played out." Nils paused releasing his hands from Josette's shoulders and turned, staring into the distance shaking his head. He couldn't look at her for fear of rejection.

"I thought she might have crashed her car on purpose because of getting pregnant. I found out later that Zach had no intention of marrying her. He didn't want anything to do with her or a baby. That worthless piece of trash just disappeared from Yasemin's life. She must have felt lost and alone. Before Zach, I really enjoyed being with her. Nora and I looked up to her." He turned again to Josette exploring her expression before going on.

"When we visited my dad in the hospital last week, he told us about that night and how Yasemin brought Zach home with her to tell him she was pregnant. When I walked in that evening, I had no idea what they had been discussing. It never came up again. She was pregnant before I messed with her pills."

"So in the end it didn't matter about the birth control pills," said Josette.

"Yes and no. Last week when Dad told us everything, I was relieved. Still, I couldn't shake the guilt for what I'd tried to do to my own sister and what could have contributed to her death. I'm angry with myself for having been so selfish and vindictive."

Josette took it all in, finally understanding why he'd created a hard shell to shield himself from close relationships. She pulled him to her and gave him a loving squeeze, then eased herself back so she could look at him. "Nils, you were just a young boy with a dream. Young people make bad decisions sometimes. I don't judge you. *Je t'aime.*"

He pulled her to him and wrapped her in his arms. With her head against his shoulder, she couldn't see the tears that pooled in his eyes. Tears that drained from them when he closed his eyes and whispered to her. "I love you too, Josette. I long to have you and Martin with me always."

They held each other for a long time without saying anything. After a short while, they started the walk back to Josette's family home on the hill. As they were leaving the park they saw another couple about their age. The man was pushing a lavender colored pram and the young woman had her elbow hooked on his arm with her head leaning on his shoulder as they slowly walked up the incline into the park. They were both quiet and smiling, as their baby girl slept in the pram.

"That could have been us a couple years ago," said Nils.

"Who says it can't be us now?" Josette asked.

Nils broke into a broad smile and looked at Josette. "I have some other news," he said.

"Good news?" She chuckled knowing it could only be something cheerful after the flood of emotion that poured out from him earlier.

"I'm going to pilot training. I got orders just before all of this with my dad happened. I'm not returning to Cyprus." He was trying to gage what must have been running through Josette's mind with this additional piece of news.

"That's wonderful. Where?"

"Valdosta, Georgia. Moody Air Force Base. It isn't New York, but you can get there easy enough." Nils knew his wife always wanted to come to the U.S. to visit New York City.

During the rest of their walk back they discussed the possibilities and practicalities of Josette and Martin coming to the States. Nils explained to Josette that if they were married before a judge in the United States, she'd become a citizen. He also expressed concern about the location and that he'd be devoted to a hard year of training with very little time off. Josette explained that in spite of the comforts of living at her family's villa, she was beginning to feel like the place was too small for her and Martin to share with her parents. She loved her parents and their generosity, but with motherhood, she was becoming a mature woman and no longer wanted their interference when it came to raising Martin.

"Let's all go there together," Josette said.

"Really? Just like that?"

"Yes. Really. Unless of course you feel a need to discuss details." She gave him a look indicating that she knew this was what he had been hoping for.

"OK. It is settled then. You know, we don't have a lot of time to get your things organized."

"It won't be difficult. I finished the last of the courses for my nursing degree two weeks ago. Martin and I don't need to bring a lot. Whatever we are missing, I have some money saved and we can get what we need when we are settled."

Nils was speechless. He came to a halt. Josette continued walking a few steps before noticing he wasn't keeping up. When she turned looking for him, he closed the steps between them with his arms wide. He embraced her and gave her a long loving kiss. As he released her he said. "I love you so much Josette. I've missed you and I never want us to be apart like we have been ever again."

"I love you too, father of our son. Let's get back so I can tell *maman and papa* our plans. They'll be happy Martin will be learning his English in an American school."

By the time they returned to the Neveu's villa, the sun had long set. It didn't seem they'd been gone that long, but they had a lot to catch up on. When they came in, Claire was finishing up in the kitchen showing them where she had remnants of dinner plated up for them in the oven.

"I put Martin down about a half hour ago. He was so tired from all the excitement." Claire looked up at Nils. "Your sister is very good with him, but it is easy to see she has no experience with toddlers."

Nils nodded but didn't comment. He turned to Josette who was already gesturing for him to come along with her. "Let's look in on him," she said.

As the two young parents stood over the crib of their son, they realized they were going to be enjoying many more moments like this in the days ahead. They both gave him a soft kiss before eating their dinner meal and then heading for bed themselves.

The next morning over *petit déjeuner* with *pain-grillé*, c*omfiture* and coffee, Josette shared the news with everyone about the plans she and Nils made to settle in the U.S. and live as a family. They both laid out the chores that needed to be accomplished before Nils's training started and announced that they'd be departing France at the end of the week.

The Neveu's weren't entirely surprised by this news. It was something they'd both hoped for, but somehow the timing caught them off guard. Claire turned around from the kitchen sink where she was drying her hands on a dishtowel. "Nilsson, Alain and I will be expecting you to visit more often. We've gotten so used to having Josette and Martin, I'm afraid Alain will drive me crazy around here." She said.

Nils sensed this was Josette's mother's way of giving them her blessing and assured her that she and Alain would have plenty of visits from their daughter and grandson.

"You as well Nilsson. You need to think of yourself as part of this family also," said his future mother-in-law.

After breakfast, while Nils was helping Claire clear off the table, Nora came over to him and did something she hadn't felt comfortable with since they were in high school. She gave him a big hug.

"I'm happy for you and your family, Nils. You all are so brilliant together. I'm proud of you. Proud to be your twin." She gave him a peck on the cheek before joining her father on the back patio by the pool.

CHAPTER 12

Cyprus

May 2001

Nils borrowed the Peugeot from Josette to drive Sven and Nora to the airport in Marseille where their Lufthansa flight would deliver them to Larnaca in time for dinner. The afternoon before, Sven had called Gavin Hart who insisted on hosting the two of them.

"I only had the pleasure of visiting with your daughter for a short while when she was last here," said Gavin. "It will be wonderful to see you again after all this time. Are you well?" He asked. Sven kept the conversation short stating that they'd have plenty of time to catch up over a tall cold Pimms on the rocks.

On the ride to the airport, Sven sat up front with Nils. Once they got on the main road, they talked about preparing for pilot training and how challenging the year would be. Nils assured his dad that Lieutenant Colonel Spade and his visiting U-2 pilots invested quite a bit of time and expertise coaching him to make sure he would ace the course. Both of them were satisfied with Nils's prospects for a budding career as a USAF pilot.

While the men were chatting, Nora was lost in pleasant thoughts of her own. Nils glanced in the rear-view mirror and noticed her leaning her head against the window frame gazing at the passing countryside.

"Hey sis, where are you? You look a thousand miles away."

Nora didn't respond. Sven turned around in his seat to look at her and noticed the corners of her mouth turned up in a happy expression. Just like her mother used to look when she was daydreaming. He then turned to Nils and said, "She's dreaming about her beau. I'm glad she was able to reach him last evening. Fortunately he was at the Hart Gallery when I called yesterday. She said he doesn't have a phone."

Sensing they were talking about her, Nora snapped out of her daydream. "I'm sorry, what were you saying? Were you asking me something?"

Nils laughed quietly to himself before answering. "Sis, you should have seen yourself deep in thought." He was looking back at her through the rear view mirror as he spoke, still keeping an eye on the road.

"I'm looking forward to meeting this young man of yours, but since Nils won't be joining us on this little jaunt, maybe it is time you tell us a little about him," Sven said.

"I can't wait to see Aydın again. He was very understanding about my sudden departure. We made plans to visit the Akamas but never made it there. I still want to go."

"What's he like? I mean what do you like about him? Sven asked knowing if he could get Nora started, that her description would be pretty thorough.

Nora started by stating. "He isn't anything like either of the two of you."

The two men sitting in the front seat exchanged glances, then laughed and said almost at the same time, "That's good to hear." Her dad then urged her to continue.

She gave a brief description of Aydın's easygoing character and casual attractiveness. She told them how he makes his living playing guitar and singing at small clubs and restaurants during the tourist season, and in the offseason, he works working odd jobs. Then she told them Aydın was raised by his late uncle because his parents were killed when he was a baby. He was a refugee from the north of the island.

While she was talking about him, she realized that there was so much more she didn't know about Aydın and his experience growing up as a Greek Cypriot. Instead she went on about the many little things he does for her when they are together. How genuine he is and how he listens to everything she says as if at that moment, she is the most important person in the world to him.

Nora's commentary went on and on like a flood of yearning. "Alright, alright, we get it," said Nils. "He's prince charming." He looked at his sister in the mirror again and said, "I'm really happy for you Nora."

Nora knew this to be a big stretch for her brother to say these things to her, given her dating history. "Thanks Nils. Coming from you, that means a lot."

"Well, I can't wait to meet him," said Sven. "Does he know how to cook?" Sven asked, knowing from experience that Greek Cypriot men take pride in preparing delicious meals.

"You'll see." Nora replied. When they spoke on the phone the day before, Aydın told her that he and Gavin would prepare a *meze* for when they arrived.

The flight was smooth and when they arrived in Larnaca, to Nora's relief, both of their bags were there. No lost luggage this time. Nora drove the rental car they'd picked up at the airport. Another Opel Astra similar to the one she drove on her last trip.

"You sure you don't want to drive?" she asked.

"Maybe tomorrow. It's been awhile since I've had to drive on the wrong side."

"Not wrong dad, just different."

As they drove onto the highway, Sven was amazed at how much the island had seemed to change and at the same time, how much of it seemed exactly the same. He noticed the large homes alongside the highway, all belonging to rich Russians and probably paid for with aid money that was originally marked for something less ostentatious. To the left he could see the Mediterranean coast and on the right, the terraced foothills of Troodos.

"This really brings me back," he said to his daughter and smiled.

"I'm glad. We can visit your old haunts and you can tell me about the places you and mom went together." When she spoke of her mother, it still felt strange to her. Nora wasn't used to talking about her. The more she learned about her, the easier it was for Nora to talk about her mother as a person connected to her own life.

Sven smiled and said. "I wasn't sure I'd want to do that, but now because we can take this journey together, I think I'm ready."

Nora reached across and gave her father's shoulder a reassuring squeeze. "No need to explain. I know what you mean Dad." She nodded and repeated to herself, "Yep I know what you mean." Then they were both quiet for a while.

They drove with the windows down. Shortly after turning north on the B-8 leading up to Laneia Village, Sven broke the silence.

"This road looks just as it did thirty years ago. You know, I can't say I remember any specific aspect to it other than the familiar landscape around here. These terraces are amazing. Just thinking about the labor involved over all the years. The work of human hands." He moved his left hand across the view out the left side of the car as if holding a paint brush and adding a few strokes of his own to emphasize the timelessness of the landscape.

"Maybe when we get to Laneia your memories will be more vivid. Even though I was only here for a short while, I had the chance to make this drive a few times. It grows on you. Being here, that is." She reflected on her own impressions, taking in what she could while concentrating on the winding road.

As they approached the village, Sven commented. "I don't recognize some of these buildings. They seem newer, like the holiday villas with the big swimming pools we saw just on the outskirts." A little further on, the road delivered them to the center of the village, where there was a well and some mature palms. "Now this I recognize. It is in much better shape then I remember, but the place generally looks the same. Gavin's is just ahead and to the left if I'm not mistaken."

"You're not mistaken Dad. We'll park along the rock wall on the dirt track and walk the rest of the way. How about it?"

Sven smiled at his daughter as he grabbed his knapsack and the ancient leather satchel. He reached across for Nora's bag as well. Nora opened the opposite door and said, "I got it Dad. Come on, let's go." She shut the door and locked the Astra with the key fob.

Sven looked around and with a deep breath exclaimed, "I can smell the *suvala* grilling over a barbecue." They both picked up the pace knowing Gavin would probably be in the garden tending to the meat.

When they entered the garden, Nora saw that Aydın was the one grilling the chunks of lamb over the grill. She dropped her bag and dashed across the garden to greet him.

Over the sounds of the sizzling meat on the grill, he sensed a presence and caught a glimpse of Nora's hurried form. He put down the fork he was holding, stepped away from the grill and closed the distance between them with arms spread wide.

"I missed you," he said.

"And I missed you. Come meet my dad." She led him over to where she left her father still standing at the entry to the gallery grounds.

"Dad, this is Aydın. Aydın, meet my dad."

"It is a great pleasure Mr. Johansson. Welcome back to Cyprus."

As they were exchanging greetings, Gavin Hart emerged from the kitchen holding a tray with four tall glasses. He wasn't prepared for seeing the changes in his old friend Sven who had become thin, gaunt, and appeared much older than his age. Gavin set the tray of drinks down on the table beneath the eaves in front of the house and strode over to Sven.

As the two men exchanged handshakes, it was Gavin who pulled Sven in close for a bear hug. "It has been awhile mate. You're looking well."

"Thanks old friend. It is good seeing you and thanks for having us."

"It's been what, twenty-five years?" Gavin asked.

"Something like that. I see the place hasn't changed much. At least not here in Laneia."

"As they say, the more things change, the more they stay the same." Gavin then turned to Nora who had her arm snuggled around Aydın. "I'm glad you could convince him to come visit young lady. It has been entirely too long and we have a lot to catch up on."

"It didn't take much convincing," she said smiling.

"The meat is ready to come off the fire." Aydın said as he excused himself.

Nora and Sven spent their first week touring around Cyprus starting with a day hike along the Akamas. It was Gavin's idea so he led them on the trek starting with a visit to the place where he painted the picture of the rocks now hanging in the main gallery in Laneia. Since it was a weekday, Aydın was free from his weekend gigs with his traditional music ensemble, so he joined them.

As they drove, Aydın pointed out some of the older villages on their way over the high ridge past Polis. They stopped the car on the windy road so that they could get a better look at one of them. Tucked away in an upper valley on the northern slope of the ridge they could see the abandoned village of Theletra. Sven commented that it looked similar to some of the run down abandoned villages left by Turkish Cypriots in their flight from the inter-communal violence of '63-64.

Aydın pointed out the location of an old Eastern Orthodox Church up on the hill in the center of the village and explained that even though it had a similar appearance to other villages they'd seen earlier, that Theletra was actually a Greek Cypriot village abandoned after a severe earthquake sometime in the late 1960s.

"I took a short trip into Turkey when I was working in Azerbaijan," said Nora. "During a school break, I joined an excursion to Fethiye Turkey and we visited a village called Kayaköy, which is also abandoned and has a similar history.

Before the population exchange after The Great War, Kayaköy was an inter-communal village with Christians and Muslims living together. When I think of those people being ripped apart by someone else's version of political stability, it is very sad. Later, locals from Fethiye and others from elsewhere occupied the dwellings left by the Christians who were forced from their homes during the exchange. Some years later an earthquake caused the demise of the village and today it looks very much like this one."

Aydın put his arm around Nora and gave her a squeeze before they all settled back into the car for the remainder of the trip down to the shores of the Akamas.

It was still cool and comfortable in the mid morning hour when they arrived at the Akamas trail head at the far end of the car park for "The Baths of Aphrodite."

They all got out of the car and retrieved their knapsacks, which contained several bottles of water and trail snacks then they began the walk along the rocky path.

"Wow this really brings me back," said Sven as he turned toward Gavin.

"It is indeed a beautiful spot. I'm sure you'll remember it gets much better a bit farther up the trail. Shall we get moving then?" asked Gavin as he looked at each of them in turn.

Aydın shrugged his shoulders and gave Nora a gentle nudge at the small of her back suggesting they should get moving before it got too hot. At his touch, Nora turned to him and winked.

"Have I told you lately that I love you?" she asked.

"Not lately, but I like hearing you say it." He gave her forehead a brush with his lips and they continued up the path already several paces behind Gavin and Sven.

A few kilometers later they rounded a bend at the top of a steep rocky rise overlooking the azure sea. A thin white rocky shoreline stretched to the West just below the green and olive scrub interspersed with acacia and low cypress trees. Though still a dry climate, the vegetation along the Akamas was much more alive than the bondu scrub in the southern region and in particular the Akrotiri peninsula. When Nora reached the point where her father was gazing at the view she noticed there was nobody around but the four of them. She said, "This is so beautiful and peaceful."

Sven pointed to a spot along the rocky shore, "Your mother

and I came here once shortly after we first met. She told me that when she was a teenager living with the Zavos family, they used to come here in the spring and picnic along the shore in the shade in the corner of that cove below."

Speculating, Nora asked her father, "She must have always found the good in everything. Am I safe in assuming Mom was an eternal optimist?"

"I'd say you're safe. She never told me specifically, but I could tell from the way she talked of Cyprus in the early times before her parents were killed that she had hopes that one day Cypriots would again live together in peace."

Aydın put the idea of Cypriot unity out of his mind long ago. He was used to the divide having been born in the midst of conflict. However, something Sven just said triggered his mind. "I'm sad that my country is divided. It is embarrassing to me that our capitol is cut in two and that we no longer mix with our neighbors." He turned his head from side to side as he said this.

They continued their walk along the path and about a half hour later Gavin took them up a different path that looked like a goat trail heading south away from the shore and up to a high ridge.

"Don't worry, it looks steep, but we aren't going far," he said.

"This area is very dry." Aydın commented.

"We're right on the National Park Boundary. That is one of

the reasons there are no homes or villas up here. The reason for the peacefulness is that drilling a well for water here is impossible. There isn't enough rain in the winter months to collect much to store for the dry season." Gavin stopped and turned around suggesting the others do the same.

"Is that Turkey over there across the water?" Nora asked.

"It is much closer than Greece," said Aydın. "This view is very special. Maybe it is good there is no water here to entice developers to spoil the tranquility."

"Precisely," added Gavin as he continued up the path.

They crested the hill a short while later and saw among the brown and golden grasses, a cluster of dark rock spires reaching up to the cloudless sky.

"Gavin, the place hasn't changed a bit. It looks exactly is it did thirty years ago," said Sven. "Gavin drew me a map and I took your mother here for a picnic."

"Sounds like you and Mom did a lot of things together."

"Every moment I could get away we went out exploring together. The Zavos only had one vehicle. A small pickup truck dedicated to supporting the supply needs of their restaurant. As a result, they spent most of their time in and around Parimali. Your mom always said that going on our outings was 'romantic.'"

Aydın had been to the property several times with Gavin already. Instead of enjoying the view, the two of them surveyed the area, curious if there were any signs of erosion caused by overgrazing herds of goats. Gavin had an agreement with some of the locals that they could graze their goats on his land in exchange for information on the location of artifacts in need of preservation.

Nora sat with her dad on an ancient wood plank set across a couple of boulders, enjoying the view north across the water and into Turkey. "I made a call yesterday to Colonel Barrows."

"Colonel Barrows?" asked Sven.

"Colonel Jake Barrows, the Defense Attaché in Nicosia," she said.

"Ah, that Colonel Barrows. Yes we've met several times. Small world," he said.

"Nils set me up to see him on my last trip. He gave me a tour of the Green Line and offered to take me to see the sights in Northern Cyprus when I returned. I called last evening to take him up on his offer," Nora said.

"I've never been there. I've always wanted to though. I'd like to visit Kyrenia, Bellapais, Salamis, Saint Hilarion Castle…Have I missed anything?"

"Maybe Morphou, but those are all the places we should see anyway. Colonel Barrows won't be able to show us around, but he said his wife Tammy is the real expert when it comes to touring the north and she offered to have us stay in the guest room of their home in Nicosia in order to get an early start. Nils has been in their home and was impressed with the way our diplomats live while posted overseas."

Sven smiled at his daughter and said, "This trip is getting better with each passing day. When will be going up there?"

"We've been invited to their place for dinner tomorrow. Tammy said there will be others and to dress casual."

Sven nodded and said, "Sounds good. You'll see tomorrow's dinner engagement will be something you'll get used to as a foreign service officer. Are you excited about the program?"

Nora should have been beaming about her plans to begin her Masters program and the Foreign Service Institute training that would follow, all leading to an overseas posting at a U.S. Embassy.

"Dad, to be honest I'm torn. I'm in love with Aydın. I don't know if we can stand the separation and I don't know if he would ever want to leave Cyprus. I'm afraid to bring it up and spoil what is left of the summer."

Sven knew not to say too much. He wrapped his arm around her shoulder and gave her a hug and said, "When the time comes, you'll know what to do. Try to enjoy what you have while you have it."

"Is that something Mom would have said?" she asked.

"I don't know, but it is something I'm saying." He smiled at her.

"Thanks Dad." She nestled her head on his shoulder. "This sure is a beautiful view."

Moments later Aydın and Gavin approached to grab some water from their packs they left beside the makeshift bench.

"Blimey it is really getting to feel like the summer heat has come on strong," said Gavin. "What do you say we head on back? I know a nice spot on the way home where we can take in an early dinner or late lunch if you like."

"Isn't the proper British term for that called Tea?" Sven asked.

"Nice to see you still have some humor left in you mate."

Aydın grabbed the pack he was carrying for himself and Nora, pulled a bottle from it and offered Nora some water before they set off back toward the car park.

Two hours later they were in the car winding down to the small fishing village of Saint Georgios on the western end of the island. The tranquil village is nestled above a small cove. A manmade jetty curves around the outer edge of the cove protecting a modest fleet of traditional fishing vessels from the afternoon westerly winds and waves.

The restaurant Gavin had in mind was nothing more than a shack built around a charcoal grill with a primitive sink that had running water supplied from a large tank braced up on the roof. The patio had a sufficient number of umbrella tables anchored down so they wouldn't blow over in the wind. Like everywhere in Cyprus the view overlooking the cove and out across sparkling waves of turquoise blue was breathtaking.

CHAPTER 13

The "Turkish Republic of Northern Cyprus"

In the warmth of the morning sun in the back garden of the Barrows residence in Nicosia, Nora sat with her father enjoying coffee and a breakfast of fresh tomato, cucumber, *beyaz peynir* or white cheese, and flat bread. She turned to him and said, "You were right, I really enjoyed last evening and meeting such interesting people. It seemed intimate having dinner together after meeting for the first time. The food was also amazing."

"I knew you'd be impressed."

"How are they able to live like this? And those Turkish officers and their wives, I wonder how Colonel Barrows became so well connected."

"It's his job. Let's just leave it at that."

"And Mrs. Barrows. I've never been around a woman so elegant. She had every one of her guests completely at ease. Do you think she really knows all of them as well as it seemed?"

"In their line of work, nothing is ever really as it seems."

"Dad, you are starting to sound like a spook. Anyway, maybe Mrs. Barrows can help us find Mom's sister."

"That could be much harder than you think. How about we take things one-step at a time and see what there is to see? I'm looking forward to finally getting to the places I've never had the chance to see."

Tammy Barrows returned to her back patio. She was dressed fashionably for their day together. She unfolded a tourist map, which she spread on the table for Sven and Nora to follow as she laid out her proposal for seeing the sights.

"Jake will drop us off at Ledra Palace Hotel here in Nicosia on his way to the embassy. We'll process through immigration and customs, then walk over to the car rental a couple of blocks further on." She pointed to the location on the map before continuing. "The rental is already set up. I was thinking we might have just hopped a *dolmuş* to head straight to Kyrenia, but then we'd miss Saint Hilarion and Bellepais. Anyway, it should only take a few minutes to retrieve the keys to the compact, and we can be on our way." Tammy proceeded to show her guests the entire route she had planned for the day before folding the map.

Checking through at Ledra Palace Hotel was surprisingly smooth. Again it appeared that Tammy Barrows was well known among the immigration staff at the crossing point. The three of them were in their rental car a short while later enjoying the sights.

"Mrs. Barrows?" asked Nora.

"What is it dear?"

"I'm just taking a shot in the dark. You see, my mother Hanife had a sister when she lived on Cyprus…"

"Nora, Mrs. Barrows probably has other things to do rather

than to involve herself in our family history," Sven said.

"Please both of you, call me Tammy, and Sven, you shouldn't assume I'd be indifferent to the fact that your wife was Cypriot. Jake gave me a brief idea of what he'd learned from your son Nils and his recent discovery that you met Hanife here and spirited her away by marrying her during the 'troubles.' Even though Nils only provided us with the basics, my imagination tells me that it must have been an incredibly romantic yet unsettling time for the two of you. I had no idea Hanife had a sister."

Sven's eyes glassed over at the mention of Hanife and the circumstances of their marriage. He drifted deep into thought at the memory of those wonderful days.

"Sven. Did you hear me? I said I never knew Hanife had a sister."

Before he could say anything, Nora jumped in and asked. "Have you ever heard of anyone with a surname Yılmaz?"

"Heard of yes, but know anyone by that name, I'm afraid not. Yılmaz is a very common Turkish Cypriot name here, especially since '74. Aside from the large number of Turkish Army occupants, there has been more than thirty years of Turkish immigrants coming to the TRNC."

"TRNC?"

"Yes, the Turkish Republic of Northern Cyprus. It is not a diplomatically recognized name for Northern Cyprus, but that is what they call it here. Sven, I didn't know that your wife's maiden name was Yılmaz. I'll be sure to keep my eyes and ears open in case someone I run across has knowledge of Hanife's sister."

"I never met her. Hanife told me a little about how they became separated when they were just young girls. It must have been a tragic story because she could only give me the barest details when she told me shortly after we met. I know very little about her family," said Sven.

They pulled into the car park at Saint Hilarion Castle and assumed the role of tourists, sipping from water bottles and taking turns photographing each other. Like everywhere in Cyprus, the view was tremendous, especially from the rocky heights of the castle. They saw the Bellepais Abbey and a number of other smaller sights along the way to Kyrenia where they lunched in the shade of a covered patio at a taverna beside the harbor.

Although the language was different, the Cypriot cuisine was nearly identical to that of the south. While they were ordering their meals, Nora noticed that the dialect was different than the Turkish dialects she'd encountered during her time in Azerbaijan. Regardless, she attempted to converse with the young man who was waiting on their table. *"Türkçeyiniz biraz farklı ama anladım,"* said the young waiter acknowledging that understood her.

"I recall now that Jake mentioned you knew Turkish. It is

really quite fortunate you'll be able to enjoy your time here in the north." Tammy commented in fluid Turkish. The two ladies engaged in a brief conversation with Nora explaining that she was actually speaking in Azeri to the best of her ability and probably sounded like an American struggling with Turkish.

Shifting back to English so as not to leave Sven out of the conversation, Tammy told them, "When we're finished with lunch, I have someone I'd like to introduce you to."

"Will we then have time afterward to get out to Salamis?" asked Sven.

"Of course. My friend Bahar Demir is a researcher for the Kyrenia Folk Art Museum. Her office is just the other side of the castle wall. She's probably very busy with the height of the tourist season upon her, but she'll make time for us. Shall we?"

They paid the bill for the lunch in Turkish lira then Tammy led them to her friend's office at the museum.

At the door to her friend's office, Tammy greeted her friend. *"Merhaba Bahar!"*

"Merhaba en yakın arkadaşım," Bahar replied.

"I brought along some friends visiting from the United States."

Bahar rose from behind her desk. The petite older woman gave Tammy a gentle hug as they said their hellos. Dressed in practical cotton blend slacks and elegant silk blouse, she gave off the impression that there was always more work to do. She stretched her arms out gesturing a welcome to her domain.

"Welcome to our museum. I'm very pleased to meet you." said Bahar.

Tammy explained to her friend that she was giving Sven and Nora the whirlwind tour of the north.

"You must be very busy with the tourist season upon you," Tammy said.

"Oh not at all. You will see that the pace of tourism here is quite different than in the south."

While Sven was distracted by a mural in Bahar's office, Tammy gave her friend a brief background of the Johanssons' connection to Cyprus and their desire to possibly reconnect with their relative Dedim Yılmaz.

Bahar listened intently putting the pieces of the story together while at the same time wrestling with demons from her own recollection of those turbulent years. She turned to Nora full of emotion.

"I'm sorry about your mother." Bahar whispered putting a gentle hand on Nora's forearm. "You'll excuse me. We Cypriots struggle to keep the past in the past. I have many friends and will ask about your lost aunt. Where are you staying? In case I hear something, I'd like to be able to reach you."

At a loss, Nora gave her Gavin Hart's telephone number and explained what lay ahead in her future. "I plan to come back to Cyprus often. I love the tranquility and beauty of the north, so taking the time to come back here will always be part of my plan."

"You'll be sure to stay in touch then. Next time we meet, I'll give you the full tour of the museum." Bahar reached for her calling card and handed it to Nora who noticed with relief that there was an email address printed at the bottom.

"Çok teşekkür ederim," said Nora taking the card and thanking Bahar.

Bahar gave Nora a hug then turned to Sven. "You make sure she remembers to call me. I want to get to know your daughter better when we have more time. Where will you be off to next?"

Sven turned to Tammy and shrugged his shoulders. "I thought we'd go to Salamis and loop back to Nicosia for dinner," said Tammy.

"Sounds like you have an ambitious afternoon ahead. I won't keep you."

They took the coast road to Küçükerenköy where they turned south to rejoin the main highway to Famagusta. The terrain was beautiful but the road was slow going. Both Nora and Sven were surprised at the number of signs posted in various places along the route that said that photography was prohibited. They noticed in several places large fenced and secure areas hidden in the trees that appeared to be Turkish Army encampments.

Tammy noticed that both Sven and Nora were intrigued by the large presence of Turkish military throughout the area and said, "There are upwards of thirty-thousand Turkish military personnel still occupying this side of the island. Surprisingly it is a sore point with the Turkish Cypriots just as it is with Greek Cypriots."

"I don't follow." Sven said.

"You're familiar with The Treaty of Guarantee and what the Turkish still refer to as the rescue mission in July of '74?" Both Nora and Sven nodded in the affirmative as she continued.

"Back then, Turkish Cypriots had recently experienced violence and political instabilities. They feared for their safety just ten short years after the inter-communal conflicts in the mid-'60s. You already know this but the timeframe is important. You see, it has been over thirty-five years and as you saw, the Turkish Army still maintains an occupational force. At this point in time the safety of Turkish Cypriots is no longer in question. Turkish Cypriots fear they are losing their culture to mainland Turkey."

Until then, both Nora and Sven hadn't considered the facts as Tammy laid them out. Nora contemplated all that she was learning from the excursion to the north.

A couple of hours later, they arrived at another of Cyprus's famous historical sites. The ruins of Salamis date back to 1100 B.C. when it was in fact the capital city of the island.

"I've always wanted to come here," said Sven after the three of them got out of the car. Even though the tourist season was spinning up, the car park was virtually empty as was the site itself. Tammy escorted them to the area where the columns and staircase ruins had been preserved.

They strolled through the ruins and took in the view. The site overlooked the aquiline colored tranquility of Famagusta Bay. The white stone provided a sharp contrast to the blue with sparse patches of olive colored low shrub. Unlike Curium, the amphitheater at Salamis is smaller and not used regularly.

While Tammy took a call on her mobile phone, Sven sat down on a large block of limestone where Nora was already sitting transfixed by the view and enjoying the warm breeze blowing offshore.

"Amazing isn't it?" Sven asked his daughter.

"Gorgeous. Dad, I don't think there are words to describe the feeling I get when I'm in a place like this."

"OK then, I won't ask if you've seen enough. I wanted to tell you something."

She looked at him trying to anticipate what he was going to say but was at a loss.

"Go ahead. Tell me."

"I like your friend Aydın. He seems like the genuine article. Different than other Greek Cypriots I've met. Like I said yesterday, when the time comes you'll know what to do."

242

Nora sensed her dad was aware of her conflicting emotions. After all, he met her mother under more pressing circumstances.

When Tammy was done talking on her mobile phone, she strode over to where the two of them were sitting.

"Well, what do you think so far? Is it what you expected?"

"Actually, no," Sven said. "I thought there would have been more to it and maybe there would be throngs of tourists. It sure is beautiful though."

"That it is," said Tammy. "We're about two hours from being back home. There is still some daylight. We could stop for an afternoon coffee or head on back. Your choice."

Nora chimed in. "I spent an evening at the home of a refugee from Famagusta a few weeks ago. She is an acquaintance of my brother and married to a British Expat. We had dinner with them. Would it be out of the way to go to Varosha on the way back?"

"Varosha? It isn't too far out of the way, but why? It isn't a place one can visit," Tammy said.

"Let's say it is a curiosity for me. You don't mind do you?"

"No problem. We should be off then if we want to take in any of the scenery on the drive back to Nicosia."

Varosha wasn't what Nora or Sven expected. As they drove down the beach road of Famagusta, signs redirected them inland and around a large complex of what looked like bombed out and decaying luxury high rises.

"What a waste," commented Sven as they drove along a corrugated barrier wall were there were signs posted in three languages with skull and crossbones warning to keep out.

"It isn't entirely secure. This holiday haven was caught in the middle of the combat in '74 and is now part of the demilitarized Green Zone. There are rumors of booby traps in some of the buildings and land mines still buried in the sand. Jake says he doesn't think so though. He said things happened too fast and that the people who fled were too scared and in too big of a hurry to have done such things."

"That wasn't the case in other places," added Nora. During her undergraduate studies, she recalled that clearing land mines in war torn countries was a hot topic for journalists throughout the world.

"Sven, you've been rather silent. Penny for your thoughts?" asked Tammy.

Sven sat in the front seat as Tammy drove along the neighborhood road skirting the rusted barriers and barbed wire coiled over every wall as they passed. A whirlwind of emotions filled his mind, as they continued toward Nicosia.

"This has been almost an overwhelming but welcome trip for me," he said still deep in thought. "It seems like just yesterday when Hanife and I met here in Cyprus and now I'm imagining how it must have been for her during the times of the troubles.

When we left Cyprus in '74, it was a relief that she and Yasemin survived. What does a young Cypriot woman with a baby do when she has no place to go? There must have been many others who lost loved ones in the conflict and left broken lives with little hope of making a better future for their families."

"Sven, I don't know if you've noticed, but Cypriots are pretty resilient in spite of the barbed wire that cuts through the center of their capitol," said Tammy. She looked over at Sven as she drove and asked, "Have you seen any 'homeless' Cypriots since you've been here?"

"To be honest, I haven't been looking," said Sven.

"When Jake and I came here it took me awhile to put my finger on it, but after awhile it occurred to both of us that in other large cities where we lived there were always 'street people' and large populations of them seemed to be without homes. In Nicosia, Limassol, Paphos, Morphou, or any other large settlement here, you don't see homelessness the same way you see it in other places. You know why?"

Sven shook his head in the negative.

"The wars have forced them to rely upon each other for protection and survival," said Tammy. "The rest of the world could learn a thing or two from those who know how to take care of their own."

Sitting in back and watching the scenery fly by as they drove, Nora mulled over what Tammy was saying about the Cypriot people. She leaned forward and squeezed her dad's shoulder and neck. "How are you feeling, Dad?"

He patted her hand, "Better than ever. Thanks." He reached for his water bottle and took a swig as Nora settled herself back into her seat.

"Dad I'm beginning to see what you meant when you said if a person understood Cyprus, then there would be hope for preventing conflict in other places. Seeing is believing I guess."

Tammy looked at Nora through the rear view mirror. "You start your program in September I hear," she said.

"Yes. I'm very excited. But now I am feeling impatient and want to get to the field as soon as possible."

"You'll do very well I'm sure. Oh and don't worry, there will be plenty of problems to work through when you do get to the field. Enjoy the freedom of academia while you have the chance." Tammy paused for a moment. "I wish I was in your position with the world ahead of you and the energy to take it all on. With your compassion, just don't let it beat you down."

"Don't worry, I have no intention of allowing that to happen. People deserve a chance for happiness." As she said this she felt more torn than ever. She was in love with her gentle and handsome man. In love really for the first time, and excited about setting her course for her professional future, neither of which seem to fit well together.

As they drove past the several road signs indicating the

direction to Nicosia, Nora noticed they were approaching a roundabout with a road leading to Ercan Airport. They slowed down as they got into the circular interchange and a sign caught Nora's eye.

"Balıkeşir." She shouted. Both Sven and Tammy were startled.

"What?" Tammy asked.

"Balıkeşir is the village where Aydın came from."

"My daughter has been smitten by the curse of Aphrodite's Isle," said Sven. "It must run in the family, to fall in love with someone on Cyprus. I've met him. He's OK by me. Good enough for my only daughter." As he said this he was thinking about his life with Hanife and then what happened to Yasemin and Zach and how tragedy carved its path in every age regardless of where people live.

Tammy was a bit perplexed. "So you've been to the north before?"

Nora understood her confusion right away. She remembered that Nils thought Aydın was a Turkish Cypriot living in the south, when he first heard the name.

"Aydın is a Greek Cypriot refugee. He was an infant when he came to a village in the south, near Kantou or Çanakkale. I just learned my Mom grew up near there."

"I see. Well, you seem to be discovering that whenever you look just below the surface, everything is connected on Cyprus," said Tammy.

CHAPTER 14

Nostalgia

It was very late by the time they returned to the Barrows home in Nicosia. Sven and Nora thanked them for their hospitality and prepared to leave early the next morning.

Over breakfast Sven commented on Jake's service dress uniform. "I've got the weekly country team update with Ambassador Bandler's staff this morning," he said. Turning to Nora he said, "Next time you come up, I'll have to introduce you to the ambassador. He's really a great guy and I think he'd be impressed that you'll soon be joining the Foreign Service."

"Thanks. I'll look forward to it." Nora shook his hand and then when Sven was finished saying goodbye to Tammy, she gave the older woman a long embrace. "Thank you so much for opening your home to us and showing us around the north. Next time you see Bahar, please tell her I enjoyed meeting her and that I plan to return to the museum."

"I'll do just that. I'm sure Bahar would love to see you again. Our door is always open." Tammy waved to both of them as they set off on their return to Laneia.

They took their time on the way back. The road up to Laneia was becoming familiar to Nora. The cool breeze descending from Troodos was a welcome change from the heat of Nicosia and the sticky humidity of the southern coast of

Cyprus. When they arrived in Laneia at mid-day it had become hot and the whole village seemed lethargic. Shutters were closed shading the interiors of the houses from the afternoon heat.

Kaplan was stretched out on a cool slab of patio under the shade of the overhanging roof in front of the main gallery entrance. The garden was still flourishing with begonias and other drought resistant ornamental flowers that lined the open grounds where the native grasses were taking on the golden brown colors of the Cypriot summer.

"Dad, how are you doing?" She had no idea what it must be like for a person experiencing terminal cancer.

"You know, I really don't feel much different than ever. In fact, compared to when I was undergoing treatment back when you were in college, I feel almost healthy," said Sven.

"I just worry. I'm finally really getting to know you and I'm getting used to having you around. I don't want to miss you." She looked at him with deep compassion and longing for a childhood she never got to enjoy. "Dad, Nils and I used to avoid you because you never said much to us. We didn't know whether you loved us or wished we weren't around, so we just avoided you. It was an instinct. Not something we did consciously. Anyway, I'm sorry we missed the chance to be close like this."

Sven put his arm around her. "It was all my fault. I was the adult and could have manned up, but chose instead to wallow in self-pity. Amazing I didn't become an alcoholic. I immersed myself in a dead end job instead."

Gavin was in the back of the studio working on a frame for one of his latest watercolors when his guests returned and came inside to get out of the hot sun.

"There's lemon squash in a pitcher in the icebox if you need something cool," shouted Gavin. He saw them through the window earlier when they came up the path. "I'll be with you shortly. Just a few things here to finish up."

Nora and Sven sat on the wooden chairs surrounding the kitchen table, each with a tall glass of refreshing lemonade. "Now what will you do Dad? Seems like we've done just about everything."

"Not everything…not yet anyway. I have had nearly all my fill of sightseeing though. Before I leave this Friday, I've got one other stop I'd like to make."

"Which is?" goaded Nora.

"Would you take me to Melanda tomorrow? Maybe early before it gets too hot?"

"Can I bring Aydın?"

"Absolutely."

"Good. I'll convince him to bring his guitar. He's really quite a musician and he's got an incredible voice, Dad. It makes me melt when I hear him sing."

Sven couldn't contain his happiness for his daughter and

laughed aloud.

"What's so funny?"

"Nothing. Can't a dad be happy for his daughter?"

"I love you Dad."

Just then Gavin walked in, oblivious to the family moment he was interrupting. Wiping his hands on the front of his shirt he said, "Welcome back. Isn't the north wonderful? I love the colors and the light. Did you manage to get out to the Karpass Peninsula?"

"It was a wonderful outing," said Nora.

"The Barrows treated us well and we got a full dose of the north for such a short visit. But unfortunately, the Karpass was too far off the beaten track," added Sven.

"Well, perhaps next time then," said Gavin.

"Dad's going to be leaving in a couple of days, so tomorrow we're going down to Melanda. I haven't had the chance to see if Aydın is free yet, but I'm hopeful. You wanna join us?"

"I haven't really thought about my plans for tomorrow, but if there is room, I think I would enjoy tagging along," said Gavin.

"Good, then it is settled. We will be heading out early." Nora paused looking to Gavin for a reaction then continued. "We want to get there before it gets hot and the beach fills up with tourists."

"That sounds fine by me," said Gavin. "I don't think you need worry too much about tourists though. I've been there every summer at the height of the season and always see the same locals year after year. Rarely a tourist."

"Great. If you'll excuse me, I'll be back in a bit. I'm going over to Aydın's to let him know we're back and see if he's free tomorrow." Nora rushed off down the path toward the coffee house and Aydın's place.

The following morning when they turned off the main road and down the track to Melanda Bay, there was enough dew left from the cool humid night so that the ride down was relatively free of dust. Gavin drove with Sven beside him up front. Nora and Aydın sat in the back with Aydın's guitar lying safely across their laps.

"Dad, does this road look the same as it did when you came here back in the '70s?" Nora asked.

"Surprisingly, yes, except for that dilapidated billboard advertising a fish house that wasn't here before."

Gavin chimed in, "Yes that sign is a bit of an eye sore. There is a fork in the track up ahead leading to a different section of the bay. That restaurant has been struggling since it was built. It's in a bad spot actually. There was a winter storm a few years back that flooded the place and they've never really recovered.. No, Makis's place is nicely protected from the elements. He's never really needed to advertise either."

"Well, I can't wait to see the place again," said Sven.

They took the right turn at the road fork and skirted the

olive grove before descending the track leading to the western corner of Melanda Bay. Nora noticed her father taking a deep breath before getting out of the car. When Sven got out he began walking down toward the path leading out onto the rise overlooking the bay. The others took their time getting things out of the car, leaving Sven to explore the beauty and reconnect his memories to better times.

"It's still early enough. Let's say we grab a table on the patio and have a coffee," Gavin said.

Aydın slung the strap of his guitar over his right shoulder and hooked his left arm around Nora, as they followed Gavin to the outdoor patio of Makis's cafe.

"Your father looks like he's lost in another world in another time," said Aydın.

"He needed to come here. He must really miss my mother. It was so hard to tell while growing up. There were no signs of her anywhere in our lives. Just the watercolor I told you about that Gavin painted for them when they met. Somewhere along the way that painting was taken down and stored away. Anyway, I'm glad he came here."

Gavin put his artists field kit on the low wall next to a table where all of them could enjoy the view and sip their Cypriot coffee. "I'll go order. *Metreo* for everyone?"

"That will be fine. Thanks Gavin," said Nora settling into the plastic chair that Aydın pulled out for her.

"For me as well, thanks," Aydın added.

After awhile when they'd finished their coffee, Gavin pulled out his sketchpad and began working. Aydın grabbed his guitar and Nora's hand and guided her down to the sandy beach.

The air was completely still without a breath of wind. Tiny waves lapped against the sand and gurgled along the rocky shore on the west end of the undisturbed stretch of beach. There was a pile of decaying seaweed that swirled in the current at the corner of the beach. Other than that, the place was pristine.

The water was so clear that it was hard to determine the depth. Varying colors of rock reflected different shades of turquoise and deep blues. The morning summer sun shimmering on the water rapidly warmed the humid air. With the humidity, the surface of the sea blended with the hazy air making the horizon indistinguishable. Overhead the sky was clear and blue.

Aydın grabbed a cushion from one of the plastic chaises leaning up against the wall below Makis's cafe. He laid it in the sand so the two of them could sit comfortably and then began playing his guitar. First tuning it briefly and then picking a rhythm with a folk harmony before adding some lyrics.

He paused between songs and Nora said, "It is perfect. Your singing, the beach, I want to hold this moment in my heart forever."

"You can. Just etch it in right now."

"I'm afraid I'll forget."

Aydın looked up and along the rise where he and Nora drank wine and kissed the first time they came to Melanda. He saw Sven near a slab of rock looking back toward the beach. "Do you think your father has forgotten his moments with your mother? They must have had some just like ours. After all, look where we are."

"Perhaps you're right. I shouldn't be afraid then. Of forgetting I mean." She tugged his sleeve. "Do you think we should go join him?"

"No, let him embrace his memories. He'll be back soon enough."

Aydın was right. Sven came back by way of the beach taking off his sandals and rolling up the pant legs of his khakis so he could walk in the ankle deep water along the sand back toward the cafe where his daughter was sitting with the man she loved. As he looked up and saw them together, he reflected on the times he'd spent at the same spot with Hanife. The memory warmed his heart.

Before Sven reached them, Aydın said to Nora, "I've been meaning to tell you some of my latest good news. While you were away, our band got a regular gig at a posh club in Limassol. Two of us arranged to lease a flat. I've been packing and plan to leave Laneia later this week. It shouldn't be too difficult. I don't have much."

Nora wasn't sure what it all meant. "That sounds like great

news. I guess I should be happy for you with the gig and all."

Aydın really was excited just talking about it with her. "There is plenty of room. The bedrooms are opposite each other with a big sitting room and bath in between. The balcony overlooks the sea. You can stay with me there until you have to go back."

She gave him a big hug and kissed him, assuring him that she was happy with his invitation. "I'll help you with the move after Dad leaves. Deal?"

Just then Sven walked up on them. "Hello lovebirds. Anyone up for a swim?"

"You go ahead Dad. Aydın is going to play another song for me."

Sven lowered himself to the sand sitting across from them. "Maybe I'll have a listen instead," he said.

The three of them sat in the sand. Waves lapped lightly upon the shore keeping time with Aydın's strumming. A little while later they made their way back up to the patio at Makis's Cafe and saw Gavin putting the finishing touches on another of his local masterpieces.

The four of them rode in silence on the trip back to Laneia. Nora drove with Sven riding beside her. Gavin was snoring in the back and Aydın was scribbling some lyrics into a notebook. "We're playing tomorrow night in town," he said. "I guess I should have told you earlier but I didn't want to upset anyone's plans."

Nora grinned to herself thinking that was so much like Aydın to put others first. "We'd love to come hear you. Wouldn't we Dad?" she said.

Startled away from his inner thoughts Sven heard Nora attempt to get his attention. "What was that?"

"About tomorrow night, you'll want to come along to hear Aydın's band play. Doesn't that sound like fun?"

"It's been a wonderful day. I got to see my most favorite place in the world," he said almost to himself. "If Aydın's band sounds anything like the wonderful music he played for us on the beach, I'm sure the performance tomorrow night will be pretty special."

"Well, how about it then? Let's plan on going?"

"Sure Nora. I look forward to it."

They were on the main road approaching the turnoff that leads into the village. Nobody spoke for several minutes. Aydın folded his notepapers and slipped them into his shirt pocket. He leaned forward and put his hand on Nora's shoulder to get her attention.

"Could you drop me at the square. I've got some arranging to do in the flat. I'll come by later, OK?" Aydın said.

Nora gave him a positive nod and looked at his face through the rear view mirror as she drove.

"Everything will be fine," he whispered to her before sitting back.

A few moments later, Nora stopped the car across from the village fountain. Gavin awoke in a start. "What, where are we?"

"Home," said Nora. "Just dropping off Aydın on the way to your place."

She pulled the lever for the boot so that Aydın could retrieve his things and then opened her door and got out. She stood in front of him and accepted a reassuring hug.

"See you later," he said. Then she kissed him before getting back in the car.

The bottle of Mount Olympus Red table wine stood half empty on Gavin's kitchen table. Both he and Nora were in a festive mood while chopping fresh vegetables for the evening meal. Only a few words were exchanged as they both were chopping and sampling bits of vegetable, fresh flatbread, and local cheese. Gavin noticed that both of their wine glasses were in dire need of recharging.

"Where is your father?" Gavin asked half heartedly while enjoying the smells emanating from his oven where Nora had a *moussaka* baking.

"I haven't seen him since we got back. Gosh I feel a little bit bad. We didn't even pour a glass for him and the wine is nearly gone already."

"No worry, I poured him a Pimms earlier. He should be alright, but maybe you should go check on him and let him know we're close to sitting down for a bite."

When Nora stepped out from the kitchen and into the courtyard to look for her father, she noticed light coming from the desk lamp on the counter of the main gallery. Sven was standing behind the small desk near the main door. Nora noticed he was replacing the antiquated telephone handset back in its cradle when she entered the gallery.

"*Moussaka* is in the oven. It should be ready soon. Who were you talking to?" she asked surprised her father would be using the telephone.

"Just making some travel arrangements."

"Travel arrangements? We just got here. We still have more places to visit and the whole summer ahead of us before I've got to be back. Where are you going then?"

Sven set down the tall glass that contained the remnants of his cocktail and approached his daughter. He put both his hands gently on Nora's shoulders and said, "This has been wonderful and fulfilling. I can't tell you how proud I am that you've embraced Cyprus as profoundly as you have, but I'm ready to go home." He guided Nora out of the gallery and into the courtyard. "I'm going home tomorrow."

"Dad, I don't understand. I thought there were more places you wanted to go. What about Caledonia Falls, Kakopetria, and the Karpas in the north? Tammy Barrows said that Bahar from the museum is expecting to hear from us."

Nora shivered a bit. In spite of the warmth of the summer season, the chill of the late evening was a shock to her sun burned body. "Gets cool fast once that sun goes down doesn't it?" said Sven.

"Dad, don't beat around the bush, are you feeling OK. Why leave so soon?"

He turned to look into her eyes, "It's a small island sweetheart. Not much has changed. I've seen enough for all the memories to pour back in and believe it or not, it can be emotionally overwhelming."

Nora stepped closer. Without saying a word, she gave him a long hug. The two of them stood in the courtyard like that for several minutes before she released her hold on him and stepped backward. "What will you do?"

"You'll be pleased. I'm going to swing through D.C. to close down the condo and grab what little I have there. I spoke to your aunt Roni earlier and she insists that I come live with her in Omaha. The man she was dating decided to return to Sweden. She said she's tired of rattling around in her house alone and promised she'd see me through the tough times ahead. Hospice is what Roni said they call the arrangement she's set up for me."

"You didn't answer the question though. What will you do with your time Dad? I can't picture you hanging around watching reruns of Hogan's Heroes and hanging out with guys you don't really like at the VFW."

"I'm going to document it, all of it. Everything I failed to tell you about your mother. Her life was a story of warm color and happy sounds. It was full of close relationships and was torn apart by forces that she had no control over. I want to get it all written down, like a family history of sorts, so I can remember everything and never forget anything."

Tears began to well in Sven's eyes. He swallowed choking back the tears and looked at his daughter in the fading light of the late evening. "You look just like her right now." He reached over to a lock of Nora's auburn hair resting on her shoulder. "Your hair may be a little lighter then hers was, but your eyes and nose are hers, that is for certain. Your mom was the most courageous young woman and I'm still madly in love with the memory of her. You see that don't you?"

Nora stood before her father as long as she could before turning back toward the house. She was suddenly filled with emotion, conflicted with finally getting to know her father and realizing this new relationship would end soon. She left him standing alone in the courtyard and ran up to the guest room to cry in privacy.

CHAPTER 15

Institutions of Higher Learning

2001-2003

Nora thought the most difficult thing she'd ever had to do was go to a funeral. The family didn't think that Sven would pass before the year was out. She had just returned from Omaha where she celebrated Thanksgiving with her dad, Aunt Roni, Nils, and a pregnant Josette with their son Martin clutching her skirts. She was in her Arlington apartment when she got the call from Nils in the late evening.

"Aunt Roni just called. She told me that Dad passed peacefully. She said there was no indication that it was going to happen so suddenly, or she'd have called us both. She's broken up about him being gone and that we weren't able to be with him at the end," explained Nils.

The death of their dad wasn't unexpected, but the timing is never good for this kind of news. Nora was speechless and felt the pressure of a grieving cry building within. "Nora? Say something. You're still there right?" Nils asked.

"Yes, I'm still here Nils," she whispered in a trembling voice.

"I understand Sis. Listen, Roni said Dad's wishes were for him to be buried in Arlington. She's going to accompany the body. I've already booked a flight and taken emergency leave. Can I bunk at your place?" asked Nils.

"Sure." Nora was still unable to process the sudden news. She knew Nils was like a rock and couldn't wait for him to arrive. "When will you be here? You can take a cab to my place. It doesn't matter what time. I'd just like to know. That's all."

"Early tomorrow morning. Aunt Roni said she's got folks at Offutt assisting with the arrangements. She and Dad will be there in a couple days. I'll call when I get in. Are you going to be alright?"

"I'll be OK Nils. I can't wait for you to get here." After she hung up the phone. Nora looked at the clock on the small space above the counter in her apartment's kitchen. She calculated the seven hour time difference and determined it was still too early in Cyprus to call Aydın. She spent the remainder of the evening sitting on her sofa staring at the wall with a textbook open on her lap. "The History of U.S. Pacts, Treaties, and Diplomacy" would have to wait until another day. Even if she were to get enough sleep, Nora knew she'd miss her morning classes.

It was fitting that Sven's final resting place would be Arlington National Cemetery. The memorial came and went before Aydın could arrange to come to the United States. Even so, he insisted on coming to be with Nora in her time of need. She didn't argue with him but managed to convince him that she had to focus on completing her first semester of courses before the winter holiday break and that he should plan to come during that time.

"I can't wait to see you. I miss you terribly and don't want to think of you being alone," he told her.

"Life is finite Aydın. We've both experienced the finality of it. I can't wait until you can come and hold me. It is cold here, so bring warm cloths. It'll be just a couple weeks before we're together," she said.

"I love you," said Aydın before they cut the connection.

In the morning, Nora received a reassuring email from him. She knew Aydın didn't have an internet connection, so she imagined that when he hung up, he'd had to walk down the boulevard in Limassol to an internet cafe where he'd sit and compose the wonderful brief note he sent her. She thought he was the most compassionate man on earth and she was the lucky recipient of his affections.

Three weeks later, Aydın showed up at Nora's door.

Even though she knew to expect him, Nora was surprised when he knocked on her door. "I didn't expect you without a call first. I'd have met you at the airport," she said.

"I don't have a cell phone and there were no phone boxes. I'm here now. That is the important thing," he said as she jumped into his arms.

Throughout the course of her graduate work, there were fits and starts in their long distance relationship. Her dad's life insurance provided her with a comfortable sum when he passed. However, as much as she wanted to, Nora couldn't break away from her studies long enough to make the trip to Cyprus. During Aydın's first trip to the U.S., Nora could tell he was uneasy with all the traffic and noises of the city. Even so, they couldn't stand to be apart for long, so Aydın made several trips to include celebrating the Master's Degree Nora earned in International Relations.

"I can't believe you have no time off between your studies." Aydın protested.

"Well, I sure could have used the break, but A-100 starts Monday." Nora wasn't disappointed about having to attend her first formal course in diplomacy at the National Foreign Affairs Training Center so much as the disappointment of not having enough time to introduce Aydın to her favorite places.

It wasn't long before Nora was singled out during the final week of the thirteen-week A-100 course required of all of the U.S. State Department's Foreign Service Officers. She was scheduled to begin a year of language training sometime after completion of the course, but instead was chosen for enrollment into a fast language course in Turkish. After only two months, her instructor was impressed with her progress and recommended her for early evaluation.

It wasn't until she tested out with solid "threes" in both oral and written that she discovered why she received the special treatment. For the uninitiated, language courses taught at the Foreign Service Institute in Arlington, Virginia were among the best in the world and similarly, so were the students. A score of three out of a possible four where a score of four is equivalent to the ability of a native speaker in a graduate level degree program, was remarkable for the amount of time Nora put into the course.

"It would seem someone you know has some influence," said her desk supervisor, an older woman with dark hair wearing a frumpy conservative grey skirt and blazer combo. "Welcome to the Middle East Section," said Amanda Rutledge.

"Thank you, but honestly I don't know anyone in the Department with influence," said Nora.

"Apparently you do," said Ms. Rutledge as she handed Nora a jacket folder containing the order to her first post.

When Nora opened the folder, she read among the words at the top of the first page "Press and Cultural Attaché, Republic of Cyprus, U.S. Embassy, Nicosia." She could barely contain the elation she felt at her luck. "Nicosia!" she said out loud still not looking up from the folder. She noticed further down the page there were instructions to "Report Immediately."

"The order came from Ambassador Bandler himself. Apparently you do know people. You're Sven Johansson's daughter aren't you?" Ms. Rutledge asked.

"I am, I mean was, still am I guess." Nora still hadn't gotten used to the idea that her father had died.

"My condolences. Your dad made some inroads back in his day apparently, but things are different in Cyprus these days, exciting I should say. Congratulations are in order then." Ms. Rutledge thrust out her hand for Nora to shake as an acceptance of her first choice of postings.

"Thank you. Thank you very much. I'll do my best."

"Oh, don't thank me. I had nothing to do with this. However, if you must, give my best to the Barrows when you see them. Tammy and I had such good times in Kyrenia." The former Foreign Service officer turned back toward the large chair behind her desk, indicating that the meeting was over.

As Nora left she whispered to herself under her breath, "Thank you Jake Barrows. I'll owe you one for that." She quickened her pace as she departed the offices at Foggy Bottom checking her watch and doing a quick time zone calculation determining how soon she could phone Aydın to share the good news.

CHAPTER 16

Nicosia Cyprus

Spring 2004

The one thing Nora could always count on was Aydin's rock steady easygoing personality. For him it was always a simple matter to pick up where they'd left off during their long separations over the previous years. For Nora things were a bit more involved. She had been hoping for a marriage proposal during one of his visits to the States while she was in school.

Living as a young diplomat in Nicosia meant her lifestyle would be packed with events. She also considered that the U.S. State Department provided much more comfortable accommodations for those who were married. Once she returned to Cyprus, convincing Aydin that they should be married was less complicated than cutting through the red tape to arrange a civil marriage while still maintaining her embassy post.

Since neither Nora nor Aydin had any family members available to celebrate a wedding, Nora asked Gavin Hart to be present when they stood before the magistrate. They were married within a month of her return and living in a beautiful flat a short walk from the embassy.

Following the marriage formalities, they held a small reception on the back lawn at the embassy. Several of Nora's colleagues were there to toast the bride and groom. After the party, Gavin Hart insisted on chauffeuring them back to their Nicosia apartment before they packed and set off for a brief honeymoon in Latchi on the Akamas Peninsula.

Gavin's motives had more to do with a request from an old friend than Nora's assumption that he was attempting to fill the void in her life left behind when her father passed. Gavin stood out on the landing while Aydın carried his bride across the threshold.

"You can come in now," shouted Aydın after lowering Nora onto the loveseat in the main room.

Gavin was waiting for them to notice the wedding gift he had propped up on their dining room table before handing Nora the item he was compelled to give her before leaving the honeymooners on their own. It took only a moment for Nora to rise from the loveseat in order to get a better look at the framed watercolor propped up on the dining room table. It was the original that Gavin painted for Sven and Hanife over forty years earlier. Nora was barely able to contained her emotions long enough to thank Gavin.

"How did you...?" she whispered to Gavin.

"Your dad arranged for your aunt Ronella to have it sent here after he passed. Your father wrote a note with instructions for me." Gavin pulled an envelope from his coat pocket. It was addressed to the Laneia Gallery in Sven's handwriting with a return address in Omaha, Nebraska. He handed it to Nora.

She carefully pulled out the two pages from the already opened envelope. The first was very short instructing Gavin what to do with the painting. The second was for Nora. It read:

Dearest Nora,

Seeing you and Aydın together, I knew that it would only be a matter of time before your special day. I would have wanted to be there with you in body, but instead, think of me present in spirit. Your mother loved this painting because it was so representative of her home and the love we both shared when we met on Cyprus. I hope you and Aydın will enjoy it as your mother and I would have wanted.

Love,

Dad

"Thank you Gavin. Thank you for being such a good friend to my dad and making me feel just as special." She gave Gavin a big hug before kissing him on the cheek.

After the long weekend of their honeymoon, Nora and Aydın settled into their routines as husband and wife. Married life wasn't much an adjustment for them. They'd been living together since Nora's return to Cyprus, before the pace of her work increased. Nora changed her surname to Kostas-Johansson. It was Aydın's idea that she keep her family name while adopting his at the same time. It was characteristic of their relationship and practical from a professional standpoint.

Nora's days were long but she and Aydın were able to attend

formal embassy events together. Aydın quickly became the heartthrob of many spouses of the foreign diplomats. His role as sound engineer and part time DJ at a cutting edge radio station in Nicosia didn't hurt his reputation either.

As those early months of her posting to Cyprus blew by in a flash, Nora became absorbed in the hopeful direction the government of Cyprus was heading. Talks between Rauf Denktaş and Glafcos Clarides resulted in the relaxation of Green Zone restrictions, and a border crossing between north and south opened at Ledra Palace for the first time in nearly thirty years. Nora took advantage of these latest developments and continued her search for her aunt. With her father's passing, her need to connect with a living relative deepened and caused strain in her relationship with Aydın.

Nora wanted Aydın to be one of the first Greek Cypriot visitors to cross to the north when the checkpoint opened on 16 April. It took nearly two weeks to convince him to come with her. She couldn't understand his apprehension. For him it was a matter of principle.

Two weeks earlier they discussed a visit to the north of Cyprus over dinner on the balcony of their Nicosia apartment.

"Nora, I know you've been there several times. I've seen all the pictures you took. It is Cyprus. It is beautiful, and the people are no different. I understand this. They are Cypriot too."

"So why the hesitation. I have little hope in finding my aunt but I have not given up. Before I leave Cyprus, I want to have accomplished something…personal, something for us. Aren't you the least bit curious about the place where you were born?

When we talked about this trip in the past, you were all excited and now, when we're about to go, you get all weird on me. Is there anything you can share with me to help me understand? Getting reconnected with a part of your life would be good for you."

"Yes, I want to see Balıkeşir. I want to find out if I have memory of it and memory of my blood relatives. Now that the possibility is real, there are so many other things to consider. I'm tired of being alone." He regretted it as soon as he said it. Aydın adored Nora like no other person he'd ever known in his life. He could see the pain in her expression.

"That hurt Aydın," Nora stated in a flat tone and rose from the table and went to the kitchen.

She busied herself with the few dishes that had accumulated on the counter and experienced a moment of uncertainty for the first time in a long while. She thought to herself, "What the hell am I doing. My posting at the embassy is finished in less than two months, then we head to Turkey."

One month earlier she received a cable from State informing her that her next post would be as Press Attaché in Ankara, Turkey. Normally she'd have been thrilled. She hadn't told

Aydın yet because she wanted him to be totally focused and committed to his work developing the radio station.

"It is the formality of the passport stamping that I have a hard time with," said Aydın finally.

To her it seemed so simple. "Really, that's it? You have a problem with having your passport stamped? Come on Aydın it's just a slip of paper and some ink. Who cares! You'll see it won't matter once you see for yourself that the people in the north want the same things you do."

"You of all people should know this. That little bit of ink stamped on the paper of my passport is almost like me saying I think it is OK for the illegitimate government of the Turkish Republic of Northern Cyprus to exist and exercise international conventions as if they were an officially recognized country." He tried not to sound exasperated as he slapped his open hands on his denim covered thighs.

Nora stood and walked behind the wooden chair he was sitting on and began massaging his shoulders. She whispered from behind as she kneaded the knots near his neck and said, "You'll do it anyway, for us. Not for me and not for you, but for us. You'll come for all of us who want the same thing. To heal and be unified and to know our past." That was all she said before quietly stepping away leaving him there to contemplate.

With the recent talks between the Turkish and Greek Cypriot government leaders, a group of Aydın's musician friends became interested in the various ways of breaking down the walls of division that plagued their lives.

As performers, most of them had traveled the regions outside of Cyprus and as a result had embraced the similarities of international culture as opposed to perpetuating fear from the differences between them. The older generations of Greek Cypriots did not view their future with the same degree of optimism.

Aydın and his musician friends, along with the support of the technical expertise from their backstage production crews, cobbled together equipment and obtained licenses to launch their own radio station. He and his friends were also able to leverage Nora's connections with the embassy and contacts in the northern part of the island.

Eventually, their work resulted in a simulcast radio program broadcast daily in both Greek and Turkish all over Cyprus, without borders. There were talk shows hosting interviews with youth from both sides of the divide, all of them embraced a similar desire for a unified Cyprus. Both modern and traditional music was broadcast and a climate of hope was beginning to take hold.

Nora was impatient to renew her search and made plans to visit Bahar in the north. Nora and Aydın arrived at the Ledra Palace Hotel Green Zone crossing post in the early hours of the morning. They decided a Tuesday would be least crowded, giving them more time to find Nora's Aunt Dedim and more time to visit with her. They had no idea what they would discover.

Arm in arm they walked toward the processing desk in the old Ledra Palace. It was easier than Aydın thought it would be. After the official clerk stamped both their passports, they both reached over to retrieve them and continued through the foyer and into northern Cyprus.

Nora stuffed her passport into her pack. Aydın opened his, leafing through the pages as he walked. Stamps from Egypt, Lebanon, Syria, and even Turkey surrounded the modest stamp of the TRNC. He took another look at it before closing the pages and stuffing the passport into his shirt pocket. Then he shrugged his shoulders. Nora hooked her arm in his and leaned her head on his shoulder as they walked out the doors on the other side of Ledra Palace.

As they stepped back out into the bright sun, the spring morning air felt warm. Under the open sky and the bright sun, Nora was proud to be on Aydın's arm.

"Not so hard now was that?" she asked him.

"No. Not anymore. What is done is done and this is my home. Cyprus. North or south, it is my home."

One of Nora's acquaintances, a journalist writing for the cultural editorial corner of the daily paper, *Kıbrıs Gazetesi*, offered to meet them and take them to Balıkeşir and then to Kyrenia for a late lunch.

Earlier Aydın entertained the idea of taking the bus for the short journey but Nora convinced him that the schedule wasn't reliable enough outside of Nicosia, so he conceded to allow Nora's friend to chauffeur them around.

At Balıkeşir Aydın felt a sense of well-being, but didn't recognize anything familiar. The white flowering asphodels and sungolds were in bloom everywhere.

"Balıkeşir, just as I pictured," he said.

"Am I hearing a bit of sarcasm?" asked Nora.

"No. I just thought there would be something more. I thought maybe I'd feel something or remember something. But this place? It is like so many of the others. Just another island village."

"Not just any other village, your village and the place you were born."

He stood looking around the open area where the roads came together and thought about what Nora just said. Then he started walking toward one of the narrow streets that weaved through the center of the village.

"Come. Let's look around a bit. It will only take a few minutes, then we can be on our way," he said to Nora.

Nora checked in with her buddy the journalist who was reading the morning paper by the car. Then she joined Aydın for a stroll around the village. It had a feel to it similar to Laneia, but with a much better view. From the high open area, you could see the Mediterranean over the rooftops of the small village dwellings.

"I like the smells here. It must be the flowers because the scrub brush is the same as everywhere else on the island," said Aydın.

"It is nice isn't it? Whenever I come to places like this, I have a hard time imagining that there was ever fighting, explosions, combat, and the screams of frightened people."

"I was just a newborn. I don't remember any of those things. There are of course the stories, but the ones I heard growing up were different then the ones that people from this area probably told."

"I don't know, maybe not so different," said Nora. "Frightened people, refugees, they all probably felt the same when they left their homes."

"We should go. I've seen what I need to see. Kyrenia awaits," said Aydın.

They were ready for a meal when they arrived in Kyrenia. Before heading back to Nicosia on his own, Nora's journalist friend handed them off to Nora's closest friend in northern Cyprus, Bahar Demir.

Bahar was waiting for Nora under the veranda of Güler's Fish Restaurant. She recognized Nora getting out of the car and correctly assumed the gorgeous man she was with was Aydın.

Nora had shared so much about him during her visits since returning to Cyprus that Bahar knew she couldn't be mistaken.

As the young couple climbed the stairs leading to the restaurant's outdoor seating area, Bahar rose from her seat and waved to her friends, *"Buradayım. Buraya gel!"*

"Merhaba. İyi günler! Nora replied waving with a smile.

The women hugged one another. Bahar held Nora out at arms length and said, "You look so lovely and happy." Then she turned to Aydın releasing Nora's shoulders from her grip. She gently reached for Aydın's right hand with both of hers.

"You must be Aydın," she said. "Nora has told me so much about you."

"It is a pleasure to meet you Miss Demir," he said lifting her hands to his lips and kissing the one closest.

"Please, Bahar," she said pointing to herself. "Call me Bahar. All of my friends do. Oh and you do sound just exactly as you do on the radio! I love your show. We listen to it here everyday," she said with conviction.

With introductions over with, Bahar signaled them both to sit where they enjoyed a fulfilling lunch. The afternoon breeze blew through the leaves of the acacia carrying a briny bite of salt from the Med. The wind had been whipping up whitecaps on the sea in the afternoons, bringing with it a slight humidity.

"Nora tells me this is your first trip to the north. How are you finding it so far?" Bahar asked Aydın.

"Technically it isn't my first trip. I was born here. I mean I was born in Balıkeşir village."

"We stopped by there on the way here this morning," said Nora.

"Yes, but I don't remember it at all. I was an infant when I left. I spent my whole life in the south, up until now anyway. I have visited other places outside of Cyprus touring with my folk band. We went to Turkey and Lebanon, but this is the first time I've been in the north."

"Yes, I've heard your music on the radio. Your sound is timeless and I must say, you have one of the best young male voices I've ever heard. One of these days you'll have to put on a private concert just for us," Bahar said this with a slight laugh as she pulled Nora into her shoulder-to-shoulder then let her go and smiled.

Bahar paused briefly and immediately changed her expression indicating she had something more serious to discuss. "Getting back to historical things, I have some news of developments related to our little project Nora."

"I'm listening." Nora said leaning forward on both elbows.

"You might find this interesting as well Aydın. One of my colleagues who had been working on a genealogy project heard that I've been inquiring about people with the surname Yılmaz. She said records had been found from some of the smaller villages between Nicosia and Famagusta. These records had been stored in a repository in Nicosia."

"I don't follow," said Nora with a puzzled expression.

"My colleague brought up the possibility that these records might include the names of people moving to and from these villages during the war. Coincidently, Aydın, Balıkeşir was one of the villages on the list of records."

"You said these records are at a repository. In Nicosia?" asked Nora.

"Yes." Bahar reached for her stylish leather purse and pulled out a matching note pad. On the top page an official looking government name and an address in Nicosia were written. She tore the notepaper from the pad and handed it across the table to Nora.

Nora read the name and address. "Cyprus National Library, Eleftheria Square, Nicosia. I've been there several times and never heard of any such records.

"You weren't looking for birth records," Bahar said.

"Now I'm really confused," said Nora.

"If we have our facts lined up, it would appear that your lost aunt's name is Dedim Yılmaz and she was or still is a health professional, a midwife to be more precise. Her name was listed next to the names of the family names of those who were born with her assistance," Bahar explained.

"Thank you so much. Bahar. This is really a breakthrough." Nora leaned over and gave her friend a fond hug.

"Do you have a ride back or will you be taking the bus?" Bahar asked.

"The friend who drove us up here had to get back, so we're going to take our chances with the bus," said Nora.

"We should go then. You have a long trip back to Nicosia and if you miss the next bus, it will be hours before the next one leaves," suggested Bahar.

Aydın took care of the bill. Then they all left the restaurant and walked the four long blocks to the bus depot.

"Bahar. Thanks so much for meeting with us and sharing the information about the records. Your help has been vital in my search," Nora said as she gave her friend a hug goodbye.

"It was a pleasure meeting you Bahar," said Aydın.

"The pleasure was mine Aydın. Please come visit again and often." To Aydın and Nora both, Bahar seemed as if she was choking back tears as she turned and departed.

"Is your friend always so emotional when saying goodbye?" Aydın asked.

"No, it was unusual, but of course everything today was slightly out of the ordinary. After all, we visited the village where you were born and you got to meet one of my dearest friends. I think she likes you," said Nora as she winked at him.

The bus ride back to Nicosia was uneventful. It was near dark by the time they passed back through the checkpoint at Ledra Palace. This time there was no stamping of passports.

Nora wasn't able to get to the National Library for several weeks due to her intense work schedule at the embassy. The bicommunal talks between Denktaş and Clarides had gone well enough for the U.N. General Secretary Kofi Annan to sponsor the implementation of a restitution and reunification plan.

Several different parties and interests throughout the international community were working the provisions of the "Annan Plan." Some of the more complicated provisions included restitution of property. Ambassador Bandler put together a diverse group of academics and legal professionals to form a "Kitchen" Cabinet.

Nora's was invited to participate on the fringes of negotiations in case her language skills were needed. However, she ended up as nothing more than an observer since some of the Kitchen Cabinet members were of Turkish Cypriot and Greek Cypriot descent and had been living and working as expatriates in the U.S. and U.K. They came from places such as London, New York City, Baltimore and Portland, Oregon.

The dedication and effort of these extraordinary people and their contributions led to the development of over six hundred pages of provisions in the Annan Plan and provided a great deal of optimism for Cypriots. Hope was blooming on both sides of the divide that the Annan Plan Referendum would result in reunification at last.

Several weeks later, early in the morning, Aydın sat at the

worn wooden table reading the front page of the newspaper in their apartment's small kitchen. The lead article on the front page of the Cyprus Mail read, "Referendum Fails to Pass: Annan Plan Fails." Nora looked exhausted when she entered the kitchen.

The buzzing energy that consumed Cyprus over the previous weeks had taken its toll on her. She knew the result of the referendum long before the papers were published and the journalists and analysts put their spin on it.

"What are the columnists saying about the future of Cyprus this morning?" Nora asked.

"I don't understand this Nora. There was so much hope, and now this. Look at this!" He held up the front page of the paper.

There on the front page was a picture of Greek Cypriots waving their Greek Flags and above the image another of the headlines. "Annan Plan Fails: What Next For Cyprus?"

"I didn't see this coming Nora," he said while slowly shaking his head back and forth.

"Neither did any of the rest of us," said Nora.

She pulled down one of the coffee cups hanging from a hook beneath the kitchen cabinet and poured what remained of the morning coffee before joining Aydın at the table. He was in a daze still holding the front page staring at it in disbelief. Nora reached across for it and the other pages resting on the table.

She gathered them up and tossed the entire bundle of paper in the bin next to the kitchen counter.

"Nothing we can do about that," she said looking at him and taking a sip from the steaming coffee cup.

He said nothing. He looked across at her making eye contact and raised his eyebrows at the same time.

"I have something I'd like to do today that I haven't been able to get around to. Will you come?" she asked.

He knew she wouldn't have invited him to spend the day if she was planning on going to work.

"You don't have to be at the embassy? No country team meeting. No press analysis? With all of this?" he said exasperated raising his arms palms up "…won't you be missed today?"

"No, I don't think I'll be missed today. I don't think I'd let it bother me if I were. Come on, Bahar has been leaving me messages about getting together. She has some work here in Nicosia this week. Let's meet her for lunch."

Aydın liked Bahar. Even though they'd only seen each other a couple of times, he told Nora that he found being around Bahar to be inspiring. Meeting her for lunch was just what they both needed to avoid becoming depressed over the day's news.

"What time?" he asked.

"It's still too early to call her, but she is expecting to hear from me. We spoke briefly yesterday."

Around noon, Aydın and Nora sat at a sidewalk table sipping tea when Bahar arrived. They made their greetings. Bahar had her hair neatly pulled back beneath a silk scarf and wore oversized dark sunglasses. Her body language revealed a sadness that the other two understood completely.

They all ordered something to eat, but none of them were hungry enough to anticipate enjoying a big meal. They made small talk until the waiter returned with the modest plates of food.

Finally Bahar broke through the tension. "I met with one of my Greek Cypriot colleagues this morning," she said before explaining her disappointment over the referendum.

The mood around the small table was somber as evidenced by the silence that followed before Bahar collected herself long enough to elaborate on the conversation she'd had with her friend and colleague.

"Did either of you watch or listen to the speech President Tassos Papadopoullos broadcast a couple of nights ago on TV and radio?"

Both Nora and Aydın nodded in the affirmative.

"Of course you did. And what did you think at that time?"

Seeing Aydın uncharacteristically eager to answer, Nora didn't say anything but rather waited to see what had her husband so riled up.

"He mixed his messages!" Aydın was almost shouting. "I

don't see how any thinking person could allow themself to be manipulated that way. I'm embarrassed to be Greek Cypriot. Really I am. We had our chance and then Papadopoullos had to say those things after sounding supportive of the plan for so long, he switched to warning people about loosing everything and being condemned to a life of damnation if we went along with the referendum. I don't know how so many of us could be so naïve."

Nora put her hand over his and saw that he was nearly shaking with a frustration she'd never seen from him. At the same time she was proud to discover that he so strongly believed in what he thought was right for all Cypriots.

Bahar removed her sunglasses then wiped her eyes being careful not to smear her mascara any more than she'd already done. "I'm afraid I've lost some of my closest friends. Forever."

Her emotions were charged and it took awhile before she was able to continue.

"The evening after the Papadopoulos broadcast, one of my dearest and closest Greek Cypriot friends invited me here to Nicosia to meet in her home along with several of her colleagues also friends of mine. We met for cocktails beforehand to make a celebration of what was to come. There were eleven of us crowded into the common room of Eva's small apartment. Eva decided we should all have a secret ballot vote on the referendum just among ourselves.

She'd prepared some slips of paper for us to check mark a yes or no. These people I thought I knew and so did Eva. I feel so bad for her. She called me this morning. I'm going to see her this afternoon."

Nora leaned across the table and put her hand on Bahar's forearm. "Bahar, what happened with the vote then?"

"Oh, I'm sorry. I thought you'd know. Before the broadcast, it was unanimous among us. All of us were for the referendum. It was tragic to witness how an emotionally charged speech could so easily sway people. People that I thought I knew. After the speech, Eva's guests left in a mood that I couldn't put my finger on.

When Eva called, she told me that the people we thought were our friends told her they voted no. All of them changed their vote, and that they felt lucky that they heard Papadopoulos speak before voting. I still cannot come to grips with the naiveté." Bahar turned away putting her handkerchief up to her eyes again.

"I'm sorry Bahar," said Nora.

"I am too," said Aydın. "I still don't understand and am worried what will be our future."

Bahar again collected herself. She wanted to be sure that Nora and Aydın understood and shared her views. "The Turkish Army occupation in northern Cyprus has been a problem for people including Turkish Cypriots. Yes, when they came in '74 there was a sense of relief and security, but over the years things have changed.

The settlers from Turkey and the rich Turkish people have changed things. Turkish Cypriots are a shrinking population and we've gotten lost in this mix. Turkish Cypriots no longer feel they have a home. We feel like the Turks have taken it from us and that the Greek Cypriots blame us for it. What are we to become I wonder."

They'd been sitting at the table for quite awhile. None of them touched their food. Finally Aydın said, "We're not leaving here in until we can find something bright and hopeful to put our attention on. Bahar, I just want you to know that not all Greek Cypriots are narrow minded about the plight of Turkish Cypriot people."

Bahar rose from her chair and maneuvered herself around to the other side of the table where Aydın was seated. She put her hand on his shoulder and said, "I know this Aydın. I hear what you broadcast on your radio station and know there are Greek Cypriots who voted yes for the referendum. What is done is done."

"For the time being, you are right," he said as he rose to his feet and looked into the sadness of her eyes. "The question now is how we will move forward. For some of us it is too late to turn back."

Bahar stepped closer to Aydın and gave him a hug, then

looked up at him and nodded her agreement before stepping away. She grabbed her sweater and purse and turned to Nora before leaving.

"Thank you for coming dear. You will call me if you locate your aunt."

"Of course," said Nora.

"Oh, and Aydın, there is one thing you could do. Something hopeful for us to think on," added Bahar.

"Anything. It will be my pleasure," he replied.

"You are broadcasting this afternoon and I'm sure there will be lots of interviews and comments from all sides. Please if you would, there is a special song that I'd like you to play." She handed him a slip of paper with the name of a song she hoped he would play during the broadcast and then gave Nora a hug and kiss.

"Görüşürüz," she said as she left.

"Güle Güle," Aydın and Nora said and waved as Bahar left.

For a while the two of them remained at the table sitting in silence. Aydın pulled out the slip of paper that Bahar gave him and read aloud the words she'd written on it.

"It is the title of a song," he said.

"Which? Have you heard of it?" asked Nora.

"Yes of course. I'm surprised we've never had anyone request that we play it though. *'Al Yemeni Mor Yemeni-Kibrism.'* It is a folk song I think. I'll play it for you this afternoon, on the air. I want to honor Bahar's request."

"That would be lovely. I know she'll appreciate it."

Later that same evening when he returned from his work at the radio station, Aydın found Nora sitting in the kitchen with a cup of tea.

"Were you listening?" he asked her.

"You mean to the show on the radio? Yes. It was beautiful." She got up from the table and embraced him. "…And romantic."

"I wasn't sure of the meaning, but could tell by the singer's voice that it is a special song."

"It is about Cyprus and its beauty and Cypriot women."

Aydın looked a little embarrassed. "I didn't know. I just liked the way it sounded so I played it. You should have seen how the switchboard lit up with all the calls coming in. Calls from both sides."

"Really? What were people saying?"

"A mix of things. Emotional things. But most important, nobody seemed to be angry or wanted to lay blame about what happened with the referendum. The ladies at the station want to do a talk show sometime in the coming week. Do you think I could get Elaina Chandler to phone in?"

"You can ask her. I don't know if she would do it. I'll get you the number for the Chandler's."

CHAPTER 17

Late April 2004

Less than one week after the referendum and failure of the Annan Plan, Cyprus, that is "Greek Cyprus" was admitted to the European Union. Had the Annan plan passed, the whole of Cyprus would have been included. Cypriots who were previously in favor of reunification were still in shock over the referendum and the latest news hadn't set in. The mood in the southern part of the island was surprisingly tranquil.

It was as if everything remained in a time warp except for CYBN Radio and their Talk and Culture show.

Aydın managed to convince Elaina Chandler to call in and express her point of view. "This is Radio CYBN. This is Aydın Kostas back with you on today's broadcast of 'Bridging the Divide.'

We were talking with Professor Sinan Demirel who teaches Peace and Conflict Resolution Studies at Cyprus International University here in Nicosia. Dr. Demirel was sharing his view on the impact of Greek Cyprus joining the European Union.

We have callers on the line with questions and comments for Dr. Demirel. Caller, tell us who you are and where you are calling from."

"Good afternoon and thank you for taking my call. My name is Elaina Chandler my family was from Karaman. I now live with my husband, who is a British expatriate by the way. Our home is in Kolossi Village. I have some comments and a question for you Dr. Demirel. I don't have specific facts to illustrate what I have to say, but as a refugee, I have experienced quite a bit to back up my viewpoints.

I believe the Annan Plan failed because of fear and distrust, not because the Greek Cypriot and Turkish Cypriot wanted their country to remain divided, but because of fear.

Greek Cypriots remembered, not specifically, but they remembered nonetheless that outside forces caused these forty or more years of conflict. In recent times there were the British, then the Greeks and the Americans, and finally, the Turks, not Turkish Cypriots, but the Turkish Army of occupation. Different perceptions and distrust sabotaged any organized formal plan of reunification.

My question to you Dr. Demirel is this: Has the admission of Greek Cyprus into the EU caused the divide to become deeper and if so, where do we go from here?"

Later when the show was over and Aydın returned to their Nicosia apartment, Nora greeted him at the door with a big hug. "You were brilliant. I really enjoyed the show today. Mrs. Chandler sure stimulated some debate didn't she?"

Aydın exhaled a sigh of exacerbation. "I never thought I'd care so much about this issue. There were so many callers. The switchboard was overloaded and we didn't have enough student volunteers to screen them all, so I just pulled them up at random. I just wish people didn't sound so angry."

Nora reached up to massage his shoulders while leading him into the sitting room and guiding him into his favorite chair. "I thought Dr. Demirel handled it well."

"He didn't say anything though. He sounded just like your diplomat friends who produce words without committing to a position."

"What could he say though? The damage is done. Even some of the Greek Cypriot callers expressed concern that joining the EU has set back any effort to move forward. Mrs. Chandler sure came through," said Nora.

"She did make some distinctions between Turkish Cypriots and the occupation from mainland Turkey, but I think it blew over the heads of most listeners," Aydın replied.

"Maybe they weren't listening. I mean really listening."

"Some people only hear what they want to hear. Mrs. Chandler and Dr. Demirel were very clear. As a Greek Cypriot, even I can see that the Turkish Cypriots are caught in between this frustrating struggle we have all been dealing with."

"You mean you don't think all Cypriots feel caught in the struggle? " Nora asked.

"I didn't say that. No, I just think a lot of Greek Cypriots don't want to acknowledge it."

"So you agree that all Cypriots are the people in between."

Aydın didn't elaborate or respond directly to Nora's last comment. Without emotion, he simply stated, "We are a united people in a country divided."

As she continued to massage her husband's shoulders and neck, she felt him becoming even more tense with the conversation so she put her lips up close to his ear and whispered, "You can still make a difference. We all can, even if we have to do it by building one personal relationship at a time. I believe it is possible and you should too."

He reached up and gently put both his hands on hers. "Thank you. Thank you for reminding me that I love you. What made you so smart and perceptive anyway?"

She stood up and took a seat on the couch opposite him, smiled and changed the subject. "I got a call from Gavin Hart this afternoon."

"Oh, how is he?"

"He heard the show. Didn't have much to say about it. He said he had something urgent he wanted to share with me but wouldn't do it over the phone."

"Did he give you any idea what it's about?"

"He didn't want me to lose any sleep so he said everything was all good. He wanted to know if I could come to Laneia tomorrow."

"And...?"

"Of course I said I'd come but I don't want to go there

alone. Are you busy tomorrow?"

He leaned forward then rose from his chair and smiled at her closing the distance between them and replied, "Of course I'm going to be busy. Busy sitting in the front seat of the car watching the most beautiful and thoughtful person in the world drive us to Laneia village." Then he kissed her.

The late morning drive to Laneia was a welcome break for Nora. With the turmoil of the past months, her work at the embassy had been exhausting. Earlier she had made up her mind that there was no way she was going to accept the post in Turkey. She discovered she was becoming too passionate about Cyprus to maintain the objectivity necessary for a U.S. diplomat working in Turkey.

She hadn't told Aydın that she spoke with the Deputy Chief of Mission the afternoon before. She knew it would be career suicide, but the amount of effort and work that was erased in just the past week alone was disappointing enough that her passion for diplomacy needed to take a different course.

"Why are you staring at me like that?" she asked Aydın as she drove.

He smiled and rolled his head back and forth, "Can't a husband admire his wife? I'm not staring. It's no secret I like watching you drive."

Nora focused her attention on the road ahead. A delicate smile took shape at the corners of her mouth.

"Mind if I turn this up?" asked Aydın reaching for the volume knob on the old Renault's radio.

She kept smiling as she aimed the car west along the A-1 toward Limassol. "Sure. As you like. Who is that anyway?"

"American. Someone Irfan discovered when he was in America a few years back. He started playing it at the station recently. Listen you'll like this." Aydın began to sing along.

When the song ended Nora said, "I've heard that before! The band is *Little Feat*. Nils and I used to listen to this band all the time when we were in High School. I loved that song *Voices on the Wind*. Nils always said it was an ocean or beach song and since we grew up landlocked in Nebraska, we listened to it every spring imagining we were standing on the shore looking out over the water. I like the way you sing along with your Cypriot accent." She turned and winked at him than returned her attention to the road.

A short while later, they made the turn of the A-1 onto the familiar road that wound up the ridgeline toward Laneia Village. Nora turned down the radio.

"Hey what's wrong? I thought you liked listening to music while driving?" said Aydın.

" I do, it's just that I have something I need to tell you."

Nora turned toward Aydın and noticed he looked worried and hopeful all at the same time. Nora exhaled a burst of laughter when it finally registered what Aydın's look meant.

"Oh, you think I'm...I was going to tell you...." There was more laughter.

"What is so funny? There is nothing funny about any of this. Tell me what you wanted to tell me. I'm all ears."

"If I were pregnant dear husband, I wouldn't be telling you about it while driving on a dusty road. You're the romantic. What kind of wife would I be telling you that here and now?" She shook her head with a smile then out of the corner of her eye saw that Aydın was still waiting for her to tell him her news.

She switched to a more serious tone then blurted it out. "I told the DCM I don't think it would be a good idea for us to accept the posting in Ankara."

"So we don't move to Turkey. I'm not bothered. It is your decision."

"No it should be our decision, not mine alone. We go where we go together. We talked about this before and I'm telling you I'm sorry for not including you in the decision."

"So now what will we do and where will we go?" asked Aydın.

"The DCM said Ambassador Bandler would be disappointed, but assured me he'd smooth the waters. State usually has no trouble filling posts in Turkey. He also gave me a stern lecture about what this request meant for my career."

There was an awkward silence before Aydın finally got her to say more. He sat up straight and rested his hand over hers as she downshifted the Renault before reaching to spin the steering wheel to maneuver the old car around a steep mountain curve.

He leaned closer to her so that she could hear him say, "Nora, I don't care where we go. It could be Timbuktu as long as we are together."

"How does Saharan Africa sound to you?"

"Like an adventure. We'd make the most of it. Did they tell you that is where we'll go?"

"No, I still don't know. I just didn't want you to be surprised if we wind up in Mauritania by the end of summer."

He kissed her just above her ear and said, "I love you Nora. Everything will be OK, you'll see."

She smiled and looked at him still amazed at his easygoing way. "I'm so glad I found you," she said then turned up the music.

Nora parked the old Renault in her usual spot near the wall in front of the Hart Gallery in Laneia. She looked over at Aydın before they got out. "This place makes me happy. Like old times."

"Not such old times darling but happy ones, yes." He opened the car door and was on his feet stretching before Nora had the key out of the ignition. When she came around the car to join him on the path leading toward the house, he kissed her and they locked arms as they walked up to find Gavin again in the back area of the gallery.

"Have a look around if you like? Holler if you fancy any of the pieces," shouted Gavin from the back room unable to see who it was that entered the gallery.

Aydın spotted the old oil painting on the wall of "The Rocks," that Gavin painted ages ago out on the Akamas. He knew the piece was not for sale.

"What is this supposed to be, this ridiculous attempt at something resembling Stonehenge. Do you have any others like it?" boomed Aydın toward the back room with a tone he hoped Gavin would find humorous.

Nora gave Aydın a friendly nudge with her elbow and they both laughed when they heard Gavin knocking things over in the back area cursing under his breath. "By God you both gave me a start. I thought I recognized your voice young man. Good to see you both. I wasn't expecting you till later in the afternoon, but now's as good a time as any to put away the brushes and canvas."

Gavin was still holding his brushes. Both his hands were speckled with remnants of aqua colored acrylic. He remained in one spot with Nora squeezing him with her biggest hug ever. "It's been way too long. I'm sorry we've been so absent from your life lately," she said looking up at him noticing the years were taking their toll.

Gavin nodded at Aydın maintaining eye contact with him. "You look like you're finding married life agreeable."

Aydın didn't say anything. He just grinned looking at Nora

as she released Gavin from her clutches.

"I have something for the young lady," said Gavin. "It arrived last week in the post. I'll get it for you. You can put the kettle on if you like. I'll just be a minute."

Aydın followed Nora into the kitchen while Gavin disappeared to root around for the postal package. Nora set about with the kettle and mugs for tea. Kaplan, her favorite ginger colored tabby was curled up sleeping on the kitchen stool. Aydın reached down to stroke him and was greeted with the content rumbling of his purr.

"He's gained weight since we saw him last," he said as he held up the large feline so Nora could see.

"Put him back down you silly. He'll have a heart attack the way you handle him."

Aydın set the oversized cat back down on the stool. Gavin came into the kitchen holding a flat box that looked like the kind that would hold a ream of stationary. Nora noticed his presence as he set the box down on the table.

"A cup of tea for you?" she asked.

"Something stronger I think, but thanks." Gavin grabbed a glass from one of the kitchen shelves and pulled a bottle of *zivania* from the cupboard.

"A bit early for that isn't it?" It was more of a comment from Aydın than a question.

"It's after five o'clock somewhere in the world, so why not?"

Gavin responded.

Both Nora and Aydın were puzzled by Gavin's expressions and uncharacteristic behavior. He seemed happy and nervous all at the same time.

"Alright then Gavin. What is in the box and what was so urgent that you couldn't tell me over the phone?" asked Nora.

Gavin knocked back the *zivania* in one pull and squinted his eyes against the burn as the intoxicating liquid filled his insides.

"I feel like a kid on Christmas morning," he said. "This package arrived with a note from your aunt. She said she was heading back to Jönköping, Sweden to reunite with a man she'd been seeing before your dad's passing. She left this note for you and this unopened box. As you can see, I'm on the edge to know what it is." Gavin got up to pour another shot from the bottle of *zivania* he left on the counter.

"Sure you won't have one?" he asked the two of them.

Neither of them answered the question. Nora abandoned her efforts at preparing tea and stepped over to the table to pick up the envelope addressed to her. She ripped it open with her thumbnail as Aydın and Gavin looked on.

Nora,

I hope this letter finds you well. By the time you receive it, I'll be settled back in Jönköping. With both you and Nils so far away, I was getting lonely in Omaha and decided to reunite with Jannik.

I was clearing out the house to get ready to sell it when I came across a manuscript your father left in the study where he cloistered himself for hours. With all of the moving around both of you do, I thought the safest way to be sure this package would reach you was through Gavin.

I haven't read all of it, just the first few pages. That's when I found the note Sven left. You'll see it when you open the box. I hope to hear from you again. My door will always be open to you.

Best Regards,

Roni

"God she is always so formal. I love Aunt Roni, but growing up with her was like being raised by a live-in housekeeper. We spent a lot of time together but never really knew each other." Nora said rolling her eyes then she quickly turned her attention to the box on the table.

She lifted the flimsy lid from the box and on top was a note in Sven's written hand. It said,

Sis,

Nora is the writer and Nils is the historian. Please be sure the bundle of family photos gets to Nils. He'll know how to care for them and work out a way so he and his sister both can be reminded of our family. As for this manuscript, it is unfinished. I don't know how this story will end. I'd like Nora to have it. Maybe someday Cyprus will reveal an appropriate ending and she'll finish it.

Sven

Nora set the note aside and leafed through the first few pages and looked over at Gavin.

"Did you know he was working on this?" she asked Gavin.

"What is it?" Aydın broke in.

"Dad's novel." She turned back to Gavin waiting to hear his answer.

"He called a couple times and sent an email or two asking for clarification on the locations he wrote about. So, yes, I knew about it. He was hoping to have it finished and published before he passed. It was a labor of love for him. I could tell through our correspondence. Are you angry at me about something?"

"Don't be silly Gavin. Thank you for asking us to come out here to give me Dad's unfinished novel. I'll treasure it." She saw the look of relief all over Gavin Hart's face and noticed he was misting up before he left the room.

"The guest room is yours if you want to stay. The bed linens have been washed. I have a few things to attend to, but maybe we can share a meal later. Let me know your plans. I'll be in the back room."

Aydın didn't hesitate. "We'll stay old friend. I miss the village. Besides you and I have a lot to catch up on."

"Aydın I've got responsibilities at the embassy. You know I can't just blow them off," Nora said.

"Sure you can. You've been running like mad for the past several months. You owe it to yourself. Call in sick."

Nora knew he was right. The ambassador held his country team meetings on Mondays, so she had no concerns about her superiors noticing her absence. She got up from the table with the manuscript and plopped herself onto one of the chaises under the veranda. "You're right," she said over her shoulder as she left the kitchen. "I've got some reading to do."

Aydın smiled to himself then rummaged around in the kitchen occasionally stopping to stroke Kaplan. The big orange cat kept him company as he helped himself to the ingredients he needed to prepare an afternoon *meze* for Nora and Gavin.

CHAPTER 18

Dedim Yılmaz

Nora's disposition became more relaxed each and every day since she'd made her decision to request an alternative to the Ankara posting. The DCM showed some compassion when he called her in to discus the transition of her duties to her replacement.

"Your timing couldn't have been better," said the DCM. "The ambassador is taking personal vacation time and combining it with some engagements in D.C., which means he won't be back until the end of May. I wanted to give you some time to think over your decisions, but I received a cable this morning."

The DCM passed the sheet of paper across the desk for Nora. It was from the Mid-East Desk at Foggy Bottom. Before she could read the short paragraph in its entirety, her eyes were drawn to the posting location and report date. "…Baku, Azerbaijan," she read, and "…report no later than 15 May, 2004."

She looked across at the DCM who sat waiting for her comment with his practiced expressionless demeanor. "At least it isn't Chad or Mali," was all Nora could say.

"You sound surprised and disappointed. Last time we discussed your career, it sounded like you'd thought about the possible outcomes," he said.

She read the paragraph again and realized that what was done was done. "I don't have a lot of time. I've got some personal matters to put in order," she said waiting for his signal to dismiss her so she could take her leave.

Nora liked the DCM. He was a career diplomat with a fair and objective management style. "Your replacement will be here in about a week. I'll leave it up to you as to how you'd like to do the hand-off. It isn't his first posting, so I suspect things will go smoothly. Best of luck young lady." He stood and as Nora came to her feet, he extended his hand and they shook.

They were still together on the loveseat in the small living room of the Nicosia apartment. He knew he'd be hearing something soon but was still taken off guard when Nora told him her latest news that evening.

"Baku, Azerbaijan," Aydın repeated in a low voice. "Just for two years right?"

"Two years. That is what I still owe for the scholarship, then I'll tender my letter of resignation," said Nora.

"You don't have to make those kinds of decisions right now." His tone was gentle and supportive. "Let's ride this wave of adventure and see where it takes us."

"It's just that I feel bad for you. Your work at CYBN has been so amazing."

"It was grass roots, sweetheart. It will be fine. Tunç, Daphne, and Milos will keep it going. CBYN isn't going anywhere," he reassured her.

Feeling a bit awkward and eager to change the subject, he asked her about Sven's manuscript.

"I'm not finished. My dad's writing style is really different," she said while adjusting her position on the loveseat. She nestled into him resting her head on his shoulder.

"Dad must not have had a lot of experience with anything other than technical writing and political correspondence. I like it though. Aside from his struggling with some of the mechanics of fictional dialog, the story flows and has an unconstrained feel to it. Plus I'm learning about my mother's life and the kind of relationship the two of them must have had. There is a beauty that is hard to put into words."

"I'll want to read it sometime," he whispered.

The early morning spring sun bathed the floor of their small kitchen in warmth, pleasing to Nora's bare feet. The coffee, though not Cypriot, was done brewing and its aroma was irresistible to Aydın's senses.

"What are you doing up so early? I thought your boss said you could have time off," Aydın said as he emerged from the single bedroom around the corner from the living area.

Nora looked at him as if it were the morning after their wedding night. He stood beside the table wearing nothing but a pair of boxer shorts. She took pleasure in admiring his chiseled upper body.

Aydın wasn't clueless. He noticed the way she was gazing at him but didn't allow himself to succumb to self-admiration. Instead he tried to break the spell, "Yes, I know. Bad hair day." Then he noticed Nora was already for the day wearing a bright floral sundress, missing only her sandals, which were left by the front door.

"Not dressed for the embassy but ready to go out?" he said sounding as if he were solving a mystery.

"Yes and if you aren't busy, I think you should come too. We don't have much time left on the island and I'd like to make the most of it."

"Where are we going then?"

Nora handed him a small envelope addressed to "Mrs. Kostas-Johansson." Aydın pulled a small slip of paper from it.

Mrs. Kostas-Johansson - I received your letter and look forward to meeting you. Thursday 29 April at 9 a.m. for tea at my flat would be best for me. The address is 11623 Yakın Doğu Blv "C". Just across from the University Main Library.

Saygılarımla,

Dedim Yılmaz

Aydın held the note for a long time staring at the signature. When Nora thought he had more than enough time to have read it several times over, she said, "Well?"

"You are amazing," he said. How did you find her?"

"It wasn't hard. I used some connections and of course

Bahar's lead. I thought about calling first but figured there was no way to avoid an awkward conversation over the phone, so I wrote her last week."

"Connections. Hmmm, from those slippery characters who work in the political section at your embassy I presume?"

She wasn't sure if he was attempting sarcasm, so she reached for the note he was holding and asked, "So are you going to get dressed and come along?"

"I wouldn't miss an opportunity to accompany you to the ends of the earth," he said and then kissed her on the neck.

"Now that is the man I married," she said as he retreated to the bedroom to get dressed.

The Near East University complex was on the outskirts of northern Nicosia and a bit farther from Nicosia's center than Nora thought it would be. She was glad they left early. She wanted to make a good impression on the person she was sure was her lost aunt.

The bus they took from the town center dropped them in front of the main library of the university. The campus buildings and those in the surrounding area were all new and modern, so different from the aging structures of Nicosia's City Center. Nora and Aydın had no trouble locating Dedim Yılmaz's apartment block.

Nora found the buzzer next to the door to the main entrance. The tag next to apartment "C" read Yılmaz. She looked at Aydın before punching the button, he shrugged and said, "Go ahead. What are you waiting for?"

The two of them arrived at the landing on the third floor and were greeted by a well-dressed older woman standing at the threshold of her flat.

"Hoş geldiniz" said the woman.

There was a long pause before Aydın replied for the two of them. *"Hoş bulduk,"* he said.

Nora was still stunned. She couldn't take her eyes off the woman who looked like she imagined her mother would have looked at this age. The moment was even more strange because the woman kept staring into Aydın's face as if she were trying to solve a puzzle.

Nora broke the spell and ran the final steps toward her aunt. "I've been searching for you and finally...Aunt Dedim," she said with tears of emotion streaming from her smiling eyes.

Dedim opened both her arms to receive a hug from her and said, "I thought I was alone in this world and you found me." She collected herself then ushered her guests inside the modest apartment.

There were a few awkward moments at first before Dedim offered to prepare tea for everyone. She asked Nora and Aydın to make themselves comfortable in the small sitting room.

When Dedim returned with the tea, she realized that Aydın hadn't been saying much, realizing that she and Nora had been speaking Turkish, she switched to English.

"Your English is perfect," said Nora.

"It was compulsory for all of us to learn English here in the north while going to school," she said.

Nora noticed she kept looking at Aydın as if she were inspecting him. She then opened her purse and pulled out a few of the old black and white photos Nils had given her from the bundle their father left for them.

Nora showed her aunt the picture of both Hanife and Dedim in their school uniforms. Then she handed Dedim a color photo taken of Sven and Hanife while they were courting. Hanife was wearing the same dark blue dress with the white dots and sleeves that she wore the night Sven first set eyes on her. Dedim handed the photos back to Nora and brought her hands up to cover her face as she began to shake and sob. Nora put her arm around her aunt.

"We've all missed each other for too many years. I'm glad I found you," said Nora.

When Dedim collected herself she said, "I thought the worst. I was very young. The last time I saw Hanife I was hanging out the window of a bus as it pulled away from our village." She drew a handkerchief from the pocket of the apron she'd put over her fine dress when she was preparing tea earlier. "Where is she now?"

Nora reached over and rested her hand over her aunt's wrist.

"She passed away years ago. I never knew her. My father died of cancer two years ago but before he left us, he showed me and my brother Nils that photo of you and my mom when you were school girls."

Dedim was speechless and full of tears. Nora had prepared herself ahead of time for this conversation and managed to maintain her composure. At a complete loss, Aydın rose from the chair he was sitting in across from the two women and gathered the remains of the tea service and returned the cups and saucers to the kitchen.

"We don't have to talk about it if it upsets you," said Nora.

"No, it is alright. I'm crying out of joy more than sadness for lost years. I'm so happy Hanife got married and had a family."

Both women were preoccupied with telling one another the details of the lost years. Dedim wanted to know everything about her older sister's life. Nora had no difficulty explaining what she knew since Sven conveyed most of the story to her during their train trip through France.

When it was Dedim's turn to fill in the lost years for Nora, Aydın returned to the sitting room with a pitcher of water and some glasses. Dedim again noticed him and again she appeared to be inspecting the features of his face and eyes.

"Aydın." She said in a low voice.

He smiled back at her and said, "That is indeed my name."

"You are a Greek Cypriot but you are named Aydın," she said and that is when the memories flooded back to her.

"This is true, I am from the south, but I was born in Balıkeşir. I don't remember anything about it though. All my memories are of Kantou - Çanakkale, the village where I grew up with my uncle in the south."

Before Aydın finished what he was saying, Dedim raised her hands to cover her eyes for the second time that morning.

"Aunt Dedim, is anything wrong?" asked Nora puzzled by the exchange.

Dedim rose from the sofa and reached in the pocket of her apron for her handkerchief and excused herself.

"It is fine dear. Please, I'll just be a minute," she said retreating into the kitchen.

Nora and Aydın remained seated in the small living room. Aydın looked at her and shrugged. Nora was about to get up and see to her aunt but stopped herself when Dedim returned moments later.

"I have memories that were locked away for a long time. Sometimes too painful to think about because of all the events surrounding those days of the troubles." She sat down in an empty chair across from them and poured herself a glass of water.

"We don't have to talk about any of this," said Nora. "I just wanted us to meet each other since we are family. Maybe we should come back after we have some time to get used to everything."

"No dear. I'm very happy you came and I'm especially happy you brought your wonderful husband along. We live in such a small world. All of us are tied to a complicated past." She took a sip of water and set the glass down on the marble coffee table before continuing.

She leaned forward clasping both hands in her lap as she continued. "You see, I was a fresh, new midwife in the summer of '74 having just graduated from nursing school in May. I was young and proud and so very happy having assisted several women with the births of their children."

"How old were you then?" asked Nora.

"Young. I turned twenty just before I graduated." She turned to Aydın before she continued. "In those days there were placements for health professionals in the smaller villages. I accepted my first assignment in Balıkeşir because your mother and I had distant cousins living there."

Neither Nora nor her husband could have imagined the deep connections imbedded in Dedim's story but they knew she had something significant to share with them.

"Until now, I've never told anyone what happened during those times of the troubles in the village," she said looking at her hands, squeezing her fingers together before looking up at Aydın again. Balıkeşir was still a bi-communal village in those days. My cousin's family had friendly relations with Greek Cypriot families in the village." She reached for her water glass and took another draw, then continued.

"I had the pleasure and joy of assisting with the births of both Greek Cypriot and Turkish Cypriot babies. It wasn't until the troubles that July when things changed. One evening I was at home with my cousin Semma, her husband and her brother. We were preparing the evening meal and listening to the news on the radio when what looked like a ragtag group of soldiers burst into our home.

There were three of them. The leader I recognized as the husband of one of the women who lived in the Greek Cypriot area of the village near the church. It was terrifying." Dedim paused and collected herself before going on. She wouldn't look up from her lap where she was still squeezing the fingers of each of her hands in turn.

"This man, the leader, I don't think I ever knew his name. He ordered the other two to take my cousin's husband and brother from the house. We heard the shots from the side yard. The soldiers were gone by the time we went out to see what could be done. It was too late of course. Both of the men were dead in a pool of their own blood.

We didn't have much time to grieve. There was so much chaos and confusion over the next few days. I suppose our survival instincts took over. I remember the day. It was only three days after the Turkish Army arrived and our village seemed safe enough to go outside.

A young Greek Cypriot boy of maybe ten years old came calling. Semma and I were holed up in the kitchen listening intently to the radio. We noticed this boy was very frightened when I came to the door. I recognized him as a local villager, but couldn't place from which family. He told me his mother was in trouble. That is when I remembered where I'd seen him.

I grabbed my medical kit and the boy led me to his home. His mother was very distressed and barely conscious. There was no way for her to get to a hospital and I was compelled by my oath to assist her with the birth of her newborn son. When we were finished, both the woman and the boy were in good health.

I recognized the woman as the wife of the man that came into Semma's home with the soldiers, just days before. The woman must have known the terror that her husband had caused in the village. She wept and told me that she would name her newborn son for Semma's husband, Aydın." Dedim looked up from her lap into the eyes of Nora's husband. "I recognized your eyes right away when you came to the door this morning. It is something that a midwife just knows. It was you Aydın. You were the newborn."

Nora squeezed her husband's hand. Tears welled in his eyes and he took a deep breath before he thanked Dedim for having the courage to tell him about the day he was born. He wished he didn't know about the actions of his father but realized it was something that couldn't be changed.

"I don't know what happened to your mother or your brother. I'm sorry Aydın. I didn't think I'd ever be telling anyone about this. I wish it weren't true about your dad and those men coming into Semma's house," said Dedim.

"It hurts to know it was my father," he said. "I never knew him. I'm sad that he did such terrible things." Aydın rose from the sofa and came around the table to embrace Nora's aunt. He knew there was even more to this story and also knew that he was indelibly linked to his family's past, as well as hers.

"You said you grew up in Kantou - Çanakkale," Dedim said to him as he released her and kneeled beside the chair she was sitting in.

"You may have already put these pieces together and I'm not even sure what the significance might be if any...." She looked across to Nora before returning her gaze in Aydın's direction before continuing. "The village where Hanife and I lived as children was the same place you grew up. In Çanakkale our family, the Yılmaz family was very close with the Greek Cypriot family who owned a corner cafe and lived in the apartment above. The man who owned and worked in the cafe was named Kostas. I don't remember his first name."

"He was my uncle," Aydın said. "A very good man."

"He raised you to be a very good man. I can tell." Dedim

reached down and stroked his cheek with the back of her hand. "I suppose all Cypriots are bound together in some way. Most just don't know it."

For a while everyone was at a loss for conversation. Nora took it upon herself to slice through the silence and asked, "Forgive me for asking, but what became of your cousin Semma?"

"Oh, no apology is necessary dear. Semma and I still correspond. She comes to Cyprus often. She and her husband Emir live in Antalya, just across the sea to the north on the Turkish coast."

Dedim noticed both Nora and Aydın sharing puzzled looks with one another. "Emir was a Turkish Naval Officer. In those days, Turkish Cypriots thought of the Turkish military as saviors who rescued the small population of Turkish Cypriots. Emir still believes that was his mission and I agree that perhaps there was some truth to that perception. Things are different here now."

Nora said to her aunt, "Aydın and I both understand the impact these misperceptions have created over the years."

"Ah yes, your work as a diplomat has provided you with the knowledge that it isn't necessary to re-open wounds that take time to heal," said her aunt.

Nora smiled at her aunt. "You sound like you are the one that is the true diplomat." She changed the subject. "This lovely man of mine is also a professor of diplomacy."

Aydın just shrugged and smiled across at Dedim.

"In what way would that be?" Dedim asked looking to both of them for an explanation.

"He is a talented musician and celebrity radio personality. Perhaps you've heard him on the air?"

"Of course. I should have made that connection. The 'Bridging the Divide' program is very popular here among the university students. Aydın Kostas." Dedim said rolling her head back and forth. "I was so overwhelmed with everything this morning. I couldn't put two and two together."

Again there was awkward silence and they were all drained after so much emotional talk in such a short span of time. Dedim rose from the chair she was seated in and said, "I do have to supervise the interns this afternoon. I don't know how I'll stay focused, but I would like to meet again in the near future when we have more time."

"Of course." Nora said and she hugged her aunt and Dedim hugged her back.

"Thank you so much for finding me dear girl. We are a family reunited. That includes you as well young man. Thank you for being such a wonderful husband to my niece." Dedim extended her hand sealing a goodbye gesture with him.

"Sonra görüşürüz," he said as he got up and held his hand out to Nora to lead her to the door.

Nora hugged her aunt. *"Hoşça kal."*

"Güle güle," Aunt Dedim said waving as the young couple descended the stairwell.

CHAPTER 19

Baku, Azerbaijan

2005-7

The City of two million people was the largest in the Caucasus region and nothing new for Nora. Aydın, on the other hand wasn't prepared for what he saw as a black eye on the Caspian Sea. Although there were holiday resorts and hotels along the Caspian coastline of the city, he couldn't come to grips with the contrasting industrial panoramas where oil wells overwhelmed the view.

"You don't like what you see here do you?" Nora asked her husband.

"It certainly isn't Cyprus."

"That it isn't. I'd almost forgotten how depressing it can be here. When I left several years ago, Baku was famous for being one of the world's twenty-five dirtiest cities," she said.

"I'm not surprised," he said than paused, surveying the urban scenes through the window of the black painted taxi-cab that was taking them from Heydar Aliyev Airport to their new living quarters near the U.S. Embassy

"Much of what you're seeing are remnants of the Russian industrial exploitation that made Baku what it is today," said Nora, remembering almost the exact words she'd heard several years earlier when a guide commented on various aspects of the cityscape. The memory of her first trip to Azerbaijan flooded back to her and now it didn't seem much had changed since she'd left Baku years ago.

Both she and her husband looked one another in the eye and almost simultaneously they said to each other, "How bad can it be? At least we're not going to be living in a desert." They both laughed. The cab driver looked at them through the rearview mirror without any expression.

"We'll get on famously here, you'll see." Aydın said with confidence.

"What makes you so sure about that?"

"Because we can spend our spare time making babies. Don't you think that would be fun?"

Nora winked at her husband. "We've got a lot of settling in to do before I'll have much free time," she said.

Their first eighteen months together in Baku mercifully sped by. Now into their second summer in the region, Aydın was becoming fed up with the dry climate and relentless dusty wind. Fortunately he remained connected to the work he' been doing with the radio station in Cyprus. That coupled with his work as a Cultural Liaison Officer or CLO at the embassy, was his saving grace. The embassy in Baku was small, so the civilian CLO jobs often to spouses of diplomats were few and far between.

Nora's duties were similar to those she'd held in Nicosia. However, she didn't get along well with the attaché in charge of the economic section in the embassy. Nora wanted her cables to contain something besides analysis of Baku's oil production and the impact the "Baku-Tblisi-Ceyhan" pipeline would have on the European economy.

There were people in Azerbaijan who were at one time or another refugees or relatives of displaced populations. Nora also struggled with the changes within the embassy when Ambassador Harnish was replaced by Ambassador Derse. She had a great deal of respect for Harnish's concerns over the environment and the progress that was being made in dealing with pollution of the Caspian Sea and the region surrounding Baku. When Anne Derse came aboard, the focus changed and Nora wasn't sure if her own lack of focus at work was due to these changes or something all together different.

The seven months that remained of her posting to Baku suddenly dragged for Nora. She arrived home one evening feeling ill.

"Aydın dear, I hope you aren't preparing anything special for dinner this evening," she said as she walked into the small kitchen at the back of their sparsely furnished urban apartment.

"Indeed I am. Don't come in yet. I want to surprise you. Trust me, you'll love this dish," he said beaming with pride.

"Oh, you can be sure I'm not coming in there," she said rushing to the bathroom down the hall.

"Nora, what is it? Are you alright?" Aydın dropped what he was doing in the kitchen and ran to discover she was vomiting in the bathroom.

"You remember what you said when we arrived here in Baku?" she asked.

"Yes, I said we'd get on famously if I remember correctly."

"...and what else did you include in that statement? Do you remember?" Nora looked pale as she brushed a clean damp washrag over her mouth and lips before turning to see the perplexed look on her husband's face. "Morning sickness. Only in my case, we might call it evening sickness brought on by the aroma of a wonderfully prepared meal that I'm sure I won't be able to stomach."

It took Aydın a moment to process what Nora conveyed to him before he burst out, "Babies! We could make babies, is what I said." He reached for her, his face lit up with a wide grin. "Is this real, are you going to have a baby?"

"Seven months from now is what the doctor said. The timing couldn't be better either.

CHAPTER 20

Ötuken Village Cyprus 2007

Nora had kept the worn cardboard box containing her father's novel close beside her. She'd read it over several times while living in Baku and had asked Aydın to read it too.

"There is good material in here but I think you need to write the rest of the story," he'd told her.

She'd asked him, "You think that is what Dad would've wanted?"

They'd had this same conversation a few times already. Then one day Aydın picked up the slip of paper from the stack of type written pages. It had begun to yellow with age but the ink was still legible. He read Sven's note again out loud for Nora to hear his conviction that Sven wanted her to finish the novel.

"You know how the story must end. We are part of it. People need to read this story and they will like it. More importantly it will make people think about humanity with a hopeful heart. I'll help you." After he'd said this to her, Nora knew she was going to be doing some writing of her own.

Together they'd worked on Sven's novel over the two years they spent in Baku. *The People In Between*, by Sven Kjell Johansson, co-authored by Kiraz Nora Kostas-Johansson was published in the United States and Great Britain.

Their novel didn't make the New York Times bestseller list,

but it did become popular reading among university students studying conflict resolution and Mid-East Culture and History. Published in English, Greek, Turkish, and French, it was also a hit among tourists on Cyprus. The book became the staple reading available on every bookrack at every tourist attraction in Cyprus.

The royalties were sufficient to take the economic sting out of Nora's decision to leave the State Department. It was a practical decision too because Nora was pregnant with their first child. Both of them decided they wanted the baby to be born in Cyprus so they arranged their return as soon as Nora's posting to Baku was terminated.

Nora sat with her husband on the limestone steps of the ruins at Salamis looking off to the shimmering horizon of the East Mediterranean with the sun setting behind them. She had her hand over her husbands, both resting on her large belly.

"Ah, feel that? It's him. I just know it!" exclaimed Aydın.

Nora looked up at him. "I don't care if it is a boy or girl as long is there are ten fingers and ten toes. I love you."

"I love you too. Both of you," he said.

"Have you noticed how everything that happens on Cyprus happens in spring time?" she asked him.

"I've never thought of it, but now that you mention it...." He kissed the top of her head. "We should go. You and our baby need rest.

Aunt Dedim agreed to stay with Nora and Aydın in their village home in Ötuken, overlooking the small coastal forest and Famagusta Bay. When she found out Nora was going to have a baby, she insisted on helping them throughout the birthing of their first child.

When Nils and Josette heard about Nora's plans, they'd arranged to spend their spring holiday on the island with them as well. Nils's career was taking a winding path that landed him in a graduate program at Harvard.

Although he missed flying his A-10 through the mountains of Afghanistan, he wasn't thrilled about the lack of a coherent military strategy there. The multiple deployments wore on him and his young family. Academia offered them all a temporary sanctuary. The Spring Break from his first academic year was a welcome relief. Nora was proud of her brother and was thrilled he and his family were able to spend more time together and especially happy they were all coming to Cyprus for the holiday.

Martin had ten days off school and his little sister, Amélie, hadn't started kindergarten, so the timing for their visit was perfect. Josette's nursing experience as a midwife was limited, so she was thrilled to have a chance to work with a seasoned professional like Dedim. Together; the two of them had everything arranged for when the special day came.

The second week of April was typical for mid-spring on Cyprus. Cool mornings and warm afternoons. Nils returned one late afternoon with Martin and Amélie caked in sand from the beach. The house was quiet. The doors leading to the balcony were open as were the front windows, so Nils knew everyone must have been home.

"We're back," he shouted.

Josette hurried from the back bedroom waving a hand in the air putting her index finger in front of her lips. Amélie ran to her mother and wrapped her arms around her leg before Josette pulled her daughter up into her arms. When Nils and Martin joined her, she kissed Nils on the lips and whispered something.

"Come on everyone. This way, but don't be loud. Aunt Nora needs her rest," Josette said to her children and husband.

"When they entered the back room they saw Nora asleep with her head propped up on pillows. Aydın was seated in a rocker beside the bed looking down at the small form swaddled in a blue blanket. Dedim stood beside him with a hand on his shoulder. He looked up as the Johansson family came over to see the baby boy. His smile was as big as could be.

Dedim stepped aside so that Martin could peek over Aydın's shoulder at his new cousin. "Wow!" he said. "He's bigger than my sister was when she was born."

"What is his name?" asked young Amélie.

Nora stirred in the bed. She was awake with her eyes closed and didn't want to miss sharing the moment. Aydın didn't answer his niece's question right away since he noticed Nora raising herself up on one elbow.

"His name is Ümit," she said. "It means hope. Ümit Galen Kostas-Johansson will be the name on his certificate of birth. Your uncle and I agreed he would go by the name of Galen."

"I like Ümit," Amélie said. "Hope is such a good word."

Nora smiled at her niece and winked at her brother Nils. "Out of the mouths of babes," she exclaimed. "I hope we see more of the Johanssons in this house. Not just for special occasions either."

Nils gave his sister a hug and said, "We were born on the same day you and I. That means our lives and the lives of both our families will be forever linked, and the one thing that has tied us all together is Cyprus. You're going to need a bigger house with lots of room, you can be sure there will be lots of family reunions in the years ahead."

The End

NOTE FROM THE AUTHOR

Thanks for reading _The People In Between: A Cyprus Odyssey_. Please be sure to rate and review this book on your favorite site, so others will know what is in store for them. Also, feel free to friend me on Facebook at LambPDXauthor, or visit my website at http://gslambpdxauthor.webs.com/.

ABOUT THE AUTHOR

Gregory S. Lamb is a retired USAF Colonel. He lived and worked in the places mentioned in his first novel, _The People In Between: A Cyprus Odyssey_. He lives in Portland, Oregon with his wife Cindy. They have three grown sons.

Made in the USA
Charleston, SC
30 July 2012